SATIN BY NIGHT

Also available from Headline Liaison

One Summer Night by Tom Crewe and Amber Wells
Your Cheating Heart by Tom Crewe and Amber Wells
Sleepless Nights by Tom Crewe and Amber Wells
Hearts on Fire by Tom Crewe and Amber Wells
The Journal by James Allen
Love Letters by James Allen
Aphrodisia by Rebecca Ambrose
Out of Control by Rebecca Ambrose
A Private Affair by Carol Anderson
Voluptuous Voyage by Lacey Carlyle
Magnolia Moon by Lacey Carlyle
The Paradise Garden by Aurelia Clifford
The Golden Cage by Aurelia Clifford
Vermilion Gates by Lucinda Chester
Seven Days by J J Duke
Dangerous Desires by J J Duke
A Scent of Danger by Sarah Hope-Walker
Private Lessons by Cheryl Mildenhall
Intimate Strangers by Cheryl Mildenhall
Dance of Desire by Cheryl Mildenhall

Satin
By Night

Tom Crewe and Amber Wells

HEADLINE
Liaison

First published in 1996
by HEADLINE BOOK PUBLISHING

A HEADLINE LIAISON paperback

10 9 8 7 6 5 4 3 2 1

ISBN 0 7472 5509 1

Typeset at The Spartan Press Ltd,
Lymington, Hants

Printed and bound in Great Britain by
Cox & Wyman Ltd,
Reading, Berks

HEADLINE BOOK PUBLISHING
A division of Hodder Headline PLC
338 Euston Road
London NW1 3BH

Satin
By Night

Chapter One

A cold wind was whipping down the Seine and along the Quais. It gusted into the Rue Mazarine, confusing the weathervane on the church of St Germain-des-Prés. It whipped around the trunks of the plane trees and shook their branches, caught at the ankles of the pedestrians as they hurried along the pavements, bound for the theatres and restaurants over the river in the Tuileries.

It lifted up a little scrap of paper that was lying in the gutter – a butcher's bill, perhaps, or a laundry list, it matters not – and blew it this way and that until it was swept down the little passageway that led away from the avenue. It fetched up in the open doorway of a café where gaslight flared and the sound of loud conversation spilled out into the street. A man in a liveried uniform of fustian and plush, standing by the door, quickly stooped down and removed the offending scrap, brushing imaginary dust from his white gloves as he nodded to the top-hatted gentleman who came in from the pavement.

There was still a lightness in the sky, at seven-thirty on a spring evening. It could be seen in tiny, rectangular sections that were glimpsed only between tall buildings, the tower of the church dominating everything else in this arrondissement. The moon, too, was beginning to rise, in its third quarter. But the blaze of light from the Café des Artistes flooded out of the windows and spilled over on to everything, contrasting with the darkness of the surrounding buildings, the hidden recesses of doorways, the pools

1

of black that seemed dark and mysterious amid the flaring yellow.

Inside the café a group of women were seated at a table quite close to the entrance, enough to feel the evening draught of cold air as the door momentarily opened to admit the gentleman in black. Eyes looked up, expectantly. Lips parted in a smile of welcome, rouged cheeks glowed. All around was the sound of subdued laughter, the sound of glass clinking against glass, of cutlery on china. Waiters strolled to and fro, in black waistcoats and starched aprons that came right down to their feet. Orders were taken and delivered to the tables with a leisureliness that, even in Paris, had become legendary.

The gentleman paused. His eye scanned the crowd but there were no acquaintances to nod back his greeting. The maitre d' caught his eye. A table, perhaps, for monsieur? The gentleman shook his head, eyes downcast, a barely perceptible gesture. The maitre d' understood.

He studied the women at the table by the door, a half-smile playing on his face, not unhandsome. Finally his eye came to rest.

A woman rose from the group, tall and demure. She made her way to the door. A word or two was spoken, a nod, a gesture of agreement.

They went outside. The doorman nodded his salutation. The gentleman in black handed him a coin. The doorman touched his cap.

The woman and the gentleman walked down the passageway, away from the bright flaring lights of the Café des Artistes. The flagstones were still wet from the early evening rain and the air had that special city smell of night. Now it was almost dark – the night time came on quickly at that time of year. Their footsteps echoed against the façades of the tall buildings on either side of them, a furrier's premises, a dealer in optical instruments, a lawyer with a German name. They spoke very little. Both knew what was required.

Finally they found what they were seeking, a doorway set back from the thoroughfare. No one came down this lane in the evening, when all the offices were closed and shuttered, except perhaps for a priest hurrying to mass and taking the short cut that would lead him through to St Germain. But mass had been celebrated more than an hour ago. Only the café at the corner spoke of any life.

They stepped into the welcoming darkness. She could feel already how hard and insistent he was. She said something to him, something lewd and inviting perhaps, that made him laugh. She smiled too, encouraging him. He looked like the type who might give her a good tip. Her hands, practised and skilled, were quickly busy with the buttons of his trousers. He murmured some words of instruction or preference. She nodded.

She knelt down. He had his hands on her bonnet, the artificial flowers that felt surprisingly hard to his touch. She was well dressed, in a gown of bronze silk and a black shawl thrown elegantly over her shoulders. She was not a common streetwalker. She had the feeling she had been with him before but there were so many of them, especially now with the lighter evenings coming on and bringing people out at night. When it got too light, and the darkness didn't finally settle until close on ten, then it was more difficult to be unobtrusive, and many girls had to use rooms or discreet hotels, which all cost money. The streets and closes of St Germain were free, though. They were almost as good as the parks for that kind of thing.

She had his penis out of his drawers now. She could see it in the darkness, white and potent, could smell the cock-smell that she knew so well. She drew back the foreskin and tasted him experimentally. He pushed at her, anxious for her lips and mouth. He was clean, his manner gentle and conservative, almost aristocratic, a gentleman most certainly. Most of them were, who came after the girls at the Café des Artistes. He had rested his silver-tipped cane against the iron railings that flanked the entrance. If she sucked him off well, he might forget it and she could go back later and reclaim it. René at the café was very good at fencing quality things like that and would give you half of what he got for it. One of the girls at the café, Rosalie, had got lucky only that evening, filching a lovely gold watch off someone in an alleyway just off the Rue Bonaparte. Each of them had her own favourite spot in the honeycomb of streets that flanked the great, wide river.

He gasped as she took all of him in. She knew this one would not be long. She bobbed her head up and down along his length, her tongue flickering. He liked what she was doing for him. He was stroking the back of her neck gently. His hands felt soft. A gentleman, again. He didn't do any work, not with hands like that. Her pimp, Léon, had hands like a gambler's.

He asked her to stand up. She did so. He touched her breasts through the fabric of her gown. They were full and ripe. Intuitively, she took hold of his penis again, moved her hand up and down its impressive length. She wondered why he did not appear to have any great desire for intercourse with her. She felt hungry, wanted to eat soon. She hoped he would not be long.

As his hands roved over her body she murmured some delicious obscenity in his ear. He chuckled, squeezed her closer to him. A lot of them liked her to talk to them like that, she'd noticed. She was sure their wives wouldn't use words like 'suck' and 'cunt' and 'spunk'. They did not kiss, though. She bit his ear gently, whispered something else designed to excite him. She made it up as she went along. She could feel the big vein standing out along the side of his penis and then she sensed his agitation. She stood back slightly – her gown was barely a month old and she didn't want stains on it. As she moved her expert fingers up and down his sturdy shaft she could feel him pulse in her hand, looked down and saw – or thought she saw – the short arc of sperm come shooting out of him and land on the pavement.

It was done. Their business was concluded. He adjusted his clothing, stepped out of the entrance-way with her. Under a gas light he took out his bill-fold and gave her money. He was not as generous as she had hoped he would be – she wanted to ask for another ten but then she felt that, if encouraged, he could become one of her regulars. So she smiled and dimpled prettily and told him that she could usually be found at the Café des Artistes between seven and eleven. He murmured something, adjusting his clothing. Then he was gone, swinging his cane.

Cosette, the girl with whom she had been talking, was not there when she got back inside. Damn! That was a nuisance. She wanted to know if she could borrow a hat of hers. So she too must have found a gentleman – still, she would be back in half an hour, maybe less. Cosette had the use of a small room only a minute's walk away, above an umbrella shop in the Rue Jacob.

She sat down. The other girls were talking about some silly novel or other. Satin wished they might talk once in a while about something of substance, but she didn't know what. Clothes, men, apartments, scandals of the day – it was always the same at the Café des Artistes.

For a while, she and Cosette had shared rooms of their own with two of the other girls, presided over by an old bag from Abbeville who combined the function of maid and madame. But there was not the money around any longer, not even in Paris. Everyone was tightening their belts. So she worked from the café and had a constant reservation at the discreet hotel around the corner. For those who didn't have the time – or who just liked the thrill of being sucked or fucked in a shop doorway, which obviously didn't cost as much – she took them up the alley.

* * *

Satin and Felicité climbed on to the bed together, naked apart from their boots and stockings. They could scarcely stop themselves from laughing at the expression of gleeful anticipation on the face of M Chavignon, lying there on the counterpane like a beached whale. He was a pork butcher from Neuilly.

They kissed as he watched, breasts pressed together. The light in the hotel room was subdued, the wallpaper green and heavy. It was uncomfortably over-heated. Satin was glad to be naked.

Slowly her hands travelled down Felicité's body, running over the smooth curves of her ample hips, the dark cleft between her thighs. Her skin was as smooth and soft as a baby's. Propped up on the pillow, eating confits and sipping champagne, M Chavignon gurgled like a baby.

Satin's tongue probed her friend's mouth, brushing against her teeth. Felicité was cupping her buttocks, drawing her to her as they knelt on the bed facing each other. She was aware of how hard and erect her nipples were. She liked to perform like this, in front of an audience. It excited her.

They broke from their kiss.

'Pour me a glass of champagne, there's a love,' said Felicité.

M Chavignon rolled over, still looking like a boiled baby, and filled their glasses. His penis was flaccid still. Satin knew no other man who took so long to become aroused. Fortunately he paid the going price and there was always a handsome tip to be shared between herself and whichever friend she happened to be with. M Chavignon almost always preferred to take his women in twos. Sometimes it was Cosette, sometimes Felicité. Satin wondered how much it had cost him, every week like this for the past eighteen months or so.

They sipped their wine, not speaking. M Chavignon had little conversation except in so far as it related to his trade.

It was hard work, usually, coming to bed with him. She wondered if there wasn't another way of making a living – like being an actress, for one, except that being an actress was still, in many people's eyes, only one step away from being a whore, and didn't pay nearly so well.

Satin was glad of the company of Felicité. They had a lot of fun together. Sometimes they'd get drunk, go to one of the theatres in which the area abounded, maybe pick up a couple of men and squeeze a good dinner out of them. Then there might be a bit of sucking and fucking or there might not – they were adept at disappearing into the night together.

They sat on the bed, sipping the wine. Refreshed, they redoubled their efforts. Satin lay down on her back on the counterpane and parted her legs. Felicité climbed on top of her. She could feel their pubic bushes as they brushed together. She pushed up her hips to meet her friend's gentle movements, her tongue flickering. Felicité had an exquisitely furnished vagina, smooth and slick and tight. Sometimes Satin would push two or three fingers inside her and wonder how it might feel to be a man in those circumstances, his cock pushed up inside her, squeezed exquisitely in the warm wet folds.

They rubbed against each other, neither of them entirely unexcited at what they were doing, their kisses hot and slow and languid. They knew M Chavignon was watching every movement, every ripple of muscle, with the intensity of a fox. Suddenly Satin remembered something.

'I forgot the dildo,' she whispered, under the pretext of tonguing Felicité's ear. 'What do we do?'

Felicité's hands were cupping her breasts, her fingertips trailing lightly over her sensitive flesh.

'I'll think of something,' she said. 'Don't worry.'

And with those whispered words, so silently spoken they might be mistaken for the gentle noise made by their bodies on the counterpane, Felicité slid down the bed and let her tongue make gentle ministrations to Satin's body. Breasts, nipples, belly – all the time she was teasing her. They were doing all this for the benefit of M Chavignon and yet Satin found it impossible not to become aroused herself. It was one of the reasons why she was so good at what she did.

She glanced down at her friend's unpinned red hair, spread out over her thighs. Oh God, if Felicité licked her there she would come almost immediately, she knew it. She often mimicked a spend to excite her customers but with Felicité there was no need. She always came when they went to bed together, with or without a man.

Slowly, inexorably, Felicité began her work. Her tongue probed Satin's outer lips, giving up their secrets to her incessant searching. Satin could feel herself opening up like an oyster. Unconsciously her hands strayed on to her breasts and she caressed her nipples, each in turn, lush and raspberry pink. Her breasts were large and one of her most appealing features. She liked dresses that were cut to show them at their best advantage, whether she was working the Café des Artistes or frequenting the foyers of the theatres, where there would usually be a gentleman who would pay good money to squeeze them. A lot of them liked to come off over her tits, because of their size. She asked Felicité and Cosette about it – both of them, in comparison, were quite small-breasted – and they said few men ever asked for it. This rather pleased Satin's vanity, which for a nineteen-year-old was considerable.

Her eyes closed and for a moment or two she forgot M Chavignon and the hotel room, with its flickering gas mantles and throbbing tropical warmth. Now she was aware only of her own body and the blood which pounded in her temples.

There! She had it. The delicate tongue-tip touch on Satin's clitoris sent a shock wave coursing through her body. Felicité's tongue was like a tiny finger, at once gentle and urgent. She always knew how to do it so delicately, not like a man, licking and lapping in that crude way they had about them, as if they'd never been weaned from the breast. Felicité could do Satin all night if she wanted to. Sometimes she did.

Felicité's tongue was tracing little circles around Satin's labia. The feeling was divine. She hoped old M Chavignon, though she knew he was watching them like a stoat gloating over a rabbit, wouldn't want her to suck him off as he sometimes did at the same time as Felicité was licking her. She wanted this moment to be for herself, even though the pork butcher was paying for it.

She knew she shouldn't come – it would tire her, of that she was aware – but she couldn't stop herself. The feeling in her loins was too intense, the sense of abandonment that went running through her like quicksilver. She drew up her legs and felt those first flickerings of pleasure stirring deep within her, like a moth's wings fluttering in her womb.

The feeling grew, became more and more intense with every second that ticked by, and she abandoned herself to her senses, gasping out her pleasure even as she came in little purple rivulets of ecstasy, scarcely even aware of M Chavignon as he climbed up behind Felicité and thrust his now rampant cock into her from behind, pumping so furiously that the bed shook.

When the tremblings had subsided she opened her eyes and winked at Felicité. She was laying face down on Satin's stomach while the Neuilly pork butcher, red-cheeked and portly, thrust inside her. His heavy moustache was beaded with perspiration, his body glowing pink in the warm light of the room, with its heavy drapes and brocaded furniture. On his face was an expression of perfect rapture.

With a hoarse cry, he seized Felicité's rump in both red hands and pushed as hard as he could inside her. His eyes closed – was this pleasure or pain? Satin never ceased to marvel at how ridiculous most men looked at the moment of ecstasy. Felicité lay on her stomach still, her face an expression of perfect boredom.

Later, after more champagne, they bathed together. It was not a large bath and the maid had not brought them much hot water – they were so stingy in that hotel, she had a good mind to go somewhere else in the future – but somehow the three of them managed to squeeze in together, thigh against thigh, hip against hip. M Chavignon made some pretence of soaping the two women but mostly it was just larking about, as he squeezed their breasts and put his stubby butcher's fingers inside them. He'd been told that he wouldn't be able to pleasure them with the dildo this time but Felicité had promised to suck his cock for him and swallow his come, and that seemed to mollify him.

Somehow Satin managed to climb on to M Chavignon's lap and spitted herself on his cock. It was not an especially large one and, in the circumstances, with water slopping on the floor and Felicité laughing and trying to pour champagne, she was hardly aware of having it inside her. She bobbed up and down nevertheless, her large breasts crushed against his hairy chest, and reassured him about how huge he was, and all the hundred and one other lies she had told a thousand and one men, and she thrust her nipples into his face and made him lick and suck them until they stood up hard and firm. Here, in the bath, she was aware more of the sensation in her breasts than in her vagina.

'Hey, steady on!' cried M Chavignon as Felicité tried to turn round in the water and succeeded only in forming a tidal wave that threatened to engulf them all. Satin laughed and squeezed his cock hard with her vaginal muscles. He had piggy little eyes, had M Chavignon, and his lips were fleshy. She had never kissed them. She didn't want to. Someone said her own lips looked like she'd just been stung by a bee, which rather pleased her. Men liked women with sensual lips, just as they liked big breasts and generous hips.

Slowly, with practised skill, she took control of the situation. She got him where she wanted him, lying flat in the bath so he could hardly move, and then she began to bob up and down on his cock, gently at first and then with increased vigour. She could sense him beginning to relax and to enjoy having her do all the work. Felicité was sprawled back drunkenly, sitting on M Chavignon's calves, her legs splayed, her knees up against Satin's bottom cheeks. The whole situation was ridiculous. She was glad they were being paid handsomely for an evening's work. After her encounter with the gentleman in the doorway, she hadn't had another customer until M Chavignon appeared just after ten.

Just when she had begun to despair of him, M Chavignon gave a hoarse cry and grabbed hold of Satin's waist quite roughly. He buried his red moustachioed face between her breasts and then she felt his cock pulse three or four times in quick succession. Thank God for that, she thought to herself, as their bodies gently subsided into the now tepid water and his come slowly began to seep out of her and into the tepid, soapsudded water.

Three parts drunk and already paid for, Satin dressed as quickly as she could while Felicité completed the final act of their arrangement. The butcher, who must have been well into his forties, took ages to come, sitting on the edge of the bed while Felicité knelt before him and took his almost flaccid penis in her mouth. Her friend was tired, Satin could tell.

'Here,' she said at length, and knelt down beside them. Felicité was naked still, Satin in her gown. As Felicité licked his prick-stem, Satin's tongue played with his balls. Once or twice their tongues met. They squeezed hands.

He wouldn't be long now, not under their double ministrations.

He had spent twice already in the past two hours and was in no hurry to come again. Satin, however, was hungry. She wanted to go home, to have Mathilde, her maid, cook her an omelette with some radishes, and then to flop down alone in her bed and sleep until noon as she usually did.

Now the two women were sucking him together, their tongues curling wetly around him, the great purple dome of his prepuce beginning to seep the first signs of his third and final spend. It would be soon now, she knew. These old ones, they always took so much longer. The young ones, they were spilling their seed almost before they could get a hand up her drawers.

Her back felt stiff from the way she was kneeling and she was afraid of getting dust on the front of her gown but she stuck to her task. It was a challenge for her. Most of them were.

It was Felicité who took him finally in her mouth. Satin was sitting beside him on the bed now, frigging his cock up and down with increasing friction as he panted and muttered his lewd thoughts. Felicité's tongue flickered in and out of her mouth, dabbing at the little oval eye at the end of his cock, while Satin's soft and practised hand continued to move rhythmically up and down, squeezing him just the right way for him – for all men were different in the way they liked women to handle their cocks – and then finally she knew they were there. She saw, actually saw, his balls contract and she let go with her hand as Felicité took him fully in her mouth and his last, tired spurt of come came struggling out and dribbled into her mouth and down her throat.

'There,' Felicité said, swallowing hard and giving him a pat on the shoulder such as a child in the nursery might receive, 'That was nice, wasn't it?'

They all three of them rose to their feet, the business of the evening concluded. Felicité dressed quickly and then they left, the two women arm in arm together, leaving M Chavignon to finish his expensively bought champagne and to consider returning to his hard, shrewish wife in Neuilly.

Felicité spat into a cupola at the top of the hotel stairs. She was sucking her teeth vigorously, trying to dislodge something.

'I've got a pube stuck at the back of my throat,' she said. 'It's driving me mad.'

'It's an occupational hazard,' said Satin, smiling. 'I wonder whose it is?'

It was past midnight when Satin reached her apartment. She climbed the narrow, stinking stairs that smelled unpleasantly of cabbage. There was a mark on the wall running the whole height of the building, where generations of shoulders had rubbed as they ascended the narrow stairway. No one could remember the last time the stairwell had been painted and the carpet was all but worn through.

Inside, Mathilde was busy putting clothes away, despite the lateness of the hour. A whore's maid does not keep normal business hours.

'Madame Lefebre has been around again,' she said without looking round.

'Oh yes?' said Satin. 'And what did she want? The usual, I suppose?'

'You are three months behind, she says.'

'So what? Everyone's behind. I'll pay her next week, tell her.'

'She said that's what you told her last week.'

'She'll get her money. It wasn't that long ago I paid her, was it?'

'She says you've not paid her since February. She's

wanting the money now that she says she should have had in February.'

'She's been at the absinthe again, the baggage.'

'She says we'll be out if we don't pay.'

'All right, then next week she can have the money. Then she won't be behind at all, at least not from her position. In July she'll have the money she thinks she ought to have now. Can't the stupid woman see that? In the meantime, let's try and find somewhere cheaper. I'm skint.'

Satin poured herself a glass of brandy, sank into a comfortable old armchair. The fire was banked up in anticipation of her return. Mathilde attacked it with a poker.

'Get me something to eat, there's a love, will you?' said Satin. 'I haven't eaten since four.'

While Mathilde busied herself with an omelette in the tiny kitchen, Satin stared at the fire. She had left the apartment a little before two and it was now twelve-thirty. In that time she had been with four men, had earned as much as she paid Mathilde in a fortnight, and yet it still wasn't enough. She had Madame Lefebre to pay off, as well as other debts, some of them not inconsiderable. Her dressmaker had been pressing her for payment for several weeks. Only the day before yesterday that awful man from the furniture shop on the Rue St Jacques had been round, demanding a settlement by the end of the week, or he would see her in court. She'd only had a sofa and a couple of rugs from him, nothing terribly grand. That old trout, Madame Lefebre, was supposed to rent them this place furnished but there were only a pitiful few sticks, that was all. It was embarrassing, sometimes, bringing clients back here. That was why she preferred the hotels.

She could, she knew, have settled the matter there and then by sucking the irate furniture dealer off on the disputed sofa but that was not the point. A girl had her pride.

Satin was just nineteen. Her parents had died when she

was young and she had been brought up by an aunt in a small and intensely rural village in the Ile de France. She still had her given name, Chantal Delacroix. She wasn't known as Satin then – that was a name she acquired later. Even a trip to Fontainebleau had seemed like a journey to the ends of the earth, the splendid shops, the great palace with its acres and acres of grounds. How small and poky Aunt Berthe's farm had seemed after that.

Through a friend of Aunt Berthe, a Madame Dupuis, she had obtained work as a governess with a well-to-do family in the Avenue Foch. The husband was a civil servant, the wife a thin, nervous woman given to periods of prostration. At first, all had gone well. The three Laroche children were pleasant enough, her tasks comparatively undemanding. Even the serious illness of Aunt Berthe had, for the moment, scarcely disturbed her equilibrium.

Of course, the inevitable happened. She was seduced by Laroche and found herself pregnant. Madame Dupuis, with surprising discretion, secured the services of a woman in Montmartre who put things right, for a fee, arranging for the infant to be cared for. She found herself another station, with a schoolmaster and his family in another and not so comfortably off district. Then her aunt died and Madame Dupuis, not entirely charitably, seemed to drift out of her life.

She was, she then realised, almost entirely alone in the world. She was attracted to the son of her master, a strapping seventeen-year-old. It was she who made the first move. They enjoyed a dangerous liaison for some several months until they were found together one afternoon in the summer house. She was dismissed at an hour's notice.

Homeless, and with scarcely a sou in her purse, it was obvious which way her life should lead. But she did not sell herself cheap. She was far from innocent, and she knew the places to go, the places to be seen. Within a week of her dismissal from the schoolmaster's house she had emerged again, in the silk and satin from which she took her new name, to take her place in the cafés and theatres of fashionable Paris. She settled, eventually, in the St Germain district. Others were not so lucky, and she pitied those sad women of the night whom she saw huddled in doorways around the Marais, their clothes drawn around them to keep out the winter chill. No one in the Marais had any money. That was why she was in St Germain.

Her good looks and undeniable charms left her with no shortage of custom. Soon she had a room of her own, and then a bigger and better one, and then she had a couple of men whom she could think of as admirers, lovers even, and she got them to pay for an even better apartment for her. Those rooms that she now shared with Mathilde had seemed like a palace at first but now she was dissatisfied, wanted better things for herself. She felt she deserved it.

She had fallen into a doze when Mathilde came in with her omelette. She ate it quickly and without appetite, there in her armchair by the fire, and then she went through into her bedroom, the sheets already warmed by the omnipresent maid. Mathilde helped her out of her clothes, tut-tutted about the slight bite mark on her left shoulder – a legacy of a customer earlier in the week – and handed her the nightdress that had been warming by the fire. Within a matter of minutes, Satin was asleep.

She was awakened by a tapping at the door.

'Madame, madame,' she heard Mathilde cry.

'What time is it?'

'It's nearly eleven.'

'Go away. I want to sleep.'

'But M Albert is here.'

Oh God, she had quite forgotten – and Mathilde had failed to remind her. Of course, Thierry Albert, the pharmacist from Neufchatel. He came to Paris every month and he always saw Satin before lunching with friends in the Tuileries.

But something was wrong. Conscious thought came speeding back to her, in the warm folds of her bed. It was the wrong day. She'd thought he was coming tomorrow – she was meant to be seeing a senior clerk at the préfecture today at one. He always came round to her apartment so punctually, wrinkling his nose at the smells emanating from the staircase. It was a regular engagement, but this time it was more important than usual. She wanted to tap him for money. Usually he just wanted straight intercourse, man on top, the usual stuff. But if she was nice to him, really nice, suggested they do something that he might find more exciting, like sucking his prick or letting him put his finger up her bum-hole, then he might give her a little extra, might even let her persuade him to borrow a little off him – just to tide her over, of course. She knew just how much she wanted to ask him for – in spite of her fecklessness over money, Satin could be quite calculating when the need arose. He was quite a wealthy man, her little clerk, and his needs were simple ones. If only Thierry Albert hadn't shown up unexpectedly. If it had been anyone else, she'd have told them to go away. Nevertheless, she would have to do it, if only to get her creditors off her back.

But Thierry Albert! So soon! A day early! She had to see him, she must. The clerk would just have to wait, that was all. As ever, her heart ruled her head. He could not be disappointed. She told Mathilde to ask him to wait a little. Hurriedly pulling on a wrap and checking her face and hair in the mirror, she did what she could with bottles and paints. Despite her empty stomach, she asked Mathilde to bring brandy. In half an hour she was ready to face her first man of the day.

'My dear,' exclaimed Thierry Albert as he came through the narrow door that led to her boudoir. He kissed her on the cheek, a grin splitting his face from ear to ear. He gave her an enormous bouquet of flowers which she tossed down on her dressing table, unnoticed. She threw her arms around him, her tongue seeking his.

They broke, panting for breath. He could see the sparkle in her eye, the eager anticipation. They looked at each other and laughed. Then they kissed again. He was tall and dark, with curly hair, five or six years older than her. He had an impressive professional qualification.

'Did you?' she said at length, sitting down at the side of the bed and bidding him to join her. 'I mean, you haven't—'

'Would I forget? Of course I wouldn't.'

She kissed him again, little butterfly kisses down the side of his face and along his chin. He was so handsome, so dark. And he had what she wanted.

He was struggling out of his coat, tossing it over a chair. In his hand he held a little glass phial, blue and sparkling in the morning sunlight.

'I've got a glass,' said Satin, her eyes not leaving his for a second. He was busy with his cravat, his waistcoat. A button flew off and rolled under the bed.

She took the glass in which she had drunk the brandy, offered it to him.

'All in good time,' he said, a smile playing around his lips. Satin remembered the senior clerk she was seeing at one, less than an hour's time.

'How you tease me, Thierry,' she cried.

He made no reply, but continued to smile at her. She helped him with the flap of his trousers and then he was naked with her apart from his shirt. He lay down beside her, forcing her backwards on to the pillows, busy with the draw-strings of her robe.

Her nipples, like her breasts, were plump and engorged. He buried his face deep between them, breathing in the heady musk of a woman's perfume. His tongue

18

flickered out, playing with her nipples. She was almost beside herself with impatience and desire.

'Shall I suck you?' she asked.

He murmured something she couldn't catch. Her hand stole down to his groin, found him already hard and rampant, just the way she liked him to be. She was aware of how aroused he was, the curious energy that appeared to course through him like electricity.

His cock tasted clean and salty. She rolled the tip around in her mouth, as if it was a plum or a cherry. Thierry was always nice to suck like this. She would let him take her in any way he chose. Her fingernails were long and carefully trimmed and she knew he would love the way she ran them along the little ridges and furrows of his testes. His scrotum was so large she could barely get all of it in her mouth at once.

As she sucked at him, she ran the fingers of her other hand up and down his cock, feeling its blue-veined hardness against her palm. She didn't need him to do anything to her. All she wanted was for him to lie back and enjoy himself and then they could share the contents of the phial together.

The room was in chaos. There were clothes strewn everywhere, over the furniture, on the floor, under the bed. Mathilde did her best to impose some mind of order but it was a losing battle. Satin's clothes even spilled over into the maid's own room, a tiny cubby-hole by the door on the other side of the landing. And yet the men who came here did not seem to mind.

Satin looked around at the large mirror by the side of the bed. She could see her reflection, the way her gown slipped back to reveal her white night robe and her legs, long and colt-like, displayed wantonly. Thierry was watching too. She caught his eye.

Carefully, still working her hand up and down his thick shaft, she managed to undo the tiny fabric buttons on the front of her gown, almost down as far as her stomach. Her breasts were revealed now in all their glory. Thierry – like so many men – had often admired them for their snowy-white fullness. He liked to shoot his spunk all over them almost as much as he liked to come off inside her.

And all the while she sucked him, gently and rhythmically, feeling the tension building up inside him until she knew the moment to be right. When she knew the time was on him she withdrew her mouth, and, without letting go of his penis, she moved her body further up the bed until her breasts were level with his waist.

She knew what he wanted. They often played this game. She frigged him again, up and down, up and down and when she felt his breathing quicken she reached round quickly with her free hand and pressed the tip of her index finger against his arsehole. It yielded to her touch, admitting her as far as the second knuckle.

And in that instant the pharmacist from Neufchatel found his release. Pressing his hips into her soft bosom, his cock pulsed five and six times and a great flow of creamy sperm came flooding out over her breasts. Watching in the mirror, she was amazed at how fulsome his emission was. He seemed to be trying to drown her. Little silvery rivulets of sperm ran over the white, foaming lace of her gown and on to the crisply laundered sheets, while Thierry flopped back on to the pillow and sighed.

They lay silently for some moments. Outside, sparrows were squabbling on the window ledge. The sun had moved around and now it was illuminating the bottles and jars on her dressing table. In the distance, she heard the church clock chime. She had entirely forgotten about her clerk and the money she hoped to borrow from him. Thierry Albert had brought her another way of escaping her creditors.

'Do you want it now?' he said dreamily, without opening his eyes. His cock lolled against his thigh, thick and succulent.

She was on her feet in an instant. She took the phial, instinctively held it up against the light, and then pulled out the stopper. There was the customary smell of raisins and aniseed, a hint of pepper, that did not entirely disguise the chemical-sickly odour of the solution.

She poured them a glassful each. She sat down on the bed beside him, took a couple of sips and then drained her glass in one swallow. It was as unpleasant as any medicine. It could not be mixed directly with alcohol, Thierry had said, or its effect would be neutralised.

Nothing happened for a few moments. Then, a sensation began to spread around her body, a welcome numbness that quickly took control of her movements and feelings. Slightly unsteadily, she let the glass drop to the floor and lay down beside Thierry on the bed.

As usual, she felt slightly nauseous for a minute or two, but the sensation gradually passed. Her whole mind and body was now one large placid glow, permeating every facet of her being. She felt excited and enervated at the same time. The world seemed to have slowed down.

She had no idea how long they had lain like this, lost in their dream world. Whole empires seemed to rise up and fall in an instant. A moment was stretched until it seemed to go on forever, unchanging. The church clock continued to chime the quarters, unheard. All conscious thought vanished and she floated away along a deep, broad river of the psyche, lost to everything but the sensations of her own body as Thierry climbed on top of her and began to fuck her with his characteristic finesse.

Some time may have elapsed before she even realised what was happening, could sense the different pressures on her senses, could feel the rhythms change in her blood. All of a sudden, a new feeling began to take a hold of her numbed and exaggerated body, and she began to respond to his movements but in a vague and abstracted way, as

21

though they were two people sharing a common activity but without partnership.

Her body was moving automatically but her mind was revelling in the delights it released in her mind. Again, she felt the wash of nausea upon her but it was nothing; nothing compared to the heights of pleasure she knew she could reach with Thierry's drug inside her.

She whimpered a little, parted her legs more to take him deeper inside her. Her eyes were open but unseeing. She could smell the cologne on his cheeks where he had shaved but was not aware of its source. That, too, was abstract like the afternoon light that played in the room, a sense that was pleasurable but utterly devoid of association.

Almost before she knew it she was rushing along a deep, wide river, alone in a tiny boat, and yet she felt no fear, only a sense of exhilaration. Her senses were wide open now. All movement, all sense of up or down or in or out became one universal pleasure, massaging and stroking her until she felt the deep tremors begin to stir in her loins, and the river became an earthquake and she flung her arms and legs out wide and surrendered herself to his utter penetration of her body, their frantic exchange of fluids and their deep and unfathomable fantasies at last made flesh.

She dozed, whether for five minutes or thirty she could not tell. When she came around, she was aware of Mathilde standing over her. Of Thierry, there was no sign. The bed beside her was empty. She opened her eyes. It was as if her vision had been cleaned as she slept. The sunlight was almost blinding. She smelled coffee, rich and intense.

'Where—?' she began.

'Monsieur left half an hour ago. Your friend is not here yet – it's unlike him to be late, isn't it?' Mathilde pulled the curtains wide, flooding the room with a light so vibrant it hurt Satin's eyes. She sat up, a shade unsteadily, and reached for the coffee.

'I'm starving,' she announced.

'We've only got some pastries. You didn't give me the money to go to the butcher.'

'Why do you need money?'

'Because Paparambourd says everything must be paid for in cash until your account is settled. He can extend no further credit.'

'Stupid man,' said Satin. She ate the food that Mathilde brought in, ravenous now. She wanted only to sleep, to while away the long hours until evening, but her clerk from the préfecture could not be delayed and she needed the money badly. She had given the last of the ready money she had to Thierry. The phial was still on the dressing table, unobtrusive among all the other bottles and jars.

She could smell his sperm still on her robe, between her legs. She arose, splashed water over her body from the bowl that Mathilde brought in, and then dressed. It was ridiculous – in half an hour she would be naked again. The feeling of having solid food in her belly calmed her down but she was jaded and irritable, always a dangerous combination. She looked around her at the chaotic room and ordered Mathilde to do what she could to make the mess look better. Her clerk was a fastidious man and the sight of such squalor would have distressed him. If she made him feel comfortable and at home, let him sense in her some of the order in which he enveloped himself, then he would be more willing to advance her the money she sought.

She drew in a deep breath, noting without a great deal of pleasure the reflection of her generously displayed bosom in the mirror. She reached for a perfume bottle and gently wafted its spray all over herself. It made her feel slightly nauseous. She scolded Mathilde for her sloth, for the clumsy way she moved about the room, knocking into things and getting in her way – he would be here in a minute and she didn't want the place to look like a pigsty. Then she poured herself a glass of brandy and settled down to wait. Her senses were inflamed still but it was a cold and angry feeling now, far removed from the Byzantine pleasures of the morning. She never did know what it was that Thierry added to the tincture of laudanum in the phials he brought her every month.

The clerk turned up at two, apologetic. He had been interviewing applicants for a subordinate position, but need not return until three. Satin pouted and looked most put out.

He agreed to lend her the money. It was a pushover.

The café. Another evening, much like any before it. The women were sitting at their customary table, by the door.

'I tell you, she married him for love,' Babette was insisting in the teeth of ferocious opposition. It was one of their favourite sources of gossip, the stories of the women of the street who had married into the nobility and lived happily ever after.

'Nonsense,' countered Colette. The Comte de Montsavant had been her own lover once – some years ago now – and she refused to believe him capable of encouraging such niceties of feeling in any woman, let alone anyone so hard-headed and practical as the new Comtesse, a former dancer born and brought up in the rookeries of the Marais. The scandal had enraged half of Paris.

'He was a pederast, in any case,' she went on when the hubbub had died down sufficient for her to make herself heard. 'He preferred boys, I'm sure of that. My, he had a vicious streak in him. No, she couldn't have married him for love. For his money, yes – what working girl wouldn't?'

'Apparently he lost most of his money gambling.'

'They were so rich, that family, that he could lose a fortune three times over and still have enough to let his mistress drive a coach and four.'

'What does she get out of it, then?'

'What does she get out of it? I'll tell you what she gets out of it. She gets the contempt of every one of his friends and especially their wives – the ones that are still speaking to them, that is. And she also gets their envy – envy that they can't be young and gay and beautiful, like she is. And not give a damn for them and their ways. That's what Giselle gets from the deal. That and a hundred thousand a year, at least.'

'I heard two.'

'I heard three.'

'You said he had no money.'

'She certainly didn't. I had to lend her a shift once, before she could go and see that mayor of hers. She only had one and that pimp she was with, the one who died in the knife-fight, had all but torn it off her back the night before when she didn't come home with enough for him to go gambling with.'

'He was a sort, wasn't he? Guy, his name was. He came from Carcassone – and that's where they buried him. A nasty piece of work.'

'You see Giselle now, and it's as though all that was water under the bridge.'

'She won't even look at me. I see her go by in her carriage and you'd think she hadn't even seen me. But I know she has.'

'The bitch.'

'Bitch is right.'

Satin sat pressed up close with the rest of the women, but took no part in the conversation. She was tired. She had not been to bed until seven that morning and had seen two men that afternoon. Thierry's tincture was exhausted now, and so was she. All she wanted was to go to bed and sleep for a week but she had bills to pay, a child to support.

This Sunday, she promised herself, she would take the trouble to go and see him. She did not often think of little

Armand but, when she did, it was usually at times like this, half-drunk already though it was only nine. He had passed his infancy with a wet nurse in Boursy and now he was quartered with a woman in a small town about an hour's journey away. Not so far that, when the sun was shining and she was in the mood, flush with wine and money, she could not get the train and dash down to see him with a collection of toys, balloons and tops and horses. Yet not so close that, when money was tight or there was a new lover to be pleased, she could not safely postpone her visit for another week – just as she had done the week before. Sometimes she felt guilty about it.

The conversation had turned, as it always did in the end, to money. How little of it there was about. How mean men were becoming. How rare, now, the days not so long ago, when there would be parties that went on for days, hundreds of guests, dozens and dozens of whores, everyone too drunk to notice. Now everything was all so – so pinched, so mean, so tight. Some of the whores, the really old ones, the ones who were forty or more, they could even remember the days of the King. It was all so different now, with the Emperor, the little bag of shit.

Satin hated these conversations. She was too young to remember things ever being any different but she – although she never dared admit it – had few complaints. Oh, for sure there were the bills and the debts, but everyone had those. No, there was still plenty of ready money to be had, here in the cafés or outside the theatres, in the discreet hotels along the Rue de Four or in small, two-room apartments, with officers on leave or noblemen up from the country, with prosperous tradesmen and even, once in a while, some bohemian out on a spree, whom you could fleece for the full whack while he'd be out so cold he never knew what he had or hadn't bought.

No, Satin was doing quite well, all other things considering. She had her apartment, she had Mathilde, she had nice clothes on her back and food in her belly. Some of the women – Chantal, Camille, Zoe, even Cosette and Felicité, who was only twenty-two – were worrying about becoming old, losing their looks. But Satin had no such concerns. She was nineteen, would not be twenty until November. She had many years yet ahead of her. Anything might happen.

And yet. And yet. Something in her was still not satisfied, some inner yearning that left her wanting more. It was like the tincture – there was never quite enough.

She realised, with a start, that she had almost nodded off in the heat of the café, her senses dulled by wine and monotonous conversation. She was glad of the warmth, for her thin dress was cut scandalously low to display her spectacular bosom to its best advantage, but she might have been glad of a breath of fresh air. Still, any minute now someone would come in and she'd be able to go off with them.

Every little while men would come to the tables where the whores were gathered, scanning anxiously the flesh and powder and fabric before them, the fluttering eyelashes, the arch expressions, the tacit invitations.

Some would move on, others would make their choice – a nod or even less would normally suffice. There would be a quick negotiation by the door and then they would go, to hotel or room or alleyway according to inclination and pocket, and then – surprisingly soon – the woman would return, another man serviced, a few more francs earned.

There was a man hanging around their table now. He looked like the type who fancied blondes, Satin found herself thinking. She was, after two years on the game, a pretty good judge of a man's whims. She hoped she was right, that he'd go for Chantal or Desirée, not for herself.

But he was looking straight at her, from under the brim of his hat. He was quite short and heavy set, in a thick brown overcoat, well cut. His eyes twinkled above luxurious moustaches. He would want to play baby-talk, she reasoned, or to pretend to be naughty. She hated men like that, the ones with the shrivelled wives who had given up trying to be their husband's mothers.

Feigning disinterestedness, she looked away, became engrossed in conversation with Babette. A new casino was opening near the Tivoli. There would be a splendid opening, next Thursday evening. Everyone was going – a whole crowd from Madame Subritski's house on the Avenue de l'Opéra. Satin could come with her. It would be fun, a great party. And afterwards.

The man went away. Satin felt herself brightening. She liked having something to look forward to, something more than going home to the apartment and a few, inadequate hours of sleep. Yes, she told Chantal, she would go. She would wear her new dress in organdie silk. Had Chantal seen it? She hadn't? Oh, but it was lovely. Madame Fitou had made it for her herself – she didn't trust any of the girls who worked for her. The buttons were mother of pearl, fifty centimes each. It was the most beautiful—

Chantal tapped her on the shoulder, interrupting her flow of words. A man was standing behind her. It was the same man, back again, his hat pulled down over his eyes. She sighed. Perhaps he wouldn't be long, a couple of quick frigs and he'd be done. He didn't look as though he had much staying power.

Reluctantly she rose to her feet but, on her face, was a smile of decorous pleasure. He spoke well, like a gentleman, but not quite well enough. She wondered if he were Jewish. There was an inflexion in his voice that puzzled her.

'Forgive me, Madame, for interrupting you,' he began. As was the custom, they had walked out into the street together to do business, past the doorman in his impressive uniform. He pretended not to see but everyone knew what went on.

'I wished to speak with you,' he began. Satin demurred.

She had heard it all and seen it all. His politeness may have been excessive but she knew better than to make judgements about people on the acquaintance of just a few moments.

To her surprise, he led her to another café, a little further down the Boulevard. What was this? Surely he knew the usual arrangements as well as she did. The Hotel de l'Oeiul was nearby. Her own apartment was close at hand, if necessary. She was glad her furniture had not been repossessed.

They took their seats. A small orchestra was playing at one end of the room. Satin did not often come here. 'Her sort' were not welcome, the management made plain – and yet the Café des Artistes, which was an altogether grander sort of place, made no bones about what went on. The man resumed his conversation.

'My name,' he said, 'is Herman Moscato.'

Satin nodded. It was a name she had not heard before, though he seemed to think it was significant. She introduced herself with exaggerated formality.

'I am the manager of the Theatre des Etoiles,' he continued. It was a large but unpopular theatre on the far side of the Tuileries. She had been there once or twice, many months ago now. The place smelled damp and musty and the play she had seen was unmemorable.

'I have a new production, opening in a month's time. I need an actress – a particular kind of actress. An actress with special talents.'

A waiter brought them drinks, a plate of sausages each. Satin was sure he was looking down his nose at her.

'I've never been on the stage,' said Satin, before he had the chance to ask her. She was good at anticipating a man's questions.

'It doesn't matter,' he said, tucking his napkin into his collar and attacking his food with gusto.

'What do you have in mind?' she said, intrigued.

'You would have very few words,' he said through mouthfuls of sausage, 'though your part is not small. And we would pay well.'

She raised an eyebrow. He named a figure. She smiled, rather more warmly than before, and nodded.

'Let me explain, then,' he said, and poured her another glass of wine.

Chapter Two

The play in which Satin had been asked to appear was, of course, arrant nonsense. It was a bit of fun, very much in the popular taste, a burlesque. The title, *Love's Plaything*, hinted at its vacuous nature. It had been constructed by Moscato and some fool playwright that he knew, a one-eyed Marbellaise called Cocon, purely to exploit the gullibility of the audience. Spectacle they wanted, and spectacle they got, a love story in the classical vein. With, Moscato hoped, a few good belly-laughs thrown in.

They sat there now in the auditorium at the Theatre des Etoiles, excited and expectant, like any other first-night crowd. It was a hot night, both inside and outside the theatre. In the boxes and stalls there were men in evening dress, women in formal gowns. High up in the gallery there was the rabble, the usual loud and foul-mouthed men and women who, admitted into this palace of the arts for but a few sous, would keep up a steady stream of interjections, profanities, oaths and catcalls that bore no relation to what was happening on the stage before them.

People gazed idly around, at the plush red curtains that hid the stage from view. Some of them craned their necks and looked upwards, to the ceiling far beyond the pendulous gas jets, where nymphs and cherubs, Mercuries and Venuses sported in splendid plaster-of-paris wantonness. There was that unique smell of the theatre, a curious compound of wet cardboard, old stairways, generations of dust and unwashed bodies.

The chatter was at its height. Outside, in the foyer, expensive people mingled, expecting to see and be seen. They would not take their seats until the very final moment, making their entrance at the most opportune time. People with less exalted positions in life went hurrying past, tickets at the ready, heading for the circle.

Those in the lobby tried to put names to faces. There was Prétédieu, the assistant to the Minister of the Interior, and next to him the Comte de Charleroi, a noted roué. That woman over there, the one in the stunning dress in burgundy silk – wasn't she Tabin, the mistress of the Chief of the Justices? And the woman she was talking to? Oh, that was Odette, over whom the Viscomte de Beaumondais fought a duel in the Jardin des Tuileries.

Cigar smoke rose in billowing clouds, to mingle with the perfume of two hundred women in the auditorium. And yet, still, it could not entirely drown out that distinctive theatre smell, the stench of decay and neglect. It seemed like an omen for the evening ahead.

And then, irrefutably, came the three loud knocks that signalled the play was about to begin. Final bons mots were exchanged, hands secretly squeezed, assignations arranged, whispered scandals hastily brought to a conclusion. The final stragglers made their way importantly through the heavy padded doors and into the auditorium. Uniformed attendants, tickets in hand, hurried them to their seats in the stalls and in their snug private boxes. An orchestra struck up a gay polonaise. The footlights flared, the curtain drew back, and the play began.

There were no murmurings until the evening's programme had been under way for close to fifteen minutes. Everyone was too absorbed studying the scenery – a shady grove, with classical allusions evinced by a ruined pillar and a distant hilltop temple – and the costumes. There were plenty of nubile young actresses running around in diaphanous folds, pursued by equally virile young men who appeared to be wearing winding sheets. It was a scene from Antiquity, evidently. The characters had Greek names. There was a great deal of merriment and good humour among the audience. Some of the jokes, said the assistant to the Minister of the Interior, were really rather clever.

The play itself seemed sparing of plot, economical too in its characterisation and dialogue. No one seemed really sure of what it was about, despite requests whispered behind programmes and fans. It was something to do with hunting, a red-faced man cheerfully proclaimed. Diana and her nymphs, said another playgoer. The fall of the Roman empire, insisted a third. Shut up and sit down, shouted a fat old woman with a hat covered in wax fruit.

Meanwhile, as everyone turned to see what the disturbance was and add their two centimes' worth, a man dressed as a warrior delivered a long and frankly meaningless peroration from the front of the stage. At the half-way point, there was a sudden commotion in the gods. A fight had broken out. Such interruptions were a commonplace in the Theatre des Etoiles, and after craning their necks to satisfy their momentary curiosity, the audience went back to the play, though with increasing restlessness. Flagging a bit, don't you think? said the man from the Ministry.

In a box high up by the side of the stage, Victor Baltheme was growing increasingly bored. The play, it was plain to see, was absolute tosh. It had started well, but then it just seemed to collapse, like an over-egged pudding. He had only agreed to come to the opening night because his friend Chambourcy had insisted. But Chambourcy had failed to turn up and now here he was, with his lady friend Felicité at his side. They had eaten well before the play, and drunk even better, and both of them were well into a state of intoxication as midnight approached. Felicité was looking forward to seeing how well her friend Satin would fare. As the play progressed, she grew increasingly anxious.

At first, Victor had assumed it was he who was muddled. As the play ploughed on, he had grown increasingly confused. What was going on? What was this damn play about? Was it one play or several short sketches, a series of tableaux? Or was it a burlesque? Songs would suddenly interrupt the dialogue for no reason. A winged chariot, at one stage, descended from the heavens and carried away the principal nymph, singing loudly and not entirely tunefully of her love for Aeneas.

Comparing notes with Felicité, he realised it wasn't him at all. She laughingly admitted she was as muddled as he, and kissed him on the cheek. The play was gibberish, a random collage of songs and speeches and scenes that had no cohesion that they could discern. The audience, who had been appreciative at first, was becoming increasingly amused by the antics on stage. The little ripples of laughter that had greeted the first signs of dramatic inadequacy grew into waves. As the interval approached, scenes of pathos – the death of a warrior, the loss of love – were greeted with open snorts of derision. The whole thing was a hoot. It was the best comedy Baltheme had seen in ages, although not as the writer had intended. This sort of piffle might be good enough for the peasants in Abbeville, but not in Paris. People were beginning to call out.

But even this inadvertent entertainment began to pall after a while. His hand strayed towards Felicité's thigh and encountered no resistance. Emboldened – for no one could see them in their box, on the highest level above the stage, almost directly level with the arch – he felt able to take further importunities. Soon Felicité was sitting on his lap, excitedly cuddling him. The great drama unfolded unheeded below them. She hoped she wouldn't miss Satin's entrance, she whispered to her lover. She didn't want it to come before he did.

She could feel his burgeoning erection through the trousers of his formal evening suit. They whispered inconsequentially to one another. How daring it was, to be seated thus in the theatre, with five hundred people sitting close at hand, none of them aware of the kissing and cuddling that was going on in the box above the stage. In their box they were safe from the attentions of the world.

Felicité put her arm around her lover. As with all her clients, she did not kiss him – this was a part of the unspoken etiquette of prostitution. But she would suck his cock, if he asked her to, and he took great pleasure from licking her vagina and breasts.

He nuzzled against her and his fingers found their way under her dress. Soon they were cupping her pubic mound. She parted her legs for him, feeling slightly drowsy in the heat of the gas flares.

His fingers roved across her pubic bush, stroking gently. She began to relax, snuggling down in his lap, parting her legs still further for him. Underneath her drawers, his fingertips moved delicately across the firm white flesh of her upper thighs, half-tickling her, making her feel aroused. She was looking forward to being entered by him. She enjoyed sex with almost all her clients. She had fucked several of them in this very theatre.

Baltheme's long, tapering fingers probed the slick folds of her outer labia. As she relaxed, so her arousal increased. He knew how to part her lips, to seek her intimate places. Most of all, he knew how to take his time. He was one of the best. She liked to go with him. He paid her well, too.

Gently, with consummate care, he eased first one finger inside her, then two. She moaned, and pressed herself closer to him. The ball of his hand was rubbing against her clitoris, almost too hard. She made him pause momentarily, and take things more gently. She felt she was going to come.

Felicité was wearing a white gown, cut very low at the front in the current fashion – the fashion, that is, among women of her standing. She was one of the more expensive ladies of the Boulevard St Germain. Men liked a little excitement from the way she dressed but, when they went out with her, they also expected a measure of discretion. Her breasts were all but bared only in the seclusion of their box. In the foyer, in the restaurant earlier, her jacket had hidden her snowy bosom from prying eyes.

She was heavily corseted underneath her dress but somehow he managed to work his hand inside her décolletage and free her breasts. Now she felt abjectly wanton, her prominent nipples exposed to his hungry gaze. She pushed her breast at him, wanting him to lick the nipple. He did so and a thrill shot through her – she was sure her nipples were abnormally sensitive. She suddenly felt more aroused, eager, anxious to have him inside her. She was conscious of her own wetness as his fingers probed her, of the hardness of his erection pressing against her buttocks through the expensive material of their clothes.

As if he could read her mind he pushed her off him. Down below the scene was reaching a crescendo. There was a lot of shouting on the stage but they were oblivious to it. She got busy with the flap of his trousers, kneeling beside him as he sprawled in his cheap, gilded chair. His penis was thick and circumcised, the end a delicate purple. Few clients could bring her to orgasm during intercourse but Baltheme was one of them. He had a way with him, a power, a feeling for the rhythms of her body. She dipped her head down and sucked at the end of his cock. She could still taste cunt on it, her own. They had fucked in the room she rented near the church of St Germaine before coming out to the theatre.

Hiking up her skirts, she leaned forward over the edge of the box. She could see the stage below her, a hand in the box below holding a programme. The box beside theirs was unoccupied. He climbed quickly up behind her, his penis slipping inside her, pushing aside the walls of her vagina. She felt swollen with him, reached out and grasped the cushioned edge of their box. A hunting scene was in progress below.

'Fuck my cunt,' she suddenly found herself saying mechanically, without knowing why. 'I want that big, thick cock inside me.'

She often talked like this with her clients. It seemed to excite them, to hear a woman use these words certainly worked with Baltheme. He wanted to come, she could tell. He powered into her from behind, pressing her thighs, fucking her through her fine linen drawers. She liked the feel of the material against her skin; she liked to wear silk too, she had silk and satin underwear both for her own pleasure and to excite her clients. She could feel how hard his thighs were against hers, with what effort he was pressing into her. She braced herself against the edge of the box and spread her legs more to accommodate him.

He grasped her around the waist, pulling her on to his thrusting cock in a demonstration of his considerable strength. He thrust into her again and again with short, savage stabbing movements, swaggering with the thickness of his cock – she knew he was immensely proud of it – and his domination of her. She came quickly and undemonstrably – it had not been as exciting as she had anticipated. Perhaps, deep down, he was just another client to her. She felt his semen pour out in a sequence of throbs, heard him half-cry out something that was drowned in the din from the stage and the hoarse cries of the audience below them.

He pulled his penis out of her. She felt the wetness run out of her almost immediately, discreetly, she tucked the hem of her chemise between her legs. Once, she remembered fucking a client in similar circumstances and was embarrassed when his semen ran down her thighs, down her stockings and, she was quite sure, on to the floor beneath them. She sat down again, was aware of him discreetly adjusting his clothing, straightening the cravat that had been pulled askew in the passion of their love-making. Had she missed anything? No, they were just coming to the end of the first act.

The interval seemed exceptionally long. From time to time anxious faces appeared and disappeared through doors marked 'private'. In the foyer people were animatedly discussing what they had seen. Quite a few were making their way to the exits.

'Rubbish.'

'Appalling.'

'The funniest thing I've ever seen.'

'It's not meant to be funny.'

'I know.'

Everyone seemed to be in remarkably good humour, considering how much they had wasted on their admission tickets.

Baltheme and Felicité, both a trifle flushed after their exertions during the first act, were standing with a group of friends.

'It's hysterical,' proclaimed Baltheme. 'I couldn't work out what was going on.'

'Did you see that hunting scene?' asked his friend Labouche.

'Oh yes,' Baltheme agreed. In fact, he had glimpsed it only sparingly over Felicité's shoulder.

'Hilarious,' added Felicité, who was scarcely any the wiser. But she felt sorry for Satin, although she was the only one of the girls who had come to the theatre that night. 'I thought I was going to burst out of my stays just watching.'

Everyone guffawed loudly. Felicité caught Baltheme's eye and winked. Only they knew the truth in her statement.

There was time, surprisingly, for a second glass, and then a third. It seemed like the interval was going to go on indefinitely. Baltheme was feeling distinctly merry. He had quite a fancy for taking Felicité again during the second act.

A group of people pushed their way over towards them through the throng.

'We're going to the Café des Artistes,' said a gentleman that Baltheme knew well from the bordello on the Rue du Tivoli. 'Are you coming?'

Baltheme felt tempted. Felicité looked at him expectantly.

'Maybe later,' he said. 'I want to catch the next act. But if it's as bad as the first, I won't bother with the third act.'

'Maybe we'll see you later, then,' said his friend. 'Let us know what happens, won't you?'

But the second act, if anything, made an even more unpromising start than the first. The scene had changed to a garden. The setting couldn't be faulted – it was a beautiful rose-strewn bower, filled with exquisite sculpture – but the dialogue was stilted to the point of inanity. Baltheme, bored stiff and wanting a drink, sat in his box and shuffled his feet impatiently. Maybe he should have gone to the Café des Artistes with his friend, after all.

He was beginning to fondle Felicité again, exchanging delicious obscenities, when a sudden commotion caused him to divert his attentions to the stage. He peered over the balcony, craning his neck to get a better view. There was a sharp intake of breath from the audience.

On the stage, one of the statues had suddenly moved. It was, even he could tell, intended as a representation of Aphrodite, the goddess of love. She seemed to be casting some spell over the two lovers whose travails had, in among the inanities of the hunting scene and a shipwreck, occupied much of the proceedings of the first act.

That, in itself, was nothing special to an audience grown jaded with spectacles of sight and sound. What had caused such a commotion in the stalls and boxes – to say nothing of the near-pandemonium in the cheaper seats – was the fact that Aphrodite herself appeared to be totally naked.

Baltheme peered hard at the stage, wishing his vanity did

not preclude him from wearing in public the eye-glasses he had been prescribed. He felt an involuntary thrill deep in his belly, that quickly travelled the length of his penis.

She was naked, he was sure. And what an Aphrodite she was to behold, tall and full-figured, her generous breasts set off by masses of white ringlets, her thighs ample and welcoming. She was a voluptuous Venus indeed and, as she walked a few simple steps across the stage to cast flower-petals over the lovers, her breasts seemed to quiver. She turned round and displayed, to the audience's astonished gaze, her beautifully rounded buttocks, a vision of desire made flesh.

He stared hard at her, unable to believe his eyes. Her body was a delicious whiteness, so smooth, so elegant. Only when he had been staring at her for a full two minutes – during which time almost nothing of any note had taken place on the stage, so all-engrossing was this pose – did he realise that she was clad from head to toe in some clinging all-over garment, the very colour of nudity.

Whatever modesty it concealed, it left absolutely nothing to the imagination. Breasts, arms, thighs – all were revealed to Baltheme's astonished gaze. He looked across at Felicité. She was watching too, rapt, unable to believe her eyes either.

Satin had made her appearance.

A hush had fallen over the audience now. They watched in near-total silence as Aphrodite picked up a second basket of flowers – displaying, as she did so, those enticingly generous bottom-cheeks – and cast them gaily over the scene. Then she glided slowly back to the rear of the stage and the empty plinth she had so recently vacated among the other statues.

She resumed her pose, as silent and static as those other figures cast in plaster. The orchestra played on, a wistful air, quite unheeded by the audience. The curtain came down almost unnoticed.

Then all hell broke loose. There was whistling and stamping of feet, applause from the stalls, lewd shouts from the gods. Men stood up and shouted to each other, scarcely believing their eyes. Women of a respectable kind pursed their lips, while those less reputable threw back their heads and laughed aloud.

'Did you see that?' asked Baltheme when he had recovered his wits. He felt confusion and arousal in equal measure.

'Of course I did,' said Felicité, with more than a hint of jealousy in her voice.

'That wasn't in the programme, was it?'

'I don't know. But I know who she was.'

'Aphrodite? Who was she?'

'Just someone I know.'

'Who?'

'Like I said, just someone I know.'

'You're not jealous, are you?'

'Me, jealous? Why should I be jealous?'

'Nonsense. A woman with tits like that? Come on, Felicité, who is she?'

'Her name's Satin. She's a friend. You see her in the Café des Artistes. She hangs around with that crowd. She used to be kept by a man from the treasury office but not any longer. This is how she makes a crust now. Don't you think she was brilliant?'

Fuddled as he was by drink, tiredness and desire, Baltheme could nevertheless sense the slight hint of jealousy in her voice. Whatever the merits or otherwise of the play, Satin's appearance had been a sensation. In all his years of theatre-going, he had never seen anything quite so daring on the stage before. He wondered how they had ever got it past the chamberlain's men. The impression of nakedness was almost perfect, as was Satin's body.

No one left during the second interval. People saw merit in the most pathetic comings and goings on stage. Soliloquies were greeted with rapt attention, songs were applauded vigorously. And then, finally, came the moment they had all been waiting for, the reappearance of Aphrodite.

She was wearing a diaphanous robe of the sheerest material, flowing down from her shoulders. It had the effect not of hiding but rather of emphasising her evident nudity. After a few initial shouts and catcalls, she had the theatre watching in total silence as she made her way to the front of the stage.

She paused for what, in dramatic terms, would have been an embarrassingly long time. Yet not a sound broke the silence as the audience, men as well as women, drank in those stupendous breasts, the ringlets, the voluptuous hips and thighs. Her face, as pretty as a picture, was artfully made up to make the most of her huge eyes, her pretty nose.

She glanced at the conductor and the orchestra struck up. The song was trite, almost infantile, Aphrodite's voice wavering like a tight-rope walker at the circus, and she sang the second verse twice in a childlike falsetto, but people were not listening for her tone and diction.

When she finally teetered her way to the final chorus, the dying chords of the orchestra were drowned by a tidal wave of applause. If anything, the reception was even more hysterical than that which had greeted her first appearance. Baltheme clapped and drummed his feet until his palms ached and glowed red. Felicité, looking distinctly envious, merely applauded as much as politeness dictated. Before they quite knew what was happening, the final curtain came down and they found themselves out on the pavement in front of the theatre.

With almost indecent haste, Baltheme hurried Felicité into a nearly hotel that rented rooms by the hour. They were both exhilarated and half-drunk, as if they had been drinking champagne on empty stomachs (which, earlier on, they had). He was lewdly aroused, she sexually inflamed too but also driven by feelings of faint jealousy – a potentially explosive mixture. It was as if she wanted to prove herself, to show that she could match Satin, however close their friendship had once been.

They fell on each other not so much as carnal gourmets enjoying a final, exquisitely prepared course to conclude the evening's entertainments, but like hungry animals.

'Watch this,' she said as she stood at the head of the bed on which he was sprawled naked, his penis standing up to attention, swollen and potent.

Her tight, silken dress with the low-cut bodice had been attracting attention all evening. It was the colour of ripe grapes. It seemed almost sprayed on, moulded to her body as far as her hips, but then flaring sensually outwards. As she'd expected, it had drawn more than the usual number of glances – admiring, innocent and otherwise – from the men and women at the theatre.

The dress dropped lazily from her shoulders and fell in a soft heap at her feet. Underneath it she was clad in her stays, her chemise and her drawers. These came off too. Then she was entirely naked apart from her boots and stockings. Her breasts were small but perfectly proportioned.

Baltheme's eyes visibly started. Full nakedness was almost unknown, even among the recherché hedonists of Paris. This was running it very close.

'You mean –' he began, but then words failed him.

'Do you like what you see?' she asked him. 'Do you think I look better than she does?'

She loved his excited confusion.

'Of course you do,' he said, but she could see he was lying. 'I love to see you naked.'

'Sometimes I go out in the evening with just the dress on, and nothing underneath except my stockings.'

She could see him gulp. She saw his hand stray involuntarily towards his penis. Then, in a trice, he was on his feet and at her side. He kissed her passionately, hungrily, inflamed by her wickedness. He liked a streak of exhibitionism in women – that was what had got him so excited about Satin. He wished he was with her now, making her suck his cock. He wondered if he might try and afford an introduction to her. Felicité said she knew the circle she moved in, it should be easy. She didn't say she had been to bed with her herself, more than once.

As if she could sense the fever that was coursing through his brain like a red mist of passion, Felicité returned his embrace with interest, caught up in the mood of the moment, the sense of wickedness and slighted prurience and infinite possibilities. Knowing Satin, she felt she was a part of the display on stage, that she too had contributed to her friend's success. She enjoyed basking in her reflected glory. She rubbed her bare pussy against his hard thigh and he could sense the wet trail that it left against his flesh.

'Fuck me now,' she breathed. 'I want your cock up me.'

She was like an animal on heat. She all but dragged him to the bed, pulled him on top of her and into her. Her vagina was wet and welcoming, easily absorbing him on his first thrust. Her eyes were open but she hardly seemed to see anything any more, the room with its expensive furnishings, the bed linen – she was aware of the rare luxury of fresh clean sheets – even the man who was powering into her. The evening had belonged to Satin but she was determined that she should have a share in it herself. For the moment, the world could serve her. She would show what kind of woman she was. She wanted to make Baltheme want her just as badly as he seemed to want Satin. He would be her servant, though he did not know it.

And serve her Baltheme did, sometimes like a bull, sometimes tenderly and caringly – whatever the motions of her body and her words dictated. Sometimes she spoke softly, sometimes she almost snarled. She felt herself floating high over the bed, looking down on their inter-twined bodies, seeing his hard, muscular backside pumping down and into her, seeing her arms splayed across the bed, her dark hair, her long legs.

He turned her over, pushing into her from behind. His hands clasped her thighs, kneading the muscles, sliding up and down the smooth creamy flesh that was already slick with sweat. The atmosphere in the room was close and the sheets had not been aired. His wrists brushed her pubic hair and then his finger was seeking her clitoris, finding it, touching it with a gentleness that contrasted with the violence of his lovemaking. How could he be both things at once? she found herself wondering. The brute and the aesthete, and yet somehow he was.

Felicité didn't always like her men to be rough with her but tonight was one of those times. After all the consid-ered, elegant conversations in the foyer at the theatre, the murmured understatements, the hints and the innuen-does, and then the sensation that was Satin on stage – here was a chance for her to release herself, to show her own potency, to kick and struggle and bite, to suck and whimper, to writhe and claw and shout and swallow. Everything Satin was, she was too. They were friends, after all.

She needed the release, and she came in a gigantic shuddering climax of epic proportions – it seemed to go on and on and on, until she felt she had absolutely no control over her body any more. When she finally came round she found herself almost falling out of the bed, with the sheets wrapped round her calves and her body soaked with sweat and Baltheme's semen.

They had the room for an hour. Wine was brought to them, and they drank it naked in front of the fire. Then they got back on to the broad divan-bed and she sucked him to stiffness again. Climbing on top of him, amid tangled sheets, she impaled herself with her back to him, facing the fire.

'Can you see my arsehole?' she asked.

'Mmm,' he said, content just to lie there while she bobbed up and down on his shaft. I'll show you, you bastard, she said to herself. She was quite fond of Baltheme really but she was determined to revenge herself on him. She wanted to show him just what kind of woman he was dealing with. That Satin – she was all tits and thighs and big eyes, nothing at all between the ears. And her voice – it was like a sparrow squeaking, ridiculous. It was one thing to flaunt herself in front of all those lecherous men but how she had the nerve to sing in front of them as well, well that was something quite beyond her understanding.

'Do you want to put it in me there?'

He had been kneading the muscles of her upper thighs as she bent forwards over him, running his fingers over the silky material of her stockings. He suddenly stopped. She sensed a hesitancy.

She wanted him to do it to her. He liked her to put her fingers inside him but he had never penetrated her in that way before. There were two or three men she had done it with, and she had not greatly liked it. She thought she could learn. If she let other men ease her out a little first then she might get more business – things had been tight lately. She knew what to do.

'Yes,' he said. 'I'd like that.'

She climbed off him. She felt light-headed and sensed her heart was beating fast. Satin wouldn't do something like that, she told herself. Even in her business, there was from time to time the sense of the forbidden. Not many girls, even in such a liberal establishment as this, offered their arses, for payment or otherwise. She wondered, ultimately, how far she would go with these men, what forbidden fruit she would taste. She knew all about the diseases she ran the risk of contracting but this was something else. She wondered if she were descending into hell.

His penis made her gasp when he first entered her. Her head swam and she wondered if she would regret her eagerness. At first he put only the swollen tip into her but then her muscles began to relax and she felt she could absorb more of him. It was not comfortable for her but there was the raging sense of desire to fuel her and drive her onwards – not a desire for Baltheme, but a desire to show herself the equal of Satin.

To her surprise she came quickly and easily, her fingers brushing her exposed clitoris. She had only to move her hips a fraction and it seemed like she had impaled herself on a cucumber. All the while a red mist of madness ran through her mind until she was no longer kneeling by the bedside in Madame Bohou's hotel on the Boulevard St Michel, but was in some exalted place that was entirely her own.

She was just as good as Satin, when it came down to it. She knew that now, had proved it by the way she had fucked Baltheme. But she could never have done what she had done there on the stage. And it was exciting to feel that she, Felicité, had a part in her success, however small. She looked forward to seeing her again, to offer her congratulations. She sank on to her face in the covers, smiling as she thought of the time she and Satin had gone with the pork-butcher from Neuilly, and scarcely even felt it when Baltheme removed his flagging penis and began to dress.

Alphonse Duruflé, a gentleman of independent means, was almost beside himself with excitement as he climbed into the carriage outside the Theatre des Etoiles with his wife Mimi. Never, in all his years of theatre-going, had he seen a display of such wanton abandon on the stage as he had just witnessed. The play, of course was at best a farrago and at worst, the purest piffle.

But that woman, whose name he had read over and over again in the programme in mystified reverence. Satin. She had been a sensation. He had watched the whole of the final two acts with his penis almost straining to break free from his breeches and it was as much as he could do not to fall on his wife there and then in the fifth row of the stalls.

As soon as they were snug inside their carriage – though it was a hot night in the city, and the first of the heavy summer rains had fallen only last night – he had all but thrown himself upon her. His advances, he was reassured to find, were by no means repulsed. In their youth, perhaps, he and Mimi had done these things quite often – most memorably, in a first-class carriage on the Paris-Orleáns railway. But not so often now, as the middle time of life approached for both of them. They had not made love since Saturday.

Mimi answered his embraces warmly. Her tongue flickered out to seek his own. He was intoxicated both by the events he had witnessed at the theatre and by his wife's own beauty and presence. She was a tall woman, well built, with generous breasts and a slender waist. She was often assumed to be ten years younger than she really was.

Her tempting bosom was impregnable behind her coat, dress and stays but he was able to slide his hand up under her skirt without undue difficulty, despite the lurching of the carriage. He had taken the precaution of pulling down the blinds, mindful of what might ensue. Despite the stuffiness and the humid air, he didn't want prying eyes spying on their passion. This sort of thing might be fashionable among the young beaux who haunted the parks and stews of Paris but it was not the sort of thing that a man of his age and position ought to be party to.

Mimi parted her legs invitingly. His hand progressed slowly, seeking to arouse her by degrees. Their lips still together, he ran his fingers delicately over her calves and knees, touching the pretty silk garters that held her stockings in place. Then higher, across the little expanse of warm, bare flesh of her thighs before he encountered the cotton and lace of her drawers.

Mimi sighed in his arms. Her hand stole down into his lap, brushing against the hardness of his erection. He shifted his position, thrown halfway across her by the convolutions of the carriage's movements, and then she was busy with the buttons on the front of his trousers.

At that same moment his own hand stole in, like a burglar by moonlight, amid the gap in her drawers and there – as she raised up her backside from the hard, leather seat – was his prize, warm and wet and slickly inviting.

He had an overwhelming desire to pay homage to that most individual of shrines. Heedless of the dust on the floor of the carriage and its rolling motion as it rattled down the midnight streets of the city, he quickly knelt down before his wife and parted her legs. She knew what to do with practised ease. As she hiked up her skirts and petticoats he buried his face in the musky warmth between her thighs and inhaled deeply and appreciatively.

Then his tongue began to flicker forth and probe among those sweet oyster lips, the incomprehensible folds, the deep cleft that hinted at so many wonders and mysteries to enjoy together. He used just the tip of his tongue at first, the delicate taste buds responding to the familiar feisty sweetness of his wife.

She moaned, ran her hands through his hair. The carriage lurched, almost throwing him off balance. He could feel the rumble of the wheels over the cobblestones through his knees.

She spread her legs even more for him, drawing herself up on the seat to make it easier for him. Surrounded by billowing snowy lingerie he lapped on, his mouth now wide open, drinking in her sweet essences, rubbing his lips hungrily against hair and flesh, warm and slick with her secretions. She had been soaking wet even when his fingers had first probed the chink in her drawers.

And then his tongue began its slow, insidious work, gently running up and down the length of her labia as she had so patiently taught and encouraged him to do. She sighed, and gasped, and moaned, and then the folds seemed to open up like an oyster before him and the tip of his tongue found the sweet little nut of her clitoris.

He touched it delicately, barely brushing against it, as he might taste a dessert on the very tip of his spoon. He touched it again and Mimi shivered, quite still now. He was astonished – never ceased to be astonished – at the extraordinary sensitivity of his wife's anatomy. His own penis seemed positively clumsy in comparison when, as now, he reached his hand down inside his own trousers and took hold of his manhood and began to pump it up and down.

Neither of them could wait so very long now, even though it was a good twenty minutes' ride by carriage to their home in the Invalides, among the large stuccoed houses of the very wealthy. Such respectable people, such disreputable goings-on! He chuckled to himself. There was a mounting tide of excitement coursing through him and he willed his sperm to stay back in his balls until his prick could safely find its lodging inside his wife. For Mimi, the edge of a precipice seemed to be rushing up to meet her at incredible speed.

She almost hauled him on top of her, her head crushed back against the seat so that her hat tilted at a crazy angle. She pushed out her hips to greet him and then he was inside her, kneeling down on the floor of their jolting carriage as it rattled through the night-time streets of Paris.

That woman – the thought kept going through Alphonse's head, he felt a vague guilt to be thinking, as he not infrequently did, of some other woman while making love to his wife, perhaps the feeling enhanced his enjoyment all the more – those breasts, those stupendous thighs. It was all too much.

He had his hands cupped under his wife's generous buttocks as she raised up her body to meet his every thrust, strong and confident in her love-making. He could feel leather, lace, flesh and fustian, was aware of the extraordinary combination of harness and padding underneath a woman's dress, without which she dare not venture into the streets. He pumped away, again with the vision of Satin looming in his mind, and a crazy voluptuousness seemed to flood through him.

He came in a seething torrent as their carriage clipped along the Rue St Dominique, shipwrecking himself between his wife's thighs on a sea of foaming lace. He could feel her spending with him, the harsh panting gasps that escaped from her lips like the last bubbles of air from a drowning sailor.

And then both of them became lifeless and inert, their bodies flopping against one another as all will and urgency ebbed away from them. For a few moments they were like sacks of grain floating on the current, as the carriage lurched around corners and bumped over the lumpen streets, their minds sated and full.

And then consciousness returned to Alphonse with a rush. He tugged up his linen and his trousers, hastily peeked out of the window. Great heavens, the Avenue Bosquet already? They would be home in five minutes, even less. He looked at his wife, at her crooked hat above her wanton smile, and she smiled back at him and winked.

He would have Clothilde bring them champagne, he thought, once they got home, and perhaps a dish of oysters. And then they would fuck each other senseless until well into the small hours.

* * *

51

Several hours after midnight, the restaurant was still absolutely crowded. Numerous parties seemed to be going on at the same time. On the right, was a swirling hubbub of demi-mondaines, all eyes and hair and false smiles, stabbing each other in the back and laughing hugely as they did so. On the left, was a table where the theatre critics sat and shouted, their reports now filed.

The papers, when they finally arrived at a later hour of the morning, would contain some decidedly mixed reviews. Some, in fact, were quite stinging, openly contemptuous of *Love's Plaything* and its voluptuous star. But, for the moment, the critics were content to leave things very much as they were, vainly lying to each other, full of false bonhomie and gaiety while underneath the champagne-fuelled jollity, old angers and jealousies simmered like a bouillabaisse.

In the middle, where three or four tables had been hastily pushed together, were Satin and Moscato and about a hundred other assorted well-wishers and sycophants.

Moscato was beaming from ear to ear as he puffed on a fat cigar, his little eyes twinkling.

'I always knew this one would be a winner,' he said, smugness pervading his every mannerism. 'All the way.'

The audience's extreme restlessness during the first couple of acts had been conveniently forgotten. But Moscato made a mental note to speak in the morning to Cocon, the playwright – if either of them were sober enough – to get a few of the lines changed for the next performance. Nothing too drastic of course, just a little snip here and there, a word or two that might be altered. Nothing at all for Cocon to worry about. He got very upset if people meddled with his plays. His one good eye would roll around in his head and he would get very angry.

He leaned over to where Satin was sitting and planted a big wet kiss on the side of her cheek.

'And how does it feel to be a star?' he asked her for

perhaps the fifth or sixth time that evening.

Satin was sipping champagne, eating canapés and holding three conversations, all at the same time.

'Fabulous, darling,' she said, without looking at him. She'd had to sleep with him, of course, to be sure of getting her part but now, already, she felt that was behind her now. Patric Esteve, the drama critic, was paying court to her at that moment. Handsome, rich, intelligent – what did she need of Moscato's favours? She would have to humour him, though, all the same.

But the impresario would not be deterred so easily. He placed a proprietorial hand on Satin's knee. She permitted him this liberty, but there was no warmth in her heart for this man who, in the space of a few short weeks, had elevated her from prostitution to stardom.

She took another sip of champagne and flashed Moscato a beaming smile.

'How sweet of you to have the party here,' she said, gesturing at the expensive room with its gilt mirrors and twinkling chandeliers. This place made even the Café des Artistes seem like a tip. Champagne spilled from her overflowing glass all over someone's trousers, greeted with a roar of laughter.

Moscato grinned back. 'It's nothing,' he said, still beaming. 'Nothing at all. This is just the beginning.'

She reached across a minor aristocrat and placed a finger on Moscato's cheek.

'Now you be a good boy,' she whispered breathily at him. 'I'm talking to nice M Esteve here, who has just got back from his newspaper office and tells me he has said some very kind things about me.'

Satin turned again to Patric Esteve.

'Do you think I'm near enough to the front of the stage?' she asked him. 'I mean, when I come to life in the statue scene, do you think people can see me clearly enough. Surely I should be much nearer the front?'

Esteve's brow furrowed. Of course she should stay where she was, on her pedestal. If she was any further forward she would interfere with the whole dramatic course of the scene, getting in the actors' way and generally disrupting things. Not that that would matter much, in a shambles such as *Love's Plaything* had been. Besides, when the curtain came down at the end of the scene and with it the new backdrop, her plinth would be left isolated at centre stage, in the middle of the Emperor's bedchamber. Her ideas were plainly ridiculous, fuelled entirely by vanity and by her woeful ignorance of theatrical protocol. He felt contemptuous of her acting abilities but her breasts were undeniably spectacular.

Esteve smiled and his dark eyes twinkled. 'What a marvellous idea,' he said flatteringly. 'I'm surprised no one's suggested it before.'

Satin looked thrilled. 'Do you think so?' she asked. 'I mean, really?'

'Of course,' he said, still with the smile fixed on his face. 'I think it could make all the difference.'

It would make a ridiculous scene even more ridiculous, he told himself. But his eyes lingered over Satin's snowy white bosom, and in his mind he recalled those voluptuous thighs, the perfect half-moons of her backside as she walked across the stage before a spellbound audience. Here, if ever there was one, was a woman whom he was determined to conquer. He would use any of the considerable means at his disposal – money, charm, charisma – to achieve that aim.

Satin drank more champagne, secure in the sincerity of Esteve. She gazed around the room, acknowledging the smiles and gestures of others. All kinds of people were here, at least half a dozen assorted counts and viscounts, the cream of Paris society, some very well-known actors and actresses. Why, over there was Labelle, the most famous chanteuse of her day. Satin couldn't believe that she was in the same room as her idol, still less that they had exchanged a few words of congratulation with each other.

Of course, the party was not for her sole benefit. Even a woman as vain as she understood that. Names infinitely better known than hers were involved in *Love's Plaything* – Boffon, for instance, whose very presence on a playbill could draw theatre-goers in their hundreds, night after night, even though he was now so old and infirm he could only take small parts. Or the large and looming Sinbade, born to be a clown with his lugubrious face and deep, *basso profundo* voice. And she could not forget Cathérine Ventoux, the singer of risqué songs who, though she was nearly forty now, had allegedly been the lover of Montparnasse and, before him, the Duc de Benelux.

Satin's mind reeled. It was incredible, really, too much to take in on top of a dozen glasses of champagne. But even without the wine, she would have felt intoxicated. Men were hanging on her every word. She only had to pass the most inconsequential remark and they doubled up with laughter, as though she had come out with some exquisite gem of wit. How very different to sitting there at the Café des Artistes, waiting for the customers to make their choice, like a piece of meat on a butcher's slab.

She had dressed with provocative abandon for the occasion. What did they expect, this woman who could appear before six hundred people clad in a nude bodystocking? Now, she was wearing a dress of purple silk cut so low at the front that even the notoriously wanton Cathérine Ventoux had gawped for a moment before recovering her composure. Those spectacular bosoms were now thrust out invitingly. The men crowding around her, at her shoulder and at her table, had a clear view almost as far as her navel. But it was only as she had intended.

Later, she and Patric Esteve managed to slip away together, under the pretext of going their separate ways. They went to a hotel he often frequented near the Gare de Lyon, that knew better than to query the arrival of two expensively dressed guests at such an hour, being so close to the railway station, at which tired travellers might be disgorged at any hour of the day or night, seeking food, warmth and shelter.

They went at each other's bodies hungrily, Patric still in his shirt and tie, Satin naked apart from her chemise, her dress and stays tossed carelessly aside after he had all but torn them off her in his haste. His penis slid massively and immediately inside her and the shock made her gasp. There were none of the usual preliminaries. That had all been taken care of back at the restaurant, in the increasing intimacy of their conversation and in their half-dazed cab ride through the streets.

The bed at the hotel in the Rue Champetre was soft and low and Satin was aware of the scent of other women's perfume that hung around the room like an exotic cloud. Plainly, they were not the only couple to have used the room that night. It gave her that familiar feeling of illicitness, as though she were an adulteress, smuggled into the family home with all its strange scents of the occupation of others. She enjoyed the sensation. As she ground her hips against Patric, she knew how well suited she was to her vocation.

Was he married? Did he have a lover, a mistress? She hadn't asked. She was too full of the excitement at being the centre of attention to care about others. And yet she welcomed him into her like a long-lost friend, her nerve-ends alive to every last nuance of sensation. Oh, but he was handsome, those dark flashing eyes, the blue-chinned face. She sensed at once how fired up he was, how she needed to do little more than to lie back and let the urgent, remorseless waves of his passion sweep over her, carrying herself away in their wash. His immediacy surprised her – she had scarcely guessed how much he had been holding back his pent-up feelings.

He powered into her with short, sharp thrusts, his hands under her backside, pulling her hips up towards him. She let herself go with the tide and she came almost immediately, alive with sensation. Still the remorseless rhythms of his hips and thighs bore down on her, into her, and she came again and again in a mounting paroxysm of lust, scarcely noticing even the shuddering sequence of convulsions with which he climaxed inside her.

Finally his powerful shoulders were stilled, and he sank down on to her breast. His breathing, like hers, was short and ragged with all the exertion of their love-making. She could feel his chest rising and falling against hers, felt his penis slip out of her and trail wetly and plumply across her thigh.

She opened her eyes and looked at the yellowing ceiling, the gas mantle over their heads. Outside, dawn had just broken.

Patric rolled over on to his back and sat up, panting for breath.

'My God,' he exclaimed. 'I thought I was going to explode.'

She smiled, kissed him gently on the cheek. Intoxicated by champagne and sated desire, she fell back into a light doze. She awoke when she heard the door click. He had gone so soon?

She was aware of his come seeping out of her vagina. The sheets were clean and fresh, so she discreetly tucked her chemise between her legs. It did not always do to make a mess in a hotel room, especially if she might be back there again in half an hour with another man. There was nothing worse than fucking one man amid the come stains of others.

Then she heard him return. It could have been ten minutes later, or an hour. She did not know and she did not care.

'I went to get the first edition of *Paris-Express*,' he explained. 'The kiosk at the station is open.'

'Oh, do let me see,' she cried, impatient for the sight of her own name in print for the first time.

He sat down beside her but the newspaper slid to the floor. 'All in good time,' he murmured. He put his arm around her shoulders and stroked her hair, and she knew his appetites were not yet slaked. She felt herself succumbing to his charms, even as he murmured subtle little flatteries in her ear. She forgot about the review in *Paris-Express*. It would only say the kind of thing he had already said to her, a dozen times already that evening. In a few minutes she reached down and took hold of his penis. It felt sticky and heavy and yet it stiffened perceptibly under her touch. She could feel it rising and hardening under her expert touch, filling with expectancy.

She half-turned towards him, arching her back and pressing her pubic hair against his hard, masculine thigh. She began to rub herself against him in a slow, sensual, unambiguous movement. His penis, she noticed, was already stiff and ready for her.

Still she prolonged the movement, building up not just a rhythm but a mood, a strange kind of dance. His arms reached out for her and his hands were against her breasts, taking their full weight, feeling the hardness of their tips. With surprising delicacy he eased the chemise up over her shoulders and dropped it on to the floor beside them. Now she was as naked as he was.

She kissed him, still grinding her hips against him. And then, without dropping a beat, she rolled over lithely on to her front, moving like a snake, and knelt up on all fours. He half-sat beside her, mesmerised. Parting her legs as far

58

as she could, she pressed her backside against him, aware of the bouncing, jiggling movements of her breasts as she did so. She felt like a bitch on heat – lewd and sexually demanding. Patric was powerless to resist.

She reached behind herself and parted the soft cheeks of her backside, revealing to her lover's captivated gaze the pink flushed lips of her sex, engorged with blood and lust, slick with her secretions. Patric, she had noticed, was a man who liked to look. Some men preferred to do it with their eyes closed and the lights out. He was different.

'What are you waiting for?' she breathed and then she dropped forward on to her elbows. 'Can't you see my cunt's ready and waiting?'

She could feel the sweat on his body, could smell her own desire for him. He moved around behind her and she could feel his hands on her back, his penis probing her, sliding down the furrow between her cheeks, and then he was against the entrance to her vagina and she had taken him in one hand and almost pulled him into her.

He pushed hard and was almost instantly swallowed up inside her, his strong hands steadying himself on her hips. She squeezed the tight, muscular walls of her vagina around him and she felt full, satiated with him. But still he pushed on, deeper into her, forcing her head down into the pillow until she felt he must be buried into her right up to the root and she came again, just as quickly as before, shuddering uncontrollably in her delirium. He came inside her for the second time in just over an hour, as powerfully as ever but not in quite such spectacular abundance.

And then they lay back on the pillows together, gulping in air, their bodies filmed with sweat and the hypnotic scents of their coupling mingling with a rising smell like baking bread. Satin, her breast rising and falling in a heavy rhythm, looked around her at the scattered clothes, the jewellery that she had taken off in such haste and which now spilled over the dressing table. It had been a crazy night. She drifted off to sleep.

Sunlight came streaming in through the window of the hotel room. Instantly, her head began to throb.

'What time is it?' she asked Patric with sudden alarm. He was busy getting dressed.

'I have a meeting at nine,' he said apologetically, tucking his shirt into his trousers. 'I hadn't realised what time it was. I am so sorry. I hate to leave you like this but my editor is a man of punctilious habits.'

He was busy with his cuff links, then his jacket. Satin stretched out on the sheets, still naked. He came over and kissed her. She had no desire to make love and her head ached abominably. She wished, to be honest, he would go.

'Shall I see you again?' she asked him.

'I am sure,' he said. And then he was gone. She looked around and her eyes caught the paper lying on the floor. The review, of course! She had quite forgotten it. She scrambled out of bed, gathered up the sheets of paper and pored over them. It took her ages to find what she was looking for.

Patric Esteve's review of *Love's Plaything* was cold, cruel and calculating. He ridiculed the play, he ridiculed the cast, but he reserved his most special venom for the woman with whom he had just spent the night, at no expense to himself.

'*In the part of Aphrodite,*' she read, '*is a newcomer to the Paris stage. Satin's talents are as minuscule as her physical attributes are exaggerated. She can no more act than fly to the moon. An audience already grown used to one embarrassment after another found special amusement in her inept posturing. See this particular Aphrodite now, because there can be no doubt that, within the week, she will have vanished without trace.*'

You bastard, she hissed to herself between clenched teeth. And she vowed, there and then, that she would do her utmost to prove Patric Esteve wrong.

Chapter Three

For weeks afterwards, Satin's apartment was turned upside down. Vases of flowers – the gift of a myriad of well-wishers – stood on every surface until they overflowed and took over the kitchen as well. Those flowers that were relegated to the back were forgotten and ignored, and quickly began to decay. As fresh bunches arrived, the old ones – some barely hours old – were unceremonially dumped. The threadbare carpet was soon hidden from view beneath a covering of fragrant petals.

She bought new furniture with the money that came to her from the play. A huge and ornate chaise longue occupied almost half the tiny salon, along with an elaborate chest in the fashionable Chinese style. The people from the apartments downstairs stared in amazement at the items that, almost daily, were wrestled up those narrow, stinking stairs by sweating teams of workmen.

Inside, clothes were strewn everywhere, on the furniture, under the bed, in every available cupboard. Even the very apartment seemed to be gorging itself to repletion. A gown would be bought one day, worn that same evening, and by the end of the week had been given to Mathilde, who kept it for herself or passed it on to her relatives. Everyone, it seemed, was enjoying their share of Satin's good fortune.

Satin rose late each day, sometimes not until two or three in the afternoon. She would airily waft around her apartment in her peignoir for an hour or three before dressing for the theatre. After the performance, there would be supper or a party. Once, she had even been invited to a reception at the American embassy where she – and not the visiting Vice President – was the obvious centre of attention.

Of men, there were many, a steady stream who made their way up those dark, cabbage-smelling stairs. Some carried roses, other jewellery. Some wished merely to inhale the heady atmosphere of her fame, others wanted more. A few lucky ones were escorted by Mathilde through into Madame's boudoir. Some stayed for only a few minutes, others for longer. The very favoured few were allowed to stay with her all night. There was, for once, no charge for the pleasure of her company.

And then, in the early afternoon, sated with love, she would eat something – a dish of quail's eggs, perhaps, or a little poisson aux truffes – and all too soon the carriage that Moscato sent each evening would arrive. Six nights a week it was the same, the rattling journey through those familiar streets that she had walked so many times in a previous life. The carriage would decant her at the stage door of the theatre, where a crowd of admirers had long been waiting, and amid their cheers and the pressing of small gifts she would make her way up the dingy, winding stairs to her dressing room.

Here, too, were more flowers than even crowded into her apartment. There was no Mathilde to look after her here, just her dresser, a sour-faced old woman who could crack walnuts in her toothless gums. Flowers were jammed into whatever receptacle was available. Others were simply dumped on the floor, along with the discarded newspapers that she scanned so avidly for news of her latest triumph on the social circuit of Paris. She had, on the whole, been delighted by what the papers had said of the opening night, despite the unnecessary cruelty of that bastard Patric Esteve.

Now, six or seven weeks on, the papers were infinitely more complimentary about her. Almost every day there would be some trivial little item connected with her comings and goings. She had been seen at the party of M and Mme Farouche. She had dined with the great chanteuse, La Picayune. A rose was to be named after her.

Of course, Satin's appearance on the stage in a state of seeming nudity had outraged many more than it had delighted. There was a savage moral thunder of criticism, of herself, of Moscato, of everyone associated with the theatre. But there was nothing to disturb unduly the guardians of the nation's welfare, it was generally agreed. It was an age of acceptance and laissez faire, after the rigours of life under the late King. Ministers of the government were seen openly with their mistresses. The deputy head of the préfecture was widely known to maintain an establishment at Les Halles for a young lady of two-and-twenty. Only the most prudish felt themselves scandalised by Satin and her ilk. The rest of the population – from the expensively dressed ladies and gentlemen in the stalls and the boxes to the sweating throng who crammed into the gallery – thought she was wonderful.

No one knew what the play, at heart, was about. Nobody cared, really. It was a spectacle merely, a vehicle for sensation. People paid to see Satin, as Moscato had calculated. Since the opening night, the script had been extensively rewritten. Most of the third act had been ditched. Satin made another appearance in the second, in which she spoke a few faltering words. Each night the audience went wild for her. She could have recited nursery rhymes backwards and they would still have cheered her to the echo. All they were interested in was that generous bosom, those welcoming thighs, that angelic face set amid a tumble of carefree curls.

She milked them for every sou she could get, and not just in terms of the way she incited the audience. She had already negotiated a substantial bonus from Moscato in return for an extra matinee performance on Friday and Saturday. Now they were sitting in her tiny dressing room, surrounded by the sweet fragrance of flowers, discussing a new play he had in mind for her.

'Of course,' he was saying, 'we'll need to move to a bigger theatre. Everyone wants to see you, my dear. I could sell each seat in the house three times over. The Theatre des Etoiles just can't hold you, my dear.'

She had read at least ten pages of the script he had given her. It seemed such a silly play. A sailor, feared lost at sea, returns in disguise to his lady love. He courts her and woos her, he flatters her, he showers her with presents, but still she will not yield to his opportuning. He puts her to the test, persuading his friends to pay court to her. It is all to no avail. She pines for her dead lover, whose memory alone is sacred to her. Sadly, wanly, she spurns their every advance. Finally he reveals himself to her in his true identity, his confidence in their love for each other fully proven. They marry. Curtain.

Three acts to tell a story like that? It was ridiculous, Satin felt. There weren't even many good songs in it, just a couple that she liked. She quite fancied herself as a singer.

There was also the matter of the costumes to think about. The content of the play was irrelevant – how Satin looked to the paying customers in the audience was, as before, the only thing that mattered.

'I think I would like to dress all in white,' she said at length.

'How is that, my dear?' asked the impresario Moscato, a large man who was perched uncomfortably on a broken-down gilded chair that had once found a home in the foyer but was now far too disreputable – and unsafe – for anywhere other than a dressing room.

'I would like to have some costumes in white,' Satin

continued. 'Lots of silk, and brocade. A long, flowing train. A diamond head-dress.'

Moscato looked nonplussed. He was used to her whims by now. He tried to indulge them wherever possible. He could be very accommodating.

'Of course, I know I'm meant to be in mourning.' His ears pricked up, but he said nothing. Only his eyes betrayed how furiously he was now trying to think.

'But black is such a sombre colour, don't you think? Even purple? I think it would be lots more fun to wear white, and maybe a little pink. Surely, Elspeth can feel sorry for herself and still wear white.'

'Elspeth?'

'I mean, if she's moping around the place crying for her lost love, well, it's not going to be much fun for the audience, is it?'

He said nothing, but his eyes narrowed slightly.

'I think she needs to cheer herself up a little. Put on a bit of a show.'

'Elspeth?' he repeated.

'Yes. That's her name, isn't it?'

Moscato smiled, a false reptile smile, and put his hand gently on her knee.

'My dear,' he said, 'I think we're getting a little confused.'

'Confused? Who? Why?'

'I'm not asking you to play Elspeth, my dear. I was offering you the part of Bathsheba.'

Bathsheba? Satin could hardly believe her ears. That was a much smaller part, from what she could gather from her perfunctory skimming of the script. She was some kind of siren, a houri, a gypsy dancer, the one who tried to divert her long-lost sailor from the course of true love. Much more appealing than the virginal Elspeth, of course, but such a little part. Why, she only had one good scene, in a tavern, very near the end of the second act. What was

Moscato thinking of? It was he who was confused.

'No, Elspeth.'

'Bathsheba.'

'Elspeth.'

They looked at each other in frank amazement. Almost a minute of silence passed between them. Moscato spoke first.

'I'm sure you would be a marvellous Elspeth, my dear. But it's a terribly demanding part, you know. She's on the stage for almost the whole of the first act. Those long speeches – her soliloquy. Imagine learning all those lines.'

Satin pretended not to hear him. What were a few more lines over and above those she had had to learn for her role of Aphrodite? She got them right, didn't she, at least most of the time? Everyone said how good she was.

'No, it's Bathsheba that the audience want,' he continued. 'That wild Spanish dance – you'll be terrific at that. I'm having some costumes designed for you – you can see them tomorrow. You'll love them. The pirate queen, the gypsy temptress. You can make anything you like out of Bathsheba. You were born to play her. Elspeth is so pure, so virginal. But Bathsheba – well, she's the kind of woman that any red-blooded man would go for. She's the real star of the show, you mark my words.'

'She gets killed off in the third act. Right at the start.'

'But what a killing, though. An attack by pirates. A boat will arrive on stage, a real boat. Real cannons firing. Rapine and pillage. Smoke everywhere. I've got people working on it right now. It'll be a wonder we don't burn the theatre down, ha ha. It's terrific. They'll love it. You get your clothes torn off, don't you remember? That's what people will come to see. It will be a sensation. The papers will lap it up. Elspeth? They won't even remember her.'

Satin was still confused, but was beginning to feel mollified. Moscato, sensing victory, poured them both another glass of champagne, although the curtain was up in less than twenty minutes.

There was another long silence. He could see her splendid bosom heaving under her peignoir.

'So you'll do Bathsheba, then?'

'I'll think about it.'

They clinked glasses. A thought came into Satin's mind.

'Who'll play Elspeth, then?'

'I'm not sure, to be honest.'

'You've never done anything honest in your life. Who's playing her?'

'I don't know. Nothing's decided.'

'The leading lady and you don't even have anyone in mind. You must be lying to me. Who is she?'

'Well, we've got one or two actresses in mind.'

'We?'

'Not me, personally. But our backers, the people putting up the money for the play.'

'And what are their names?'

'Oh, Lartigue of the Orléans bank. Lescarboura, the manufacturer of patent remedies.'

'Not them, you fool. Which actresses?'

'I don't know.'

'Which actresses?'

'I tell you, I don't know.'

She was getting really angry now. Moscato was trying to pull a fast one on her, she knew.

'You tell me who, or I won't go on stage.'

Moscato's jaw visibly dropped. There was less than a quarter of an hour to go to curtain-up. He knew she'd do it, too. She was the wildest, most wilful woman he had ever met. She would make the perfect Bathsheba. When he'd seen the script for the first time, just a few days back, he had almost trembled with excitement at the prospect. Satin's voluptuous body wrapped up in a mantilla? It was too exciting for words.

She got to her feet, still half dressed, and took her cloak from its hanger. Involuntarily, he rose to his feet beside her.

'You tell me,' she said, 'or I'm walking out of this door and I'm not coming back.'

She'd beaten him. He sank down again on to his broken-down chair and put his head in his hands.

'La Cabache,' he said without any expression in his voice.

Satin threw her glass at the wall, and then swept the contents of the dressing table on to the floor. Jars and bottles flew everywhere. They said afterwards that you could hear the commotion in the orchestra pit.

Satin's appearance, that evening, was as sensational as ever – the nude body stocking, the carefully exaggerated walk to the front of the stage, the pouting expression. All showed precisely why the theatre had been sold out for the rest of the play's four-week run.

But her performance – if that was the right word – was execrable. She hardly bothered with it. She walked smack in front of Tartuffe, a veteran actor and for thirty years a great favourite of the Parisian audience, just as he was about to deliver his impassioned soliloquy, and stayed there, forcing him to edge sideways around her. In the last scene, one of the few genuinely memorable moments in the entire production, where the two lovers made up their rift, she assumed such an expression of arch disdain that the audience began to titter uncontrollably at her antics. She fluffed her lines with a show of indifference, sang her silly little song as if anxious to be rid of it as soon as possible. And yet the audience shouted and clapped as if they couldn't get enough of her. She felt that if she had walked on stage and vomited, they would still have cheered.

Any other night, and Moscato would have asked her, as politely as he could, if she were feeling indisposed, or if

70

there were some minor problem with which he might help. But he knew, tonight, that La Cabache was at the heart of the problem. He could see it coming. The trouble was, La Cabache had been the kind of actress who could fill a theatre for five or six years now – a beauty with no small thespian gift. Satin – well, she could be a nine-day wonder. She could no more act than she could fly to the moon. If he'd given her the role of Elspeth, he would be buying himself a disaster. People would come to see the show because of La Cabache. Satin, for all her sensual charms, was just a highly desirable extra.

These were his thoughts as he sat on one side of the stage, glass in hand. At the other side of the stage stood Satin, awaiting her cue.

That bitch, she thought, looking daggers at the man opposite her. She was nearly thirty, for a start. Her looks were disintegrating fast. She was a laughing stock. That fool Moscato – she couldn't believe he could be so naive as not to see it.

Once, though very few people knew it, La Cabache had been a streetwalker, much as Satin had been. It had been only for a few months, but the facts were well enough known among the gay ladies of Paris. Subsequently, she had made her way into the theatre, and a kind of respectability not normally accorded to women (and men) in her station in life. She was a very good actress, of that there was no doubt. But once a tart, always a tart, they used to say.

Her big mistake – or one of the biggest – had been in disowning the life she had left behind. Some of the girls, the ones who had married bankers and noblemen, had come back from time to time to drink wine and share tales and exploits. Everyone liked that kind of woman – the ones like Sophie, who had married the Duc de Marac, or Nicolette, now the wife of a Prussian nobleman with a real castle and a carriage with six white horses. They came back, just once in a while, to talk over old times. That night at the Tivoli with the Comte du Maupassant? A shriek of laughter. The crazed demands of the Abbé from Portugal. More laughter. There was nothing grand about them, no airs and graces that they put on.

But La Cabache – the bitch had simply disappeared into her chateau with her new husband, an art dealer and a distant relative of Zola, the novelist. Incredible as it may have seemed, he knew nothing of her past, the poor innocent fool. They had met at dinner somewhere and it had been love – or some such – at first sight, at least for him. She was too smart to spurn such an opportunity.

Once, when she came to Paris to act in a play specially written for her, she had actually come to the Café des Artistes with Manet and Courbet and other figures from the Parisian art world. And – this was the worst bit – she had completely snubbed the women on the table by the door, even though, only two or three years earlier, she might well have been sitting there herself.

The husband had died a couple of years back, leaving her a fortune. Now she had struck up with a painter, de Fleury, the portraitist, but she was much the same as ever. This story was handed down like a piece of folklore among the women of the Café des Artistes. Of course Satin knew it. And now she too was to have her face rubbed in it. She heard her cue, waited as long as she possibly could, and then made her entrance. Her lips were already poised in that already-famous pout but her eyes were cold to the point of hostility.

It was all Moscato's fault. She decided to make a few enquiries about him.

Pardieu, her lover of the moment, was waiting for her as usual after the performance. He was a tall, dark figure in his early thirties, a gentleman of private means. He showered her almost daily with gifts of clothes, jewellery and money. He had paid the rent – for three months in advance – on her dark little apartment on the Rue de Carmargue, even though she had no plans to remain there a minute longer than was necessary.

'Are you hungry?' he asked her, taking her into his arms in the privacy of her dressing room, once all the attendants and hangers on had been shooed out of the door.

'Hungry for what?' she asked him, a mischievous twinkle in her eyes.

'A little fish, perhaps, to begin with. I hear good things about this new restaurant in the Beaubourg – the lobster terrine is said to be divine. And then we might find other ways of amusing ourselves.'

'That sounds fine to me,' she murmured, kissing him on the cheek. He watched in rapt adulation as she stepped out of her costume, those marvellous breasts exposed to his wanton gaze. He wanted to take her in his arms there and then but there was a delicious delight to be had in postponing that moment of rapture. He smoked his cigar, watching her as she sat naked apart from a loose robe in front of her mirror, removing her stage make-up.

'Why don't we—?' she began and then faltered, as if not knowing how to continue.

'Why don't we what?'

She turned round and looked at him. Her robe fell open, exposing again those luscious melon breasts.

'There's a house we could go to. On the Rue St Michel.'

There was an instant recognition in his eyes.

'Madame Paolozzi?'

'Exactly.'

'How do you know about Madame Paolozzi?'

'Doesn't everyone?'

He laughed. It would be fun. He had often been there himself – Madame Paolozzi ran one of the most exclusive and expensive bordellos in all of Paris. It catered for many tastes.

The restaurant in the Beaubourg was extremely busy, even as midnight approached. But such was the power of money and fame that they were able to secure a little table away from the window, in an alcove all by themselves. The maitre d' presented his compliments. A waiter came and took their order.

Satin took off her gloves and the fur she wore as a wrap around her neck and laid them on the table. Both were gifts from him. He was delighted to see her wearing them. She didn't tell him, of course, that she had already pawned the gold bracelet he had given her a fortnight ago. It had settled the butcher's bill, outstanding for six months and more.

They ate a lavish meal – the famed lobster terrine, lamb cutlets, a suberb brie. The wines, too, were magnificent. For once, no one recognised her. It made a pleasant change not to have people coming up to her, total strangers, asking for a lock of her hair or something. She and Pardieu were able to devote all their attention to one another.

Their conversation was inconsequential, as usual. She found him a handsome man, an accomplished lover, but there was no other chemistry between them. He paid the bills and from time to time she let him come in her mouth, for which he seemed to have a particular fondness. It made little diffcrence to her.

'Well,' she said as the meal drew to its close. 'I think I'm in the mood to have a little fun tonight.'

She crossed her legs. She was aware already of a tingling of sexual excitement in her loins, could feel the dampness down there between her legs.

'And what kind of fun might that be?' he asked her at length.

'Oh, I don't know,' she said. 'It depends what Madame Paolozzi has to offer us, doesn't it?'

'Give me a clue.'

'Well, it might be nice to watch, or something. See how the other half lives, if you like.'

'You like to watch people making love in a bordello?'

'Doesn't everyone?'

He looked nonplussed.

'I like being hidden away, watching. And there are other things that happen there. Things that I really enjoy doing.'

He looked at her, a smile playing on her lips.

'Such as what?' he asked her.

'Beatings, punishments, that kind of thing. Do you like that?'

'No, I don't. Well, I've never tried it.'

'Would you like to watch it? Someone being beaten. With a switch?'

She could tell by the new-found brightness in his eyes that he found the idea exciting.

'Would you like to watch?' she repeated. 'I would. Let's see if Madame Paolozzi can arrange for us to watch someone being beaten. I'd like to see a man, an important man, tied down. A woman, naked apart from her boots and stockings. Perhaps wearing a mask. But not so they can see us, of course.'

'Are you sure? I mean, I'd love to. Yes, let's do it. Let's go there as soon as we've finished. I'll get the waiter to order us a cab.'

Pardieu had had a busy day but there was a strange excitement about him, she could tell. He ordered more champagne. He left his dessert almost untouched, smoked a cigar. She too felt very excited by the prospect. The conversation turned to other topics.

'You know what else goes on down there at Madame Paolozzi's, do you?' she asked. Their coffee came.

'How come you know so much?' he ventured. She lightly brushed his hand, and winked.

'Oh, let's just say a girl gets to hear about these things.'

'What kind of things?' He had been with many women in his time but he had encountered few who were as open and as explicit as Satin. His erection made him feel uncomfortable.

'Just the kind of things people like to get up to,' she said when the waiter had gone away. 'Just things I'd like to see.'

She had him on her hook. He pressed her still further.

'Women doing it with other women, for instance. Women with dildoes strapped to them. Men watching, perhaps with women on their own laps, naked.'

He swallowed hard, fiddled with his cigar, looked distracted.

'Would you like to see me with another woman, my sweet?'

She was really winding him up, she could tell. He was puffing furiously on his cigar, trying to get it to light.

'Have you?' he asked between coughs, as casually as he dared.

'Oh, that would be telling, wouldn't it?' she whispered. So she laughed, and tried to gloss over the implications of what she had been suggesting.

'But I do like men best,' she said. 'Especially big strong men like you. With nice big pricks like yours, who can keep it up all night.'

Men, she reflected, always seemed so susceptible to flattery, however much they might try and deny their vanity.

'I'm a nice strong man with a big prick, am I?'

'Yes you are. I just wish I was sucking your cock right now.'

She looked at him over the rim of her coffee cup. She had his attention. His pupils were large and black.

'Go on.'

'Sometimes I like just to lie there and suck it for as long as I like. I don't think that you're going to put it into me, or that you want to come or anything. I just like lying there sucking it.'

'You're very good at it.'

'I get a lot of practise, don't I?'

She looked around. The nearest people were twenty feet away. Nevertheless, she lowered her voice.

'Sometimes, best of all, I like to suck you as soon as we're together. I like it when you come into my dressing room with your coat and hat on, and I'm there naked, ready for you. I like to kneel down and get your cock out, feel your surprise, see how big and stiff you are, how much I've excited you.'

She was feeling aroused herself, now.

'I love it when you're sucking me and I'm licking you,' he said, his eyes never leaving hers.

She felt a warm frisson all over her. So few men wanted to tongue her out, and even fewer knew how to do it with any finesse. Pardieu was one of them.

'You lick me beautifully.'

'Do I now? Maybe I should kneel down under the table.'

'You make me go all damp just thinking about it.'

The waiter came and brought fresh cups for them. They lapsed into silence, like schoolchildren caught talking in class. Then they resumed.

'I like the way you're all warm and wet down there, the taste of you, the way you move when I'm doing it.'

'Do you do it with other women?'

'Not many,' he said. 'Most women don't like it.'

'How strange,' she said. She'd never noticed that with any of the women she'd slept with.

She felt his hand on her knee, under the tablecloth. Christ, she thought, he wants to have me in the middle of the cafe.

Pardieu turned slightly in their cramped little alcove and leaned towards her. She parted her legs to make it easier for him. His hand slid up her thighs, on to the tops of her stockings, feeling the contrast between the silk garters and the soft, cool flesh of her thighs.

For a couple of minutes or more his fingers delicately brushed across her skin, making it tingle, making her long for him. She wanted his fingers there, his tongue, his penis. She was temporarily lost for conversation.

His fingertips moved higher. She glanced anxiously around the room. No one could possibly see them, unless they knelt down on the floor and looked up. She felt reassured, and was able to relax. She parted her legs a little more, moved forward in her seat so that his fingers brushed against her drawers.

He stroked her delicately, between her legs. He was looking straight into her eyes.

She was wearing drawers of pale mauve silk, with a deep lace trim. They were the kind of thing Pardieu liked. She had been looking forward to him taking them off.

Now his fingers slid underneath the silk, against the moist lips of her pudenda, the palm of his hand cupping her pubic mound. She had to push herself almost off the edge of the chair so he could reach her and so she was leaning right back. She glanced out of the window and saw people coming and going in the street outside, the cabs passing, the breath of the horses in the cool night air. She sipped at her brandy, trying to look nonchalant. She realised her hands were shaking and she nearly dropped the glass.

Pardieu's middle finger roved around her labia, probing between the folds, finding the entrance at last and slipping inside her. She had not been particularly wet before but now she felt her juices beginning to flow, easing the passage of another finger and then another, until he had three fingers buried in her, there at their table in the restaurant, with people eating and drinking and smoking and talking only a few feet away.

'Do stop it,' she heard herself say for form's sake but she wanted him to go on, to push on into her, to push her over the edge. With the ball of his thumb he found her clitoris and he massaged it with infinite gentleness, all the while his fingers twisting and sliding and turning inside her. It was so very different to the rough and uncompromising way most men did it to her, even the more refined ones. Already she was pushing out to meet him, trying to force herself on to him, ready to be penetrated.

She didn't reach a climax, though she was close to it – she felt too inhibited by the other people in the restaurant and the waitresses hovering around the place. She whimpered and moaned and sighed quietly enough for Pardieu to think he had brought her off. He withdrew his hand, sniffed appreciatively at his fingers. She felt warm and excited.

'Come on,' she said. 'Let's go to Madame Paolozzi's.'

She smiled at him, discreetly adjusting her clothing while he sipped the last of his brandy. He looked happy. She could see the prominent erection in his trousers.

Like several of the most celebrated brothels of the day, Madame Paolozzi's establishment was very close to the Opéra. It was a large house, decorated in impeccable taste. It was known for its discretion, and for the fact that it was able to cater for particular tastes. In consequence, a visit to Madame Paolozzi could turn out to be very expensive indeed.

But Pardieu was himself a rich man. They were quickly able to realise Satin's fantasy of watching a man and a woman together in flagellation. They were ushered into a small room on one of the upper floors, not entirely unlike the box in a theatre. It opened out, below, on to a large room, opulently furnished and dimly lit. The gas jets that flickered on the walls beneath their observation point prevented anyone from looking up and seeing the watchers – unless they particularly wanted to.

They could see clearly everything that went on. Satin's mouth felt dry and there was a tingling sensation in her loins. She was excited, wicked. She wanted power and she was about to taste it. But she had little real idea of what to expect, despite what she had said to Pardieu. Of course, she had played games with some of her clients, a little playful bottom-smacking, that kind of harmless fun. She rather hoped that this would be different. She wondered what passions she might witness, how far people might want to go. She had indicated little of what was expected – and accepted.

As their eyes grew accustomed to the gloom of the room beneath, she heard movements, a door closing. She could make out a figure, a woman's. She could see her across the room, seated on a sofa. Her face looked pale and still, her bright eyes were accentuated by smoky lines of kohl. There was an unexpected redness about her mouth – her facial features seemed to be exaggerated almost to the point of grotesquerie – and her luxurious hair assumed an imposing quality from being piled up on top of her head. This woman was painted and dangerous. She was the dominatrix.

Nevertheless, Satin felt an inevitable desire welling up inside herself. She looked at Pardieu, gave his cock a quick squeeze through his trousers. It was as hard as a rock. Both of them looked back at the woman in the room below, their eyes taking in her face and hair and the generous globes of her naked breasts. She was wearing a wasp-waisted corset of black leather, as smooth and supple as her own skin. It held her soft curves like a tight-fitting glove, sculpting and moulding her contours, wickedly and enticingly exposing her pubis. Satin had never seen a woman in this kind of outfit before, and the novelty excited her. She ignored her partner, trying for the moment to blank his presence from her mind. She was concentrating on the job in hand.

The woman wore long black stockings and high, devilishly high, lace-up boots. They had been made for her, she later explained when Satin spoke to her, by a shoe-maker in Montparnasse, a specialist in such things. Her name, it transpired, was Mirabelle.

Crouched on their chairs, Pardieu aware of the erection of his penis and Satin of her own wetness, they were taken by surprise when, after a knock, the door to the room below opened and the familiar figure of the deputy mayor of Paris came in.

Taken by surprise, Satin stood up involuntarily to get a better look, and so – for different reasons – did the woman she was watching. Immediately she sensed the atmosphere in the room below them had changed. She became commanding and direct, in control of the situation. She spoke briskly to Hécaté, the deputy mayor.

He could not catch the words but the official began to take off his clothes, his eyes scarcely leaving the woman's. He placed them neatly on a chair. Pardieu too was watching Mirabelle, wondering what her next move would be. Quietly he squeezed his own cock, knowing that the best was still to come.

Pardieu looked at the other man's body with something close to disgust. He knew him from various committees and suchlike, a pompous man, almost a bully, full of his own importance. His waist was flabby and his legs were milky-white and spindly. Mirabelle spoke again, this time with a whip or riding-crop in her hand and a beak-like leather mask obscuring her features. Hécaté took off his shirt and drawers and stood there in his socks alone, naked and vulnerable.

Satin too felt an amused contempt for the man who was about to be beaten. The erect penis that jutted out aggressively from the deputy mayor's body seemed only to add to her feelings of scorn. She sensed that Mirabelle shared her emotions. A half-smile played around her lips but her eyes spoke differently. Heavy with cosmetics, they gleamed with a mixture of power and derision, like some powerful hunting animal with her quarry at her mercy. She gave Hécaté orders in a clipped, unnatural voice.

Settling back on the sofa and parting her legs so the deputy mayor could see the pouting lips of her vagina, she stabbed with her riding crop in the direction of a chest of drawers. Evidently knowing the rules of the game, Hécaté moved quickly across the room and pulled it open. He took out a large, black, ivory dildo and brought it to his mistress.

She settled back still further on the sofa, moving her backside forward until she was on the very edge, exposing her genitals to Hécaté's rapt gaze. Then, in a tantalising slow pantomime of sensuality, she inserted the dildo into herself.

Hécaté knelt down in front of her, fascinated. She pulled out the dildo and pressed it against her groin, holding it out to him like a penis. He leaned forward and began to lick it.

Intrigued by the sight of the deputy mayor's own penis as it bobbed ludicrously from side to side, Pardieu leaned even further forward in his seat. The woman's power over Hécaté – a man he knew well who, despite his failings, was respected throughout the city for his probity and high standing – seemed to have absorbed him completely. The deputy mayor devoured the dildo, still glistening with Mirabelle's secretions, with hunger and evident relish.

Satin saw Mirabelle close her eyes briefly and rest her head against the cushions. She could see the steady rise and fall of Mirabelle's breast and Satin realised what a consummate performance she was witnessing. Then Mirabelle took command of the situation once more, tapping Hécaté on the shoulder with the riding crop, bidding him stand up.

He shuffled clumsily to his feet. When his hand strayed involuntarily to his penis, she clipped him hard across the wrist. Gone was the smooth, dapper figure of authority whom Pardieu had seen so often at civic functions, pressing hands, offering a quiet word. Now Hécaté was more like a victim himself, a beaten animal cowed by one more powerful than he. He was plumbing the depths of the murky waters of his emotions, desperate only for abasement, and yet there was a bizarre kind of triumph there as well, a sense of enjoyment in his own humiliation. It was a kind of pantomime for him.

Satin glanced, wide-eyed, at the cruel black whip with which Mirabelle caressed the smooth flesh of her thighs. The image aroused Pardieu too, the uncompromising brutality of the leather, the masked face, the silk stockings, the ivory skin, cool as marble. She moved it closer and closer to her naked sex, stroking it through her pubic bush and along the lips of her labia. Hécaté simply stood there, mesmerised.

She bade him stand against the brass bedhead. His penis seemed unnaturally engorged, alive with lust. Pardieu knew what was coming next.

She commanded him to kneel.

Slowly, almost gracefully, Hécaté lowered his head on to the table and then Mirabelle cut a series of sharp, stinging blows against his backside. Pardieu could see him wince with genuine pain, his body involuntarily trying to inch away from her. Not once did Mirabelle look up from her work.

With those splendid breasts jiggling above the tight black corset, she stepped back and put her full strength into a savage assault with the whip. The blows rained down, again and again, unremitting in their harshness. Long weals sprang up on the deputy mayor's flesh and Pardieu could see Mirabelle's face was turning red with the exertion. Mirabelle closed her eyes and caught her breath for a moment. Then she resumed, drawing the full length of the whip through her fingers before raising it high and then bringing it down with stinging force on to the man before her.

He could hear Hécaté cry out, saw him squirm with fear and pain even as he pushed his backside out for more. Pardieu looked at those red bloody weals and wondered if this was the same man he had associated with for so long across polished tables in smoke-filled committee rooms. He could only guess at what Mirabelle's frame of mind must have been at that moment – or, for that matter, how Satin was reacting to the scene in front of them. He could not see much of Mirabelle's eyes through the mask but she seemed strangely exhilarated, shocked and amazed and excited by what she was doing, illuminated from deep within her psyche by a fire of passion more deadly than anything he had ever seen before.

Satin arrived at the modest house in the Marais in very good time, carrying the small portmanteau with the items that she had borrowed from Mirabelle. She was greeted by the madame; they enjoyed a demi-tasse together. The parlour was warm still from the hot summer day and there were fresh flowers in a bowl on the table. It was more like someone's house – certainly nothing like as grand as the establishment close to the Opéra where she had been a few evenings ago with Pardieu.

'I don't find many girls who are in the same line of work as you,' the madame was saying. She was a fat little woman of forty, perhaps younger. 'So when Chloe was took ill, I was glad to find a replacement. Quite a few of my gentlemen ask for chastisement.'

Chloe was only ill, of course, because Satin had arranged for her to be ill. She had found out where Moscato, the impresario, took his solitary pleasures, and what those pleasures might consist of. She was determined, in the wake of her humiliation over the casting of *Lovers' Vows*, that he would have a beating he would not forget for a long time.

'He's a very particular gentleman,' the woman went on.

'Very punctual, as a rule. He'd have been well put out if I'd have had to cancel him. He comes here every Sunday, week in, week out. He's in the theatre, I think I heard him say. Sunday's his day off.'

In the bedroom into which she had been ushered, with the curtains carefully drawn, Satin unpacked her case. She took off her own coat and dress and hung them in the wardrobe. She looked around her – everything was so normal, the washstand with its jug and ewer, the solid old bed, the fireplace in one corner.

She removed her linen, every last item. Now it was time to put on the costume. She took the corset of tight black leather and, with something of an effort, she stepped into it. Even with Mathilde's help it had been a struggle to get it on and today, on her own, it seemed especially restrictive.

She went to the door and called out. The woman came scurrying upstairs. In the room next to hers she heard giggling and a man's voice.

Together, by tugging hard and Satin drawing in her breath sharply, eventually the two of them managed it. The shoulder straps cut into her flesh but she liked the way the bodice seemed to sculpt and mould her breasts, which were much larger and more spectacular than Mirabelle's. She looked at herself in the large mirror on the wall, bending down slightly to get a better view of her cleavage. It was possible to see her areolae, which she had dusted with rouge to make them more visible. Madame admired her body as well.

Sitting on the bed, she drew on her stockings. The silk felt cool and smooth against her thighs. She loved the caress of gossamer silk. Sometimes, alone at home, she would spend a whole evening naked apart from a pair of these stockings, perhaps pleasuring herself with a godemiche.

She adjusted the garters, trimmed with black lace, then

she drew on a pair of drawers fashioned from the same material. They were utterly wicked, making little or no attempt to hide the reality of her pubic hair. There was more to come. She fastened straps around herself, tight black leather that cut into her flesh, around her buttocks and across her thighs, as if they were trying to restrain her from bursting forth in her own voluptuousness. Gradually, piece by piece, Satin began to disappear. The woman who emerged in her place, clad in leather and lace, was darker, colder, more powerful. She turned her attention to her face, expertly applying the materials she had brought with her from last night's performance. With all the kohl and rouge she was applying, she started to look like a voluptuous vampire, a creature of the night, black and red contrasting with the cold whiteness of her flesh.

All this was achieved with just a few coloured creams and pigments. It was pure theatre. Moscato would have been proud of her, the conniving bastard.

Next she put on the long leather boots that she had borrowed from Mirabelle. They rode up above her knees, black and shiny, almost to the tops of her stockings, and it took her an age to get them on and laced up. The heels were so high she could scarcely walk in them. But the effect, when she studied herself in the mirror, was staggering. She wondered if she could wear them with Pardieu – he had been so excited by what he'd seen in the room at Madame Paolozzi's that she'd had to suck him off in the carriage on their way back to his apartment.

She sat down with a feeling of relief, running her fingers over the shiny leather. It would take her some while to get used to the boots.

She hoped Moscato would like what he saw – after all, he was paying her to make his life hell, for an hour or so at least. She could do what she liked to him and she would make him love her for it, the shit.

Lounging there in her corset and those extraordinary

boots, Satin again found herself contemplating her reflection in the mirror. She wondered if any of the men she had known even six months ago would recognise her now, so much had things changed about her life in the intervening period. Where once they might have seen a typical woman of the night, all silk and feathers and ready for a few minutes of comfort, now they saw a wasp-waisted devil-woman in black, with heavy kohl-rimmed eyes and shameless scarlet lipstick – a vision of power and potency and almost infinite capability to punish, an avenging angel indeed. And the odd thing was, Satin knew which of the two was closer to her real self.

There was a knock on the door. She heard the woman's voice. She felt a little like she usually did in the last seconds before going on stage, a flutter of nerves in the pit of her stomach, a dryness in the mouth. She knew – or just about knew – the lines and the plot and her stage directions, but there was always that element of danger, the fear of failure that had to be conquered every night. She had never felt like that as a whore, supremely confident in her own abilities. But tonight Satin had the advantage of being able to work out her anxieties on her audience – an audience of one. The angrier and more frustrated she felt, the better she would perform.

She stepped out on the landing and down the stairs – not without a certain difficulty. She was ushered into a small room right at the back of the house where she put on the final items of her costume – a pair of long black gloves in the softest leather and a black beaked mask. Now she was ready for action.

Punctually at eleven – in fact a little before – she heard a tap on the door. She ignored it. There was a clock on the wall opposite her, and she let the second hand tick round the face several times while she adjusted the buckles on the straps that cut into her thighs. Again the knock. She rose to her feet and opened the door a tiny fraction.

Through the chink in the door she could see Moscato in his customary heavy overcoat and hat. He was in his mid-forties, she guessed – he had never volunteered any specific information about himself and she had never troubled herself to enquire. She understood he was married and attended mass at least twice a week.

As she ushered him in, she could sense him looking at her. Could he have known? Impossible.

'You are the new girl, then?' he said.

She lowered her eyes – what little of them he could see through the slits in the mask.

'I understand Madame has given you some indication of what is required,' he said, sniffing the air. With the most inconsequential of remarks, he took off his overcoat and hung it over a chair.

Satin bolted the door behind him, two heavy bolts that slid across and effectively cut them off from the outside world. There was no window in the room.

He took off his jacket and trousers, and then his underlinen. His thighs were as pink and cherubic as his face, and Satin could see he was already erect. To think she had allowed this man to sleep with her once, as a way of securing her part in his play – she certainly wouldn't do anything like that now, a woman in her position. He unfastened his cravat and tossed it on to the table. Standing there in his shirt-tails, still in his socks and boots, she thought he made a contemptible sight. She felt her own power surging through her, an irresistible tide.

She could sense his eyes burning into the backs of her thighs, studying the white flesh, the way her straps and stockings cut into the tops of her thighs, those stupendous breasts that seemed to be trying to burst out of the top of her corset. She was glad he didn't touch her, or want to speak to her. She had rehearsed a deep, slightly foreign voice, in case he recognised the way she spoke.

Moscato didn't talk either, or very little. In days gone by

she had flagellated several men, in a casual sort of way. All of them were especially vocal – at least at first. Always in the same hushed, hurrying monotone, they spoke of their guilt and their misdemeanours, real or imagined, as they professed their humility and contrition. It was rarely anything that would trouble even the most attentive of priests and Satin sometimes wondered whether they might better find solace in the confessional. It was all so mundane – sometimes, if she had to punish anyone, she wished it could be a sinner with a little imagination. Moscato, though, stayed almost silent throughout, alone with his concerns and preoccupations.

'Will you give me the garment?' he said quietly, not looking at her.

She carefully removed the loose-fitting drawers in black lace that she had been wearing. She commanded him to kneel and then she held them up to his face. Taking them from her, he inhaled deeply and appreciatively, burying his face in them. Then, knowing every step in this particular dance, the impresario leaned forwards over a hard leather chair placed for that precise purpose in the centre of the room. With great discretion, he slipped Satin's drawers against the cushions, like an antimacassar of wicked black lace.

He pulled up his shirt-tails, exposing plump, round buttocks.

'The straps now, please,' he commanded.

Long fastenings were attached to the arms of the chair. She bound them around his wrists, then fastened a belt around each of his ankles and tied them to the chair legs, so tightly that he could not move.

She went to the cupboard in the corner of the room, aware of her own bare buttocks and her exposed pubic bush. Inside was a selection of rods and switches, some mere canes, others with elaborate lashes. She selected one that was long and whip-like, with a decorative handle.

She came up behind him, laid the lash against his buttocks.

'Do it hard, if you would,' he said. His voice was almost inaudible.

She tested its suppleness with her thumb, flexed it at arm's length. Then she brought it down viciously against his fleshy rump. She heard him wince. Good, you bastard, she found herself thinking. There's worse to come.

She changed position slightly to make it easier for her to swing the lash. She hit him three or four times, with increasing hardness. She noticed how quickly the red marks appeared. She never liked to touch him but she fancied he had particularly sensitive skin. She would see what she could do about that. Down came the lash again.

Moscato gasped, drawing in his breath sharply. She could see the marks of old bruises on him.

Despite the tightness of the straps that bound him, he still wriggled a bit, trying to get comfortable. As she raised the switch again, she could see him rubbing against her drawers, excitedly anticipating the next stroke. She brought it down again and again, so hard it made him gasp, and he pushed backwards and forwards against the chair where her drawers lay like he was fucking them, a parody of love-making.

She was relieved he wasn't much of a talker, though he gurgled and mumbled to himself. Some of them liked to tell her about the things they enjoyed but Moscato, mercifully, seemed perfectly content with things as they stood. She could smell alcohol on him and knew he had been drinking. She wondered if it helped dull the pain – but then again, perhaps the pain was the whole point of the exercise.

She beat him again, six or seven cruel strokes in a row, and she knew she had hurt him. It pleased her, made her feel fired up inside. She enjoyed the anonymity of the mask, of the power that enabled her to dominate him.

Long familiar with ways of holding sway over men, this was a new and wholly exciting new role for her. She wondered if she might care to play the dominatrix more often.

After all, she had the motives, as she brought the lash down again and again, the anger rising in her heart. She bitterly resented this unpleasant man, who had chosen another woman in preference to herself, a woman whom she hated. No one would ever be allowed to treat her like that, no one at all. Didn't he realise who she was?

You fat shit, she hissed through clenched teeth, as the rod again swished through the air and struck him a withering blow. She knew he was close to orgasm now, could hear his breathing change, could see the way his backside quivered before each blow.

She paused for the moment, then went back to the cupboard. She took out something like a dog collar, bound it around his jaws till it cut hard into his cheeks. That would keep him quiet, she reflected.

Each time she hit him was one step towards her own release from the anger that had troubled her ever since he had told her about La Cabache. That bitch! People wanted to see her, Satin, not some old tart of thirty.

She cut him low and hard against the top of his legs and, despite the gag, he cried out loudly. This time, despite her better judgement, she stayed her hand. He grunted incomprehensibly, the strap cutting cruelly into his face, rubbing himself against the chair as best he could. She beat him again and again and again. He rubbed himself furiously against the black lace of her drawers, squirming and grunting. The red weals stood out savagely on his skin – his whole backside was criss-crossed with them. She wondered what his wife would think and then realised she was probably not the kind who had ever seen her husband naked, nor he her.

The lash cut through the air a final time and then he was still. He lay slumped over the chair, panting. She stooped down and undid the buckles and straps that restrained him, aware of the pungent smell of his semen. After a few seconds he pulled away from her and got to his feet, wiping himself with his shirt-tails. She could see the damp patch on her drawers where he had ejaculated over them.

He took off the gag and dropped it on to the floor. Without even looking at her, Moscato went over to the chair and dressed hurriedly still not looking at her. He was obviously in some distress, his eyes bloodshot and his breathing ragged. She picked up the soiled drawers and tossed them to one side, holding the cane against her booted thigh and watching him knotting his cravat.

'Get out!' she commanded.

He glanced up at her as he put on his hat. Was there a hint of recognition in those pain-filled eyes? No, it couldn't be, not through the mask and the rest of her costume. She unbolted the door and let him out, then she glanced at the clock on the wall. She had another half-hour before she met her next gentleman – a prosperous wine merchant who liked to be tied up and bitten. Satin wondered if she might be able to do this kind of a thing on a regular basis. She had done it from purely personal motives but, now that she had tried it, she realised she had rather enjoyed the experience.

Chapter Four

The enmity between the two women began to surface even before rehearsals were under way for *Lovers' Vows*.

Moscato, under the illusion that oil should be poured on waters even before the first storm clouds began to gather above a still-tranquil sea, invited them to supper with him at Chez Pascale, at that time the most fashionable restaurant in Paris. Satin was with Pardieu, though their relationship was showing clear signs of strain in consequence of her sudden rise to fame and fortune. They had bickered in the cab on their way to the restaurant. They were all but ignoring each other even as they sat down at the exquisitely laid table.

She paid little attention to Moscato either. Since that night in the house in the Marais, she felt she had bested him. Now he meant little to her, other than as a stepping stone in her career. He was disposable. Now that *Love's Plaything* had finished, she was anxious to be on her way as soon as possible, onwards and upwards. The new play would be merely a stepping stone for her.

It had been a trying day for her all round. First came the news that her new apartment would not be ready for another week at least – she had hoped to move in the day after tomorrow. After luncheon, she had made the effort – for the first time in many weeks – to go and see her little son, Thierry Armand. The little chap had scarcely recognised her, clinging to his nurse's skirts and refused to come from behind her, even when cajoled with the expensive toys that Satin had brought from Paris especially for him.

The visit had not gone well. He whimpered. She sulked. It was so ungrateful of him. At two years old, nearly three, he should have known better. She did her best for him, she told herself and Pardieu as they rattled homewards in his carriage, and this was how she was repaid. She was still pouting as she dressed and, somewhat late, made her way to Chez Pascale. The auguries were not good but Satin decided to brazen it out.

La Cabache – whom Satin was meeting for the first time – was a woman in her early thirties. Some cruel souls hinted that she might be as old as thirty-five but, whatever the truth of the situation, she was capable nevertheless of playing the part of a woman ten years younger than herself. It required but a little stretching of an audience's credibility, even from the stalls, to accept her in the title role of Elspeth, a woman – a girl, really, of no more than nineteen.

As they took their seats, Satin immediately studied those famous features. Her nose was quite large – a sign of character, no doubt – and so were her eyes, slightly slanted and a wicked green. Her hair was a deep and lustrous black, her cheekbones high. There was something undeniably Slavic about her and her striking features were emphasised by the simplicity of the black evening gown she wore.

La Cabache was perfectly civil to Satin – as she had every right to be. Here was a woman, rich and successful, an object of admiration to many, at the peak of her beauty and career. In comparison with her Satin was young, naive and – in physical terms at any rate – still not fully formed. She held out a languid hand and Satin touched it with as much grace as she could muster.

Already she hated the woman. That aristocratic nose – huge, huge. The hair – false, unquestionably. The figure – the result of careful corsetry and hours of preparation. Why, even the mincing way she spoke seemed to be entirely artificial. The woman was a fraud, an imposter. No wonder she had become an actress – being a lady of pleasure required that you put something of your real self into your work. This woman was a fake through and through.

La Cabache murmured a compliment – obviously forced out of her, Satin decided – about Satin's triumph as Aphrodite. She had not actually seen the play herself – of course not, the lazy bitch – but she had heard many good things about it from friends, especially concerning Satin's performance. Satin's heart glowed briefly but her conscious mind told her to disbelieve her words. The woman was up to something, it was plain to see. She was trying to flatter her, to make her feel small and insignificant. She could resist all that kind of thing now.

Satin turned her attention to the famous actress's companion. Frédéric de Fleury was a fashionable portrait painter, much in demand by the aristocracy and a rich fund of scandalous anecdotes concerning their peccadilloes. He was in his mid-forties, grey-haired and grey-eyed, still very handsome. He had a way of looking straight at Satin when he spoke that she rather liked. Was he admiring her décollétage, she wondered, or her hair, piled high on her head in an elegant chignon.

He mentioned the Duc de Rochelle. Satin had met him – albeit only briefly – at a supper party only the other week. He was a charming man, she observed. He and de Fleury, it turned out, were great friends, went shooting together. Satin liked this feeling of being on intimate terms with the great and the good, even though her acquaintance with the Duc de Rochelle had been at best fleeting and hardly reciprocated on his part. There was still, for a man in the duke's position, something vaguely compromising about being in the company of theatrical people. And yet, ironically, it was company that so many of them craved – so free and uninhibited, in comparison to their own staid and respectable lives. A clear corridor existed between the boudoirs of the highest in the land and the shadowy demi-mondaines who sparkled like stolen jewels in fashionable society.

Frédéric de Fleury, it turned out, had seen Satin's now-legendary Aphrodite. He had been there with two painter friends and had seen the performance three times.

'Absolutely marvellous, my dear,' he beamed as he recalled those evenings in the tiny, cramped theatre. 'And you knocked 'em all dead, that's for sure. I'm so glad you're playing Bathsheba. I'm sure you'll be a tremendous success. All of Paris loves you.'

Satin was sure that La Cabache shot him a look of disapproval. It pleased her. It meant that her ploy was working. She had determined to charm him, to force him to make unfavourable comparisons with her. What good was a fortune when your looks were fading as fast as La Cabache's were?

She turned back to Frédéric de Fleury, asked him a few inconsequential questions about his work. Men, she had noticed, were only too ready to speak of their concerns. They spoke about their property, their responsibilities, their estates – all in very material terms. Men liked to talk of things, she believed, and women of their feelings. Having been with many dozens – if not hundreds – of men in her short but eventful life, she reckoned she knew a thing or two about what made them tick.

'And who,' she ventured, 'is the most dreadful person you have ever had to paint?'

It was far more interesting to speak in this way, inviting scandal and revelation, than to ask any other question. Who cared what a nice man the Duc de Rochelle was? Satin wanted to hear about men who drank, who beat their wives, who preferred to bugger boys in greasy stews in the Moroccan quarter. Such information was always of use to a woman such as Satin.

'St Xavier,' he said immediately, without a moment's hesitation. Guy St Xavier was one of the greatest poets of the century, many were agreed, even if his fame in the world at large was not in proportion to the respect he was accorded in literary society. He was a poet of enormous sensitivity and depth of feeling, loved by the women of the salons, adored by the literati. His poems – eloquent testaments to lost innocence and unfulfilled yearnings – had moved even hard-bitten government ministers to tears.

He was also, according to Frédéric de Fleury, a man of bombast, a rude and officious poser who had become too used to getting his own way to take any notice of others. He had marched into his studio, surrounded by acolytes, and had listened impatiently while, over a glass of the finest Médoc opened especially in honour of the great man, Frédéric de Fleury had explained how he visualised the intended portrait, a commission from the Society of Arts. St Xavier had hemmed and fidgeted, scarcely listening to a word that the most respected portrait painter in all of France had said, and then began to outline some preposterous scheme of his own to immortalise himself in oils.

The ideas he put forward were ridiculous, although the artist was at pains to dismiss them as gently as possible, but the poet would not be deterred. There was no hope of a compromise. In the end, St Xavier fell ill to a bout of pleurisy and the matter of the portrait was conveniently allowed to drop. When pressed by the Society of Arts, the painter made his excuses but in private he allowed that he would steadfastly refuse to paint even a hair on that dreadful man's head, even if they offered him a million francs and the Presidency for life of the Academy.

He carried on in a similar vein, one famous name after another tumbling from his lips. Satin laughed at de Fleury's tales of lechery and infidelity among the rich.

They were just as bad, she reasoned, as the clerks and minor officials who, for so long, had helped pay her rent. And yet they put themselves up as custodians of the public good, all moralising and sermons. What a bunch of hypocrites they all were, to be sure.

She told him about the deputy mayor, about how he was supposed to have a taste for flagellation. She could see Moscato's ears prick up, sensed his discomfiture. Pardieu was talking to La Cabache and didn't hear her.

'How do you know that?' asked the painter.

'Oh, a little bird tells me these things,' she said, her eyes twinkling. She leaned forward a little, offering him a glimpse of her plunging cleavage.

'I thought he was a terribly upright man,' said the painter.

'He's not very upright after he's had a good thrashing,' replied Satin. 'I hear he can hardly walk down the stairs of Madame Paolozzi's afterwards.'

The painter roared with laughter. He and Satin were getting on famously, just as she planned they would. La Cabache was looking daggers.

Then the name of Gaspard, the philosopher, came up. Now Satin happened to know that this man, reviled and revered in equal quarter depending on whether one was a classicist or an empiricist, had once spent a great deal of time in the arms of La Cabache, way back in her street-walking days. It was obvious, from the way Frédéric de Fleury spoke of him, that he had the greatest disdain for the man and yet she was sure that this was not because of jealousy.

'I've heard,' she ventured, 'that he used to frequent a brothel in Montparnasse. The house of Madame Pitolou, I believe.'

'Did he now?' said the painter, all ears suddenly. She could see La Cabache had stopped talking to Pardieu and – as unobtrusively as she could manage – was listening intently to what the other woman was saying to her lover.

'Oh yes he did,' she breathed, her eyes sparkling mischieviously. 'And do you know what he liked best to do at the house of Madame Pitolou?'

'I'm sure I don't know what he liked best to do at the house of Madame Pitolou – but I'm damned sure you're going to tell me.'

'Well, he used to like to have not one, but several women at once.'

'Did he now?'

'Oh yes he did. Or so I'm told.'

'He always was a randy old goat.'

'Several women at once,' she repeated. This last was a direct dig at La Cabache, of whom she knew that tribadic extravagances were something of a specialism.

The painter chortled as he sipped his wine. 'Well, there's life in the old dog yet,' he exclaimed, spearing a mussel. 'Did you hear that?' he said to his companion. 'Old Gaspard used to like having half a dozen women at once.'

'Not half a dozen,' Satin was quick to interject. 'Only a couple. Sometimes three.'

She could sense the discomfiture of La Cabache. The distinguished portraitist, she was sure now, knew absolutely nothing of her colourful past.

All the men were laughing, but there was not a smile to be seen on the beautiful dark features of La Cabache.

'Oh yes,' Satin went on, now looking straight at the great actress. 'There was a woman he had regularly, and she used to procure the girls for him. And would stand and watch while he made love to them.'

The three men gathered around the table – de Fleury, Pardieu and Moscato – looked at each other in amazement. Men of the world they may have been, but this was something almost beyond their wildest expectations. Still looking straight at La Cabache, Satin seized the initiative.

'And sometimes, would you believe it, she would join in herself. He'd have one girl and she'd have the other. Or so I'm told.'

She and La Cabache exchanged a final, cold glance of hostility. It was obvious now that the other woman knew her own secret. The knowledge gave her a thrill of power, every bit as great as the feelings that had surged through her when she had thrashed Moscato in the basement of the house in the Marais.

'But still,' she ended gaily as their desserts arrived, 'I'm sure it's all hearsay. You can never believe some of the silly things you hear, can you? Why, I've even heard it said that the Emperor Napoleon prefers boys, which is plainly ridiculous.'

As rehearsals progressed, the relations between the two actresses – never cordial, even at the best of times – deteriorated almost to the point of open hostility. Everything was as bad as Moscato had feared. He had thought, for a while at least, that he had managed to soothe Satin's ruffled feathers and to channel her energies into her part. But he was a fool to think she could exist on the same stage as La Cabache. The latter was all professional poise and confidence but he could see how Satin's little subterfuges were beginning to undermine her.

They only had two scenes in which they were on stage at the same time. They were rehearsing them that afternoon. Moscato sat in the stalls, on his own, watching the drama unfold, uncomfortably shifting his scarred buttocks. He had never felt right since that night a few weeks back when that strange woman with the enormous bosoms had thrashed the daylights out of him. He had gone too far that time – or rather she had. He was glad when the regular girl came back after her bout of illness. There was something dangerous about the masked woman in the long leather boots.

The first scene that Satin and La Cabache were rehearsing was innocuous enough, a meeting in a marketplace where they barely spoke to one another. Satin was required to make overtures to Mésnel, the sailor, even as La Cabache, as Elspeth, watched events unfold before her eyes. But in the second scene, when Mésnel has plainly preferred his long-lost lover to the tempestuous gypsy beauty, Satin was required to heap scornful and angry words on her rival and then to perform her wild gypsy dance. It was obvious, even to Moscato and the others as they watched from the stalls, that she meant every word she spoke.

It was an explosive mixture. But the play was too far advanced by now to think of making any changes to the cast. Besides, Satin was not doing too badly. The play had been revised to accommodate her limited abilities as an actress but she was managing to get through most of her lines without too many mistakes. If she faltered, she had a rare gift for ad libbing. Moscato felt inwardly relieved.

What he was more concerned about was where Satin's overt sexuality was going to make its appearance. The part of Bathsheba had been tailored especially for her – a wild, tempestuous beauty, all fire and earth in comparison with Elspeth's silvery beauty. After the way she had performed at the Theatre des Etoiles, Moscato had every confidence that she would bring a rare and uninhibited sensuality to the role. But, as yet, she seemed to be holding back, not letting herself expand into her part. It wasn't the woman he had seen holding an audience in the palm of her hand, breathing out her own simmering passion. It was more like an actress playing the part of a red-blooded woman. Still, it would all come right in the end, he told himself all through that long Saturday afternoon, looking forward to his regular Sunday-night beating at Madame Subritski's. If only Satin would play her part with the same vigour that the mysterious flagellante had shown towards him that night a few weeks ago. He went back to his tortured daydreams.

That afternoon, they were also intending to rehearse the long scene where Mésnel is finally reunited with Elspeth. Satin was not required but, instead of returning to her apartment, as she normally did, she hung around in the back of the auditorium, watching the endless processes of refinement that were enacted on stage between La Cabache and her lead.

Mésnel was good, Satin had to admit. He was tall and dark and very good-looking and yet she felt little for him in the physical sense. He was, she had been able to gather from her intimates in and out of the theatre, a noted pederast. It was ironic, then, that he should be playing the part of a sailor.

La Cabache, well, she had to admit it, was not short of acting talent. Far from it – she had this uncanny ability to project herself, to fill the auditorium with her presence, even when she was whispering to Mésnel. Satin could never act like that. Everything she did had to be loud and furious, painted in violent primary colours of red and black instead of the delicate pastel shades of La Cabache. She was so engrossed in the performance taking shape on stage – the director, Fonson, was trying to get them to move about more, instead of delivering their words from a near-stationary position – that she scarcely noticed the man who unobtrusively entered the theatre and came and sat in the row behind her.

When she became aware of his presence, she turned round. To her surprise, there was Frédéric de Fleury, wearing an elegant suit of lilac cloth with a flower in his button hole. He nodded, smiled at her and indicated the developing scene on the stage with his silver-tipped cane.

'What do you think of that?' he said when the scene came to an end and the assembled troupe on stage sat down for a breather. 'Good, eh?'

She turned round and smiled at him, murmuring something inconsequential.

'Are you rehearsing today?' he went on.

'No, I've finished for the day. I'm just watching.'

He rose, came and sat next to her, kissed her hand.

'And is your friend, M Pardieu, not here too?' His small, dark eyes scanned the theatre.

'No, he's not in town. In fact, well—' she was beginning to sound quite flustered. 'We're not seeing each other at the moment.'

The portrait painter raised his eyebrows. 'Oh dear,' he murmured. 'Still, love comes and goes among the young, I dare say.'

She looked at him. She hadn't told him the whole truth. She had ditched Pardieu when he started complaining about her unreasonable demands. Another dress? More jewellery? Was she trying to milk him of every centime he had? She snorted with derision and threw him out of her apartment, the one he had been paying for.

But how handsome de Fleury looked with his grey hair and neatly trimmed beard. He made no move, by gesture or by word, to identify himself to La Cabache, whom they could see was seated on a skip full of costumes off to the side of the stage. In the back of the stalls, with the house lights down, they would have been all but invisible.

There was a silence among them. Satin could begin to feel her heart beating. She wondered how best she could urge along the inevitable moment.

'Are you—?'

'Did you—?'

They both spoke at once, and laughed. No, he wasn't staying. He had merely been passing the theatre on his way back to his studio and had dropped in on the off chance of a word with Moscato who, as it happened, had already left the theatre for the day and was not expected to return until rehearsals resumed on the Monday. He had a sitting at three, a young girl whom he was painting as a flower seller, a private commission.

It was inevitable that he should invite Satin to accompany him back to his studio. It was only a few minutes' walk from the theatre, though his own apartment was some considerable distance away, on the Rue Vignon.

'It's dreadfully boring,' he said, 'watching someone paint. Nothing happens much. You might as well sit in the park and watch the grass grow. The sitter gets a stiff neck, and that's about all there is to it.'

But Satin was nonplussed. 'I'm sure it's fascinating,' she said, lying through her teeth as she took his arm and they made their way out of the theatre. His fleeting presence had evidently not been noticed by his mistress.

Her eyes blinked in the unaccustomed brightness of day. Lost in a bizarre half-world of painted scenery and costumed actresses, rarely emerging from her apartment until after dark, and retreating to it as dawn broke, she found it difficult to adjust to the sudden sparkle of the summer sun. How rough and dirty everything looked in the harsh light of late afternoon. The people, they were so ugly. Everyone seemed so serious, so downtrodden. She was glad to reach the sanctity of his studio.

It was a large space in an imposing building occupied, for the most part, by clothiers of the highest calibre. The rent, said de Fleury, was extortionate but he had been able to secure a long lease on the premises and at least it was quiet. One of his friends, the landscape painter Seury, had a studio overlooking the Gare du Nord and he could barely work for the constant interruptions of whistles and the drifting smuts of smoke.

They made their way upstairs. The place was deserted. Satin wandered among half-finished canvases and paint-spattered furniture. The studio itself was covered in dust. It was even more untidy than her old apartment had been, despite Mathilde's constant attentions. The new place that she was renting for the whole of the summer, though three or four times the size, with a superb view towards the river from its balconies, wasn't much better. She felt immediately at home.

The painter came in with a bottle of wine and glasses. Satin was looking at the nearly completed painting of the flower girl. Her face was still incomplete but she could sense already how pretty she was. She reminded him of her friend at the Café des Artistes, Felicité. She caught a glimpse of her only the other night as she came out of a restaurant with Pardieu. She had pretended not to notice her. It wouldn't do for her to be recognised by women like that.

'Do you like it?' asked de Fleury, coming over and standing by his painting.

'It's lovely,' said Satin.

'It's nearly finished,' he explained. 'I must get it done by the end of April. My dealer is screaming for it. I have another commission, to paint Count Otto von Stalheim, and I have to travel to Bavaria. It is the only time he can see me, for the first two weeks in May.'

They sipped their wine, standing by the open window. Satin looked out over the rooftops of the city where she had lived almost all her adult life. Those days as a child in the countryside of the Ile de France suddenly seemed a long way away. She had come far, in the past few years, and the feeling was as intoxicating as the wine she sipped.

Down below, the spires and domes seemed to be crowding in on her but up here she felt free, liberated from the oppression of the streets.

The time of the flower girl's appointment drew close. De Fleury selected his paintbrushes, adjusted his easel. 'I have an assistant,' he said, laughing. 'But he doesn't usually come in on Saturdays.'

There was a knock on the door. He answered it. A small boy stood there, a little urchin of eight or nine. He spoke quickly in a hushed whisper. For a moment, de Fleury's face fell, but then he dug in his pocket and handed the boy a coin. He patted him on the head and then closed the door behind him.

'Just my luck,' he said, jangling the change in his pocket. 'Sabine – that's the little girl who's been acting as my model – has a fever. That was her brother. They're a poor family, her father's dead, her mother is a dressmaker. She works a couple of streets away – that's where I saw her. They live in the Marais. They need the money. Damn. I really must get the painting finished. Still, no use crying over spilled milk.'

He poured them both another glass. Satin saw her opportunity. She took off her hat and coat – which she had kept on throughout her visit – and sat down on the sofa by the window. She knew the soft light would outline her fine features to their best advantage, emphasise her spectacular figure by silhouetting it against the window.

He stood by the fireplace, watching her. She knew what was going through his mind.

Their conversation was stilted and artificial but that mattered little to her. She had other plans.

'I'd like to have my portrait painted one day,' she started to say but before she could go any further he'd come and sat down next to her on the sofa and kissed her full on the lips. She felt her heart melting away. She wanted him to release her, but she wanted to take him away from La Cabache too. She didn't care much about him for herself. The other woman represented something she'd known she'd wanted all her life but had never dared ask for. Now, she felt, it was within her grasp.

There was a kind of ferocious inevitability about the way she responded to his burning kisses, his roving hands. It was born of her jealousy as much as her raging lusts. She wanted to make it worth his while to seduce her, to captivate him utterly, to make him lust after her and not

La Cabache, the woman with whom he had shared his life for two years.

This was the reality of love in the modern age. This was not the kind of silly love story they acted out on stage, before a gullible audience. This was what it was really down to in the end – envy and contempt. Stealing. Hatred. Power and possession.

She snatched at the buttons of his jacket, hauling the black material down over his shoulders, burying her face in the hollow of his neck, her mouth wide open, her tongue working.

Her hands were pulling his shirt out from his trousers, holding on to the hard muscles of his stomach and back, roving over him like she'd never explored a man's body before. He had his hand up under her dress, up above her stockings, pressing against her pudenda through her drawers. She would, she knew, be soaking wet already. He looked like the kind of man who would find that exciting.

He tore his shirt off, and then his underlinen. His chest was deep and covered in a mat of greying hair. He had hard little brown nipples and she greedily sucked at each of them in turn, and she was aware of the big, powerful muscles of his chest as they rose and fell with his breathing.

She raised her face up and pulled his head down, seeking his lips, those cool grey eyes that had been watching her dispassionately as he stood by the fireplace. I want to make you want me like you've never wanted anyone before, her eyes told him. I want you to forget that other woman.

He helped her step out of her dress – a task she normally entrusted to Mathilde – and she let it fall on to the floor. It was new only last week, made for her by a dressmaker who had cut cloth for some of the most fashionable figures in Paris society. Maybe it had been made by the flower-seller's mother, who could have known? Now she stood there in her linen, snowy white and billowing, trimmed with lace, her bodice heaving above the epic construction of her stays. She let his eyes take her in for a moment, could sense them moving over her ripe, full breasts and the flat stomach, the swell of her hips. It looks good, doesn't it? her body seemed to be silently saying. You like what you see, don't you? Wait till you get a taste of it.

Breaking from his embrace, she took off her drawers and then his hand was between her legs, cupping her. She could sense again the wetness that was there, born of her frantic desire. She stood with her legs slightly apart, standing on tiptoe, with only her boots and stockings on from the waist down, and they were kissing again and he was running his fingers up and down the length of her labia – God, that felt good – and then he slipped what must have been two, no three fingers right into her.

It was exactly like having a cock in there, stretching her wide. She squeezed him hard with her vaginal muscles, holding his other hand as she did so. She thrust her breasts at him, pressing them hard against his chest, and he let go of her hand and began pawing her, releasing first one breast from her stays and then the other, evidently surprised at the size of them.

They were magnificent, full and raspberry-tipped. She could see the pleasure they gave him. She looked forward to him sucking them, taking their weight in his hands. He took his finger out of her vagina and was busy with his trouser buttons, finally hurling them to one side.

His cock was huge, one of the biggest she had ever seen. It had a big purple helmet that looked as if it was inflamed. Quite impulsively she sank to her knees and took it in her mouth, swirling her tongue around over its moist surface. He tasted salty and clean. She was sure he had lots of come in him. She knew from what the girls had said at the Café des Artistes that it took a lot to satisfy La Cabache.

Still in his socks and shoes, he was pushing her over backwards on to the couch, his cock jutting out like a weapon. He went into her straight away, with no preliminaries. There was no time for any of that, neither of them wanted it, there was just an insistent, animal urging inside them. She parted her legs as wide as she could, as if he were going to drive right inside her, and hooked them up around his hips, her arse in the air, using her legs as levers to haul herself up on to that gorgeous, thrusting cock that was buried in her right up to the hilt.

He felt as enormous as he looked, even though she was aware of how wet and floppy she was from all the hundreds of cocks she had had inside her. He was bucking and thrusting against her hips and when she looked up she could see his eyes were tight shut and he was sweating, head back, and the veins on his forehead were standing out with the effort.

'Come on, you bastard,' she called out. 'Get it up me.'

He opened his grey eyes lazily and smiled at her, and she saw how white and even his teeth were. He evidently liked a woman who spoke her mind.

'Give me that lovely thick cock now.'

He shoved hard, a harsh, stabbing movement that made her gasp. His eyes never left her face. He seemed to be asking her a question.

'Yes, like that,' she gasped. 'Do it to me. Do it to me good and hard.'

Again he thrust at her. Each time it was like being pierced by a blunt instrument but she wanted him in there, wanted this stranger to invade her, to violate her privacy. She couldn't remember when she'd last felt so excited with a man, so swept away by the rush of desire that went speeding through her veins like the tinctures that her doctor from Neufchatel brought her. It had nothing to do with La Cabache any more, it was just about her and this man. This wasn't making love or anything like that – she didn't know what the words meant, in any case – this was just fucking plain and simple.

She could feel it now, the little flutterings inside her womb, her senses teetering on the edge, her body starting to become prickly as though a series of small electric shocks were rippling over its surface. For some reason her eyes were wide open and she could see, over his heaving back, the half-completed canvas of the flower-seller and her own expensive gown lying on the floor, discarded like a snakeskin that had been sloughed.

Again and again he forced himself into her and the feeling inside her was growing, and everything began to merge until she was just one enormous vagina and he was just one enormous penis, and then something let go and she felt these huge shuddering pulses go through her. She could even sense her arsehole opening and closing in little spasms – something she'd never known before – and she was falling down into some deep and swirling pit even as she felt him come off into her, her hips moving automatically, her tongue blindly seeking his.

Afterwards, they lay together on the sofa. She felt cold, wished there was a rug or some kind of cover they could pull over each other. But she felt sated and wanton too as she lay there beside him, her hair chaotic and her body slick with sweat and sperm. She was still wearing her stays – he had gone crazy over her breasts as they spilled out of them – and she sat up and managed, with no small difficulty, to take them off, tossing them on to the heap of clothes on the floor.

She needed to piddle. He told her where the closet was, hidden behind a screen in a far corner of the room. She got up and walked naked across the room, aware of his eyes on her and that stupendous arse. As she relieved herself she felt a tingling all over her skin and all her nerve-endings seemed to be alive. She didn't feel a trace of guilt, just glad that she had taken something from La Cabache and made it hers.

When she came back into the room Frédéric was sitting up on the couch drinking wine. His penis looked smaller now that it was only half erect. He poured her a glass and made her sit on his lap. Then he fucked her hard from behind, pressing up against her arse, reaching round to fondle those large and prominent breasts as they hung down like over-ripe cherries. He made her come, twice, before he spilled his seed deep inside her womb. He loved her breasts, he said. She felt triumphant.

The affair with de Fleury continued, at intervals, throughout the rehearsals. By the time the play opened, they had slept together four or five times – once at her new apartment, once at a hotel, the remaining times at his studio during 'sittings' for the now much-postponed painting of the flower seller. The dealer continued to plead he could sell the work six times over if only it were finished but his words were to no avail – de Fleury had other concerns for the moment. La Cabache, Satin and de Fleury knew, was entirely ignorant of their dallyings. It was not the first time the painter had strayed since he had been living with her. Satin, of course, was well versed in secret intimacies and let not a slip fall to anyone with the exception of Mathilde.

Interest in the new production was mounting daily. Almost every seat for the first night was now taken. La Cabache, as ever, was the name on everyone's lips, but there was a strong swell of curiosity about the role of Satin. People who had seen her in her only previous performance spoke of it in reverential terms. The new play, it was rumoured, would be even more sensational, despite the presence on the same stage of the great actress La Cabache.

Moscato did all he could to fan these rumours and expectations. Privately, though, he was worried about the course of events. The play itself was fine. Everything was on schedule – well, only a little behind – and things looked set for a triumphant opening night. The leading characters, in particular, were coming into their parts superbly, and none more so than La Cabache. At the first dress rehearsal even an old cynic like him had been moved almost to tears, such was the intensity of her performance.

No, the problem was with Satin. Everyone knew, of course, that she couldn't act. All she could do, when she got on a stage, was to shimmer with the kind of incandescent sexuality that had been such a stunning success in the role of Aphrodite. None of that, or very little of it, was coming through into *Lovers' Vows*, even though the opening night was only four days away.

In vain did Moscato plead with her, flatter her vanity, offer little encouragements. She was as wooden as the door to his office, behind which he was sequestered for increasingly anxious hours. It was far, far too late for them to get in another actress and besides, who would believe in him any longer if he failed to deliver his promised sensation. As his Sunday-evening dominatrix beat him, he cursed his foolishness in allowing himself to be seduced by the woman's over-ripe sensuality.

There seemed to be no reason for her diffidence, though he was aware of a vague frisson between Satin and Frédéric de Fleury – although, in truth, Satin seemed to have that effect on every man who came into contact with her. Certainly La Cabache seemed entirely innocent of any machinations on the part of her lover, as she sat now in the impresario's office, still in her make-up but with a robe around her.

'I tell you,' she was saying, 'she was absolutely appalling this afternoon. She forgot half her lines, she missed her cue, she got in everyone's way. At one stage Boffon practically fell over her when she managed to get herself somewhere she had no right to be. The woman's a liability. We'll be a laughing stock if this continues.'

'I know, I know,' Moscato sighed wearily, his head in his hands. 'Believe me, my dear, I've tried almost everything. I just don't know what to do. Maybe I've made a terrible mistake. But it seemed such a good idea at the time.'

He had already called in Blanco, the playwright, to engineer a few little changes to make things easy for Satin – the timing of her entrances, the length of her already brief speeches. But nothing seeemed to work, nothing at all. He made his way down into the auditorium with a heavy heart to watch the rehearsals of the final act.

In the normal course of events he would have been hugely delighted with the way things were going. But as the scenes unfolded, he felt an increasing heaviness of heart. When Satin finally came on stage for her last scene – the one in which she contemptuously dismisses the man she has lusted after – he could hardly bear to watch.

But Satin was a revelation. Instead of her previous sluggishness and show of indifference, here was real projection of her character. Bathsheba suddenly came alive before his eyes – wilful, capricious, imbued with a dark and terrible sensuality. It wasn't so much what she said as the way she said it, the words almost spat out, the heavy air of turgid longing that accompanied her every contribution. Despite his own predilections, he felt himself becoming aroused by the way she acted on stage – that arrogant haughtiness, the huskiness in the voice, the clear impression of a woman totally at ease with herself and with her body.

When the scene was over everyone, cast included, broke into a spontaneous spattering of applause. Satin bowed and acknowledged their acclaim but remained aloof and within herself. She left the stage quickly and hurried to her dressing room.

As fast as he could, Moscato freed himself from the crowd who had clustered around him and bounded up the stairs after his new-found star. At last she had done what was wanted of her. She was wonderful. She would be the sensation of his career, rather than its destroyer. He knew he had been right all along – he just had that feeling.

He knocked on the door, made his way into the cramped little room, past the costumes that were hung untidily on rails. Satin was sitting at her rickety mirror, already scraping her face-paint off with a cloth.

'You were fabulous, darling,' he cried, his round little face positively twinkling. 'I've never seen anything like it, in thirty years in the theatre. Everyone loved you. The play will be a wonderful success.'

'That's not what you were saying earlier,' she pouted sulkily. 'I knew you were trying to get at me.'

'Nonsense, dear child, nonsense. I was simply trying to encourage you. Everything's fine. Don't worry. Everyone loves you.'

She looked levelly at him. 'I want another two hundred on top of my existing fee,' she said simply. 'Either that, or I don't act.'

Moscato was dumbstruck, he couldn't believe what he'd just heard. He was already paying her almost as much as La Cabache's agent had usurously extracted from him, and now she was asking for half as much again. It was impossible. He had to say no and yet, in his heart, he knew he couldn't. She had duped him, had duped everyone. She'd made them think she couldn't act and then, when she'd proved that she could and everyone had relaxed, she was making this ridiculous demand. Intuitively, he knew he would have to find the money, out of his own pocket if necessary. And the money was not everything. In half a sentence he agreed in principle to her every demand, and then he left her alone in her dressing room. Satin glowed with inner triumph.

* * *

She reached her apartment still in a state of elation, scarcely in need of the tinctures that her friend Thierry Albert had brought, punctually as always. He rose to his feet as she swept in, embraced her. They went almost immediately into the bedroom, more overflowing than ever now with her clothes and material possessions. The place was owned by a scion of the Rothschild family, and was not required until autumn. Satin had been able to secure it on very favourable terms. Her visitors were most impressed.

She watched like a hawk as he measured out the contents of the bottle, did the necessary business with his little glass pipettes. Oh, she was ready for it, that familiar taste of raisins and chemicals. Where once Thierry Albert had brought her release and respite from the wear and stress of late nights at the Café des Artistes, now she looked on her addiction as a means of propelling herself still further into the realms of pleasure. She craved the drug's soft enveloping of her feelings and sensations, the new awareness of being swaddled in the softest down.

They took it together, each silently lost for a few minutes in their own individual rapture. And then they looked at each other, and giggled like errant children – this highly qualified pharmacist, this streetwalker-turned-actress – and tore off each other's clothes in their raging passion for one another.

They fell naked into bed together, their bodies writhing and mingling on clean, fresh sheets but their spirits somewhere up among the clouds. He went into her straight away and she gasped as he took her, his violence tempered by the softening effect of the drug, again and again as he pushed into her. She spread her legs out wide for him, aware of the way she gaped and the lewdness with which she welcomed him inside her. Oh, but he was strong, Thierry. Frédéric de Fleury was an imaginative and inventive lover but Thierry was all power and strength, a man more like a rutting animal.

They paused, panting for breath. She had already come once, abandoning herself wildly to her passions. She could still feel the drug running through her veins, her senses beautifully numbed and distorted. She turned round on the crisp white sheets and looked at his dilated pupils.

'Put it up my arse,' she murmured dreamily.

'Suck me first.'

She slid down the bed, down his long and hairless torso. She could smell his arousal, the tangy smell of maleness that arose from his loins. With the bedclothes kicked roughly back she took hold of his penis in one hand and began to move her fingers up and down his shaft. She was fascinated by the way his foreskin drew back and forwards under her expert touch, hiding and then revealing the domed purple glans with its mysterious little eye in the middle. What a strange shape the tip of a man's prick was, she reflected. It wasn't round at all, more a collection of curves and ridges going off in different directions. She had looked at many of them and she didn't think any two were quite alike.

She swirled her tongue over him – how clean and fresh he tasted – and then took the whole length of his shaft into her mouth until she almost choked. He tried to push against her but she pushed back, bidding him resist. He might hurt her and she didn't want her pleasure to be over too soon.

Up and down she bobbed her head, lying there crouched over his body at the foot of the bed, and then she began to turn herself round, still with his penis in her mouth, so that her body was lying inverted by his side. Her pubic bush was now almost level with his face and when she parted her legs for him he showered her lower lips with kisses, his tongue flickering in and out until it found the little nibbly bud of her clitoris.

The shock was almost too much for her. 'Enough,' she sighed, and got – a little unsteadily – on to all fours on the bed, with her feet on the pillows. Thierry's cock lolled there, hugely erect after she had sucked him up to his full stiffness. His saliva and her own juices were running all over her pussy and arse.

He climbed up behind her, moistening the tip of his cock with his own spittle, though it was still wet from her ministrations. It was never difficult to get into her from this attitude. As usual, Satin took control, arching round and with her hand steering his cock until it was pressed against her tight little rosebud.

'Now,' she said and he pushed forward. Instantly she felt herself filled to repletion, that great distended cock in that narrow channel. It hurt, sometimes, but not now, the laudanum loose in her veins making her reckless, and she urged him to fuck her hard in her arse. She had never known him so big up there. Her new lover de Fleury's cock, she knew, would almost split her apart but Thierry was a more reasonable size, better suited perhaps to her little games.

As Thierry rocked backwards and forwards, his arms clasped around her waist, she basked in the warm glow of the afternoon's triumphs, her humbling of Moscato, the applause of the cast, the knowledge that she had stolen the lover of La Cabache. She felt powerful and wild and free, fucking this man in the afternoon sunlight, her mind still reeling from the drug.

His expertly probing fingers found her clitoris and this time she let him caress it, moving her towards orgasm even as he powered into her from behind. The gentleness of his fingers contrasted with the violence of his rearward attack – though to her it was all a part of the same sensation, inevitable and irresistible, her breasts swinging free as she pushed back against him, spreading herself right to the hilt on his cock even as she felt the little butterfly tremblings inside her building up into a steady fluttering roar of feeling. She was scarcely aware of the torrent of seed that came bursting out from his loins and into her violated body. Instead, she was lost in a dizzy kaleidoscope of her own senses, where pleasure and pain became one and nothing had any meaning any longer and everything was just feeling.

They lay on the bed for some while afterwards. Perhaps they even slept for a moment or two. Satin was aroused by Mathilde's frantic tapping on the door.

'Madame,' she hissed. 'M de Fleury is here.'

Satin sat up with a start. Frédéric? Here already? He wasn't due until seven. She looked at the handsome ormolu clock on her dressing table, a recent gift from an admirer. The hands pointed to seven.

'Quick, quick,' she snapped at the dozing Thierry. 'You must go. Someone is here.'

To Mathilde, she called: 'Tell him I have a headache. Tell him I've just woken up. He can come in and see me when I'm ready.'

She all but pushed Thierry out of the bed and into his clothes. The pharmacist was as confused and panic-stricken as she was.

'What shall I do?' he asked.

'Hide in my dressing room,' she replied, quick as a flash. 'I'll try to get rid of him. Then you can come out.'

The dressing room in Satin's apartment was, if anything, less than half the size of the tiny cubicle in which she attired herself at the theatre. But needs must, and Thierry quickly gathered up his clothes and disappeared among the gowns and coats while Satin frantically made up the bed and slipped into a silk night robe that de Fleury had given her only the other day.

She drew a languid hand over her brow as Mathilde, in answer to Satin's call, ushered the great portraitist into Satin's boudoir. He was, if anything, in even more of a hurry than his predessor had been. He smiled his greetings, asked anxiously after her health, was pleased to hear that she would be well for tomorrow's opening night.

'I have a little something for you,' he declared after satisfying himself that her illness was no more than a mistress's caprice.

Satin always liked to be given things. It made her feel special, wanted. The more extravagant the token of affection, the better she liked it – and the giver.

In this desire, as in so many on that fateful day, she was not to be disappointed. She opened up the box he had given her and found, nestling among padding of the palest pink silk, an ebony dildo, banded in silver. She looked at it in amazement. Set into the end, in a filigree mount, was a single diamond.

'Do you like it?' he asked, anxiously.

'Like it?' she said. 'It's wonderful. Where on earth did you get it?'

In answer he tapped her lips. 'No need to ask too many questions, my sweet,' he said simply. 'Sometimes it's best not to know these things. I am not the only artist with a reputation at stake. There are some remarkable artists in Paris, as you well know.'

Already his hands were busy under her silken nightrobe, cupping her generous breasts. She kissed him open-mouthed, passionate and urgent, her eyes on the gleaming black godemiche on the bed beside her. She wondered how it would feel inside her, whether Frédéric had had it modelled on his own generous member or whether the sculptor had simply used his imagination. Surely it was the work of various hands, the man who fashioned it in hard ebony, turning it on a lathe presumably, the silversmith who added the delicate filigree work and the lavishly engraved banding.

He lowered his head and kissed each of her nipples in turn. For a moment she forgot that Thierry was secreted in the closet beside them. The hunger of her suitor was obvious and immediate. His tongue roved over her

119

breasts, over her neck, down her body. His agile fingers undid the tiny pearl buttons that ran down the front of her robe and then he pulled it down from her shoulders, her plump breasts now free and magnificent. For a moment he looked at her, rapt in admiration, and then he clasped her to his side as he busied himself with his own buttons and hooks. She noticed that the closet door was slightly ajar, could sense Thierry's presence in there, watching them.

'Lie down,' said Satin as soon as he was as naked as her. He did as he was told, his head on the pillow beside her. Quickly she clambered up on to his lap, offering him again first one breast and then the other. He licked and lapped at them until her nipples stood out hard and red, glistening with his saliva. She pushed his head down further on to the pillow and then climbed up on top of him until she was practically sitting on his face.

'Eat me out, you wicked man,' she commanded. Frédéric de Fleury, one of the greatest painters of his generation, needed no second bidding. His probing tongue lapped against her pubic bush, seeking out her dark and sopping folds. His skill was breathtaking but Satin was more aware of Thierry's eyes, peering round the crack in the door.

She caught his eye, nodded her head vigorously in the direction of the door, all the time pushing down hard on de Fleury's face lest he look up and see the man who, as agile as a fox, stole out of the tiny dressing room and tiptoed fully clothed across the bedroom floor. Satin, squatting naked over her other lover, her large breasts jiggling, even blew him a kiss. And then the door clicked and he was gone. Mathilde knew better than to ask questions, and now Satin could enjoy the pleasures of the great portraitist's tongue without further distraction.

Still feeling the effects of the drug inside her, she floated ever nearer to that magical moment of release. His tongue seeming to stretch deep inside her, licking and lapping, exploring all her most sensitive and secret folds. Oh, but de Fleury knew how to pleasure a woman. Thierry, the man with whom she had made love not an hour before, had the strength and the staying power but Frédéric had literally the skills of an artist. He was touching her clitoris with just the very tip of his tongue and yet the sensations that he was able to release in her were almost unbearable. She drew in a deep breath, tensed her thighs and came in a great shuddering wave of pleasure until she almost seemed to rise up above herself, looking down from somewhere on high at their two bodies there on the bed beneath them, so intimately conjoined.

Mathilde brought them champagne while they lay there, the covers pulled lightly over their nakedness to spare them from the chill air of early evening. There was no fire in the room, now that spring was slowly giving way to summer. They sipped and made pleasant conversation. Then, while she handled his once-more burgeoning penis, he took hold of the dildo and handed it to her to lick.

Her tongue roved over its exemplary smoothness, a perfection of finish that was exquisite. It even tasted real, alive. She longed to have it inside her, lying there on the tangled white sheets, making sure de Fleury could see her tongue as it snaked over the delicate silverware, played with the glittering jewel in the end.

With one hand she stroked this exciting new toy while, with the other, she caressed his penis until both were of equal hardness.

'Put it up me,' she breathed at length.

He ran a gentle finger along the ridge of her nose. 'Which one, my dear?'

'Whichever one you'd like. The dildo first, perhaps.'

He smiled to himself, used his knee to part her legs. They opened willingly for him. Then, with gentle force, he inserted the jewelled tip of that great black thing. To Satin it felt eager and hard, just like a real prick, but cool also, so she was aware of how heated her cunt had become, could feel how easily its polished surface slipped between her welcoming lips and swallowed it up. Soon it was buried in her almost to the hilt.

Frédéric moved it about inside her with consummate delicacy, long slow strokes alternating with movements that were almost like caresses. The feeling was extraordinary, the size and the hardness that were equal to if not greater than that of any penis she had ever taken before. She wondered sometimes, having taken so many men in her life, whether she might be beginning to lose her celebrated tightness – 'like fucking a virgin', a distant scion of the Saxe-Coburg dynasty had once told her – but the dildo quelled all her fears. She felt full and sated, stretched to the limit. She knew she was imminently going to come again.

She took hold of Frédéric's prick, frigging him vigorously up and down. No time for subleties now. As both of them, lying cheek to cheek, their lips almost touching, murmured sweet obscenities to one another, she could feel his muscles beginning to tense. He called out something unintelligible and then, right at the moment when the first wave of her own orgasm hit her, he spouted out a thick stream of creamy-white spunk all over those spectacular breasts.

Little rivulets of semen were running down the soft flanks of her body as she withdrew the dildo and tasted it experimentally. It was rich and salty. She dipped it in the deep pool of semen that lay still in the valley between her breasts. Then she licked the dildo again, the familiar ammoniacal smell of a man's spending, the unmistakable taste. She made Frédéric lick it too, dipping the jewel-studded godemiche again and again into that slowly spreading lake of sperm. When it had finally seeped away, she made him do it all over again, starting with her nipples.

Chapter Five

Lovers' Vows; or, The Testing of Elspeth was certainly the making of Satin. Systematically, and with a cunning that was almost reckless in its audacity, she turned her new-found status to her advantage. Largely on credit that couturiers were only too willing to provide, she acquired an entire wardrobe of new clothes – in the very van of fashion, of course – and took a lease on a new apartment, on the equally fashionable Boulevard de la Madeleine. She was even able to afford a carriage – a modest one, perhaps, but a carriage nevertheless. It gave her immense pride to stand on the balcony that overlooked the busy thoroughfare so many floors beneath and to see it waiting there, ready at her beck and call. On Sundays she would often go riding in the park, to see and be seen. Her name appeared in the society papers with a regularity that was becoming monotonous and yet it seemed the public could not have enough of her, in Paris at any rate.

The faithful Mathilde was joined by a young footman, a black boy from Africa called M'Barki – Satin simply called him Mu. His duties were not onerous and were more decorative than functional – for the most part he just hung around the apartment, ushering in visitors and serving drinks. She also acquired a new lover, the Comte de Loury, and dumped the faithful Moscato – the man who had hauled her up from the streets – for a new impresario, Alain Hubert. Surrounded by furs and the favours of a wealthy elite, the old days at the Café des

Artistes suddenly seemed a long way away.

As all great actresses – in which category she would unquestionably now have placed herself – like to do by volition, and lesser ones do because they have no choice, she rested for a substantial period after the completion of the current run of *Lovers' Vows*. There had been plans for a revival early the following year if there was sufficient demand, even to take it on a provincial tour – the name of Satin was, as yet, but little known in the provinces – but these were now in abeyance with the hasty departure of Moscato. La Cabache, too, had other commitments – or rather, she hastily managed to arrange them. She did not take kindly to the way Satin seemed to consume everything that lay before her.

Satin had triumphed over her infinitely more experienced and infinitely more gifted rival. Her performance as Bathsheba had set a new standard in sensation – on stage, she lived and breathed a disturbing sensuality that came from deep within herself. There was no way that La Cabache could compete with that. In bed with de Fleury, too, she showed herself to be a gifted and innovative partner, an exciting adjunct to La Cabache, a welcome and increasingly indispensible distraction. She never knew quite when La Cabache began to realise the nature of the dalliance between her companion and the young actress – he had dallied before, but never for very long – but during the lengthy and highly lucrative run of the play she could tell by the other woman's deepening moods and burgeoning hostility that her arrows had struck home.

As soon as she had driven a deep wedge between the actress and the portraitist she dropped him. One afternoon he came to her apartment – the old one she had rented for the summer from the Rothschild family – and she refused to see him. He returned the following day with flowers and gifts and she consented to see him for an hour. They had made love, with great passion on his part and with a show of bored indifference on hers. That evening they ate together at Antoine's. She flirted openly with a young barrister, a friend of de Fleury's. In the cab back to her apartment the great painter was almost apoplectic with fury. To madden him further, she refused to let him take her in her backside again. That was the last time they slept together. He would call on her almost daily but she was not at home to him, despite the increasingly extravagent gifts he showered on her – and which she was cynical enough to accept. Finally he got the message, and took up with a young girl who modelled for him. The portrait of the flower seller was never completed.

The dumping of Moscato was brutal. He had an option on her next play. She didn't want to do it – it was, in many ways, a rehash of her role as Bathsheba in *Lovers' Vows*. The playwright he had brought in was the indefatiguably third-rate Cocon, a writer of little imagination. The play that he outlined had absolutely no merit, Satin insisted. It was simply a blatantly calculating attempt to cash in on her popularity in the previous play. What was so dreadfully wrong with that? he argued. She simply refused to countenance it. Friends – she refused to name them – insisted she try for something much better. Molière was becoming increasingly popular once more, she said. Moscato knew the great playwright's work well and could not think of a single role in all the huge volume of his work that would be even remotely suitable for an actress of Satin's extremely limited abilities.

When it seemed she was refusing to do another play with him, he showed her the clause in her contract that tied her to him for two more plays over the next twelve months. She flatly refused to honour them. He suggested their lawyers discuss the matter. She was just waiting for the opportunity to mention the evening at that small, quiet house in the Marais when, in disguise, she had beaten him until his buttocks were crossed with flaming, angry weals. To have a weapon to use against him later was one of the reasons why she had gone through with it.

She told him all about it, in precise and lavish detail.

Moscato had turned bright red, looked down at the threadbare carpet of his office, tried to say a few words. He was a strong man of the church and the revelation of such news – should Satin care to reveal it – would destroy him. He had a wife in Vincennes, an invalid. He prayed for her every day.

'How do you know all this?' he finally managed to say.

'I just do, that's all.'

'How can you prove it?'

'I don't need to. You know exactly what I'm talking about.'

'You haven't any witnesses. It's just hearsay. You didn't see anything yourself of what you say happened.'

'Didn't I?'

He turned to look at her. The woman in the mask and the leather corset, those long black gloves? He tried to look her in the eyes, tried to imagine the savagery that must have been there for her to have beaten him so viciously on that painful night. 'No actress has ever been paid so highly, not even La Cabache. You could have the same again, you know.'

'I deserved it,' said Satin, her eyes like steel. 'It was me that people paid to see, not that old bag. I only took what was fairly due to me.'

'I'm sure you did,' retorted Moscato, desperately trying to recover his composure. 'But part of the arrangement was that you would appear in the next play I put on.'

'I never said that.'

'You signed a contract.'

'Did I?'

'Of course you did.'

'I'm sure I didn't read it, then.'

'But you knew about the option. You knew you had two

126

more plays to do. We talked about it, don't you remember? That was why we let you have the extra money.'

'I don't remember a single word of it. I think you're making this up.'

'I'll say it to you again – would you like to talk about it with a lawyer?' He waved a sheaf of papers in her face, trying to call her bluff. 'After all, you could afford a good one now.'

'You talk to them,' she said. 'I'm not doing your new play, and that's final. It's rubbish, anyway. Cocon is a lousy writer, everyone says so. You try and force me, and I'll let it be known about your little soirée with the lady in black.'

'You wouldn't dare.' He was angry too now.

'Wouldn't I? You just try me.'

'And even then they wouldn't believe you.'

'What makes you say that?'

'A man in my position – and a woman in yours, a former streetwalker.' He managed an ironic, cynical laugh. 'It would be your word against mine. Your career would be over before it began. They'd wipe the floor with you in a court of law. Your word against mine, remember.'

'Like I said, I've got witnesses.'

The silence that descended on the room was palpable.

'Witnesses?'

'Witnesses.'

'Who?'

'Someone was watching.'

'Who?'

'Never you mind. But he's a very respectable gentleman. He knows you. You know him.'

'He wouldn't compromise himself, not in court. No gentleman would admit to frequenting a house such as that.'

'Then you're no gentleman yourself. And he wouldn't need to compromise himself. It wouldn't ever get to court, would it?'

Moscato knew it wouldn't. He tore up the contract. Satin had called his bluff and come up trumps. There was no witness, of course. She just made it up, to add spice to her argument. It was another way she had become aware of her increasing power – people believed what she said. She just had to say something – anything – and they took it at face value.

Moscato was devastated. The extra money he had paid Satin for her part in the *Lovers' Vows* had been provided by one of his backers, in anticipation of a long and profitable association with the new star. Those three plays that she had been contracted for were only the beginning. As things stood, the play had actually lost money, including some of Moscato's own, because of Satin's excessive demands. It would have had to have run for over six months to show a profit, instead of six weeks. These men were not fools; they knew about short-term losses and long-term gains. Now there would be no profits, not for themselves at any rate. Moscato would have an awful lot of explaining to do.

That evening, at his house in Vincennes, he quietly locked himself away in his study. He took the contract from a locked drawer and burned it in the fireplace, crushing the ash between his fingers. Then, from another drawer, he took a pistol. His final act was to write a note to his wife.

Satin and Thierry Albert lay naked on the bed together, the huge Louis XVI four-poster that, Satin had been told, had once occupied the bedroom of the king's mistress at Versailles. Exhilarated by his love-making and by the tincture that slowly seeped through her veins, she felt like she was royalty herself.

Idly, she glanced through a book of engravings that she had acquired, images of men and women in poses of wanton abandonment. Here, a group of gentlemen in a brothel showed more than a passing interest in the way one of their number was openly fucking a young courtesan in full view of everyone. In another picture, a woman – a servant girl, evidently – knelt to suck a man's cock while he peered through the keyhole at the amorous antics of the newly married couple in the next room. The book was full of tempting ideas and possibilities – women dancing naked before an appreciative audience, that kind of thing. It would be nice to do something like that herself, to throw a really wild party like the ones in the pictures. She felt aroused once more.

She nudged Thierry Albert awake.

'Come on,' she said. 'I need to be fucked.'

She ran her fingers along the not inconsiderable length of his penis until it began to stiffen. Then she knelt down, took its sugar-plum end in her mouth just as the servant girl in the picture had, and brought him up to full erection.

She climbed on top of him, guiding him into her. Her pussy was still sticky from his earlier spendings. She remembered one of her regulars from the old days at the Café des Artistes, a man who liked her to come to him immediately after she had been fucked by another. A senior official at the Préfecture, he greatly enjoyed the sensation of fucking in another man's spunk.

She bobbed up and down, those snowy white breasts bouncing enticingly in front of the pharmacist's face. He stretched forward on the pillows, took one of her nipples in his mouth, rolled it around between his lips, caressed it with his tongue.

How lovely her own breasts were, she thought, studying herself in the mirrors that lay on either side of the bed. She was twenty years old, going on twenty-one, and her body was magnificent, fecund and irresistible. She was glad she had not breast-fed little Armand when he was a baby but had put him out to a wet nurse. It did things to a woman's body, giving a child the breast. She herself had been back on the streets within a fortnight of giving birth.

She must go and see him more often, she really must, she told herself. Guilt was an emotion to which Satin was, by and large, a stranger. But some almost forgotten maternal instinct still drew her to that house in the little town outside Paris where, for an afternoon, perhaps less, she would spend what time she could spare – which was not much – with her son.

She looked down at Thierry Albert as he nuzzled succulently on her breasts, tonguing her nipples until she squealed with delight.

'Hey!' she said. 'Let's try some more of that tincture.'

He brought it to her, as he always had done, every second Tuesday of the month. She was using it more than ever now, welcoming the relief it brought her. Often, after a night of champagne and dancing, she would feel too exhausted to do anything much beyond lie around in bed and wait for that evening's round of parties to start. The tinctures kept her going, led her through her dreamy afternoons so that she did not need to do anything to amuse herself, just to take a little phial full and transport herself to her own private arcadia. It was better than champagne, better even than shopping. It was almost as nice as making love with a rich man – and the only men with whom Satin made love these days were very rich indeed.

Later, still unsteady on their feet, they dressed. Satin wanted to go out riding, to take the carriage with little Mu perched on top. The ornamental ponds and terraces of the Jardin des Tuileries suddenly seemed very desirable to her. Everyone would be there at that time of day! She spent an age dressing, trying on one outfit and then another, choosing one hat and then discarding it. Finally she was satisfied.

They soon reached the gardens. They left the carriage in the Place de la Concorde, walked along the elegant box-lined avenues, admiring the statues and the formal plantings, from time to time nodding and exchanging greetings with passing acquaintances. The shadows of evening were beginning to lengthen now. They left the broad main avenue behind, strolling along the narrower terraces towards the river.

A woman approached, walking arm-in-arm with a gentleman. Satin had been admiring her hat – a spectacular creation of silk and ostrich feathers that she would very much have liked to own herself, were it not for the fact that it were so obviously the kind of millinery that a streetwalker would have adopted.

The woman was plainly a tart, Satin could tell from the cut of her dress. That pink parasol too – there were so many subtle codes that gay ladies could adopt. She had obviously just picked up the man. They were presumably walking towards one of the hotels just off the Rue de Rivoli that catered for pleasure-seekers, whatever the time of day.

As they drew level, the woman in the ostrich-feather hat looked up. Her face was immediately familiar. It was Felicité, the girl she had known so well at the Café des Artistes. Satin felt confused, uncertain. She did not need to be reminded of her past life, not at this stage. She tried to look away but Felicité had already spotted her. She affected not to have seen her, looking disdainfully away.

Satin caught Thierry Albert's arm.

'I feel faint,' she said, leaning on him for good effect. 'I've had such a headache all afternoon. You must take me back to the carriage, right now.'

Thierry Albert did as he was bade. Felicité and her gentleman admirer simply stood there, watching.

The man turned to the tart he'd just picked up and with whom he had struck a very acceptable bargain.

'Wasn't that Satin, the actress?' he said, excited by this momentary contact with celebrity.

Felicité took his arm and propelled him firmly towards the hotel.

'It certainly was Satin,' she said in a quiet voice so he could not hear the anger in her words. 'But whether she still is, is quite another matter.'

Satin had been approached by Hubert after *Lovers' Vows; or, The Testing of Elspeth* had been running for barely a week – enough to establish itself as the most sensational play of the season. When he casually mentioned her future arrangements, she had equally casually forgotten to mention her deal with Moscato. That, she felt, would take care of itself when the time came. She hadn't beaten the shit out of him just for the fun of it. That too had been an investment whose value she hoped to realise with time. She had a dividend sooner than she dared expect.

Alain Hubert had not long been in the theatre. He was young, full of ideas, more of a businessman than a showman. To men like Moscato, the theatre was a way of life. To Hubert, it was a way of making a profit. He came from a family of bankers but had independent means. He was rich enough, by the age of thirty, to dabble in such a speculative venture as a new play with Satin.

She did not allow him to bed her. She knew he wanted to, at first desperately, but there could be no advantage to her in it. Gradually his ardour seemed to cool. Eventually, he seemed satisfied simply to be with her. She could get anything she wanted out of him just by being herself. She didn't want his body, not in the least. So she gave him her presence instead. It seemed to keep him happy.

'I want,' she said one day to the Comte de Loury, 'to buy a house in the country.'

The Comte was astonished at what he heard. He had been sleeping with her for nearly a month now. They had met at a dinner hosted by de Loury, had arranged a discreet assignation. Quickly captivated by her beauty and her exceptional talents in the bedchamber, he had helped her buy and furnish the apartment on the Boulevard de la Madeleine. He sat on a brocade sofa, looking at an ormolu clock that Satin had bought – with his money – from Fabergé. His penis was still throbbing from the previous night. He knew why he let her spend his money with such reckless abandon.

'My dear,' he said, glancing at her. 'You would go into a decline if you ever left Paris.'

Everyone in the room looked up and laughed. It was five in the afternoon and people were drinking champagne. Satin had got out of bed only an hour ago.

'No, I want a house in the country. A big house, so we can have parties. People can come and stay with us.'

'What a marvellous idea,' said a foppish young man of eighteen or nineteen, whom Satin had been playing with for the previous week. There were never many women around in Satin's apartment, and certainly none who could be considered in any way a rival to her. Nor, after her chance encounter with Felicité in the Jardin des Tuileries, were there any who had any contact with the old days at the Café des Artistes. The only other woman present was Véronique, a dancer whom she had met through her pharmacist friend.

Mu passed silently to and fro with drinks. The air was heavy and slow with tobacco smoke. The room, though expensively furnished, was untidy. Satin had acquired a dog, a tiny little ball of fluff called Nana, which was busy at that moment worrying the costly Persian carpet, quite ignored by everyone and especially by Satin, who after a month was growing more than a little bored with her. It was Mathilde who fed and cared for her. The dog never left the apartment except as an accessory for Satin to appear at some reception or when promenading in the public parks on a Sunday afternoon. Sometimes her little son, Armand, was allowed to spend a few days here with Maman, but he seemed to pine for his nurse and always seemed to be glad when the carriage arrived to take him home. Satin was annoyed by his selfishness.

Smoothing out her long dress in pale blue organdie silk, she sat down beside Antoine, her young man, and ran her hands through his hair. It was incredible to think that he was actually older than she was. She had been in the company of older men for so long that she actually began to think of herself as being far older than her comparatively tender years.

'It would be lovely to have a house in the country,' Antoine was saying. He had ambitions as a sculptor, was enrolled at the Academy. 'I would make you statues for your garden, a fountain even.'

'Yes, a fountain,' cried Satin. 'I've always wanted a fountain. Really, Antoine, you're too clever. Yes, a fountain it must be.'

The Comte de Loury looked on indulgently. His estates – and his wife – were far away in the Vosges. Satin was but one in a long line of mistresses he had taken over the years. Actresses, ladies of pleasure, even shop girls – unknown to Satin, he still had a pretty little thing of seventeen installed in one of the several properties that his family owned in town. But a house – and especially the kind of house that Satin would want – was something he would have to think very seriously about. He was a wealthy man, perhaps one of the thousand wealthiest men in all of France, but he knew she would settle for nothing less than a small chateau. Why not a sweet little house in Chantilly such as he had kept for his plump mistress of these past fifteen years? But Satin, as he had learned even after so brief an acquaintance, was not the kind of woman to be satisfied with a sweet little house in Neuilly. He would have to see his people, see what might discreetly be arranged. Purely as an investment, of course . . .

Gradually the gathering in the smoke-filled room began to thin out. People drifted off, to dress for dinner, to prepare for the evening ahead. Satin bade young Antoine a tender farewell – he was so dear, that boy, such a little sweetie. When everyone had gone, she and the Comte made their way into the bedroom together.

A tap on the door roused Satin from her reverie.

'Yes,' she called, thinking it was Mu or Mathilde.

The door opened. It was Véronique. She hastily pulled the covers around herself. She was naked in bed apart from her stockings. It was a hot evening.

'I thought you'd gone,' said Satin. Beside her, the Comte stirred and sat up.

'I fell asleep,' said the other girl, who was the same age as Satin, practically shared the same birthday. 'When I woke up, everyone had gone. Would you like some more champagne?'

She had a bottle in her hand. She seemed quite drunk. Why not? thought Satin. She could drink champagne all night and not feel particularly tiddly. She and the Comte were eating that night in their usual private room at Victor's. There was plenty of time left.

Véronique brought in some glasses and sat on the edge of the bed. If the drawing-room had seemed ostentatious then Satin's bedroom was something else entirely. The bed itself, allegedly liberated from the Palace during the Revolution, was like its own little room, heavily swagged with curtains and raised up on a dais at one end of the room. The carpets were white and very thick, the furniture abundant and elaborate in the extreme.

Their talk was inconsequential. Soon it became plain silly. Satin had Mu bring them another bottle of champagne. They were laughing uproariously at nothing in particular, Satin sitting up in bed, wantonly bare-breasted, the Comte showing more modesty, as befitted his station in life. The world seemed a very jolly place. As night fell outside, Satin and Véronique and the

Comte de Loury were in high spirits.

Afterwards, Satin could never quite recall how Véronique came to be in bed with herself and her lover. One minute they were lying on the covers, laughing their heads off at some idiotic joke, the next the three of them were engaged in frantic love-making. Satin had been involved in such tribadic extravagances before, of course, but always for money. To do so out of her own volition was a new experience for her, and helped her realise a new and deeper facet of her own sexuality.

Soon Véronique and the Comte were naked on the bed together. Satin, sipping wine, was happy to watch. Véronique was short and blonde and full-busted, with delicate pink nipples. She had small gold rings in her ears, cheap and insubstantial, quite unlike the elaborate jewellery that Satin wore.

Very quickly, the Comte was on top of her and inside her. Pouring champagne for herself, Satin could actually see his penis being swallowed up inside the other woman. She was, she now realised, drunker than she had thought and was amazed at the arousal that coursed through her like a fire. It was like looking at those engravings in the book, only better. She noticed, as if she were staring down the wrong end of a telescope, how hard and muscular his rump looked, how his thighs twisted and turned as he thrust into her. She could see his balls hanging between his legs, heavy and potent. It made her feel excited, especially when Véronique wrapped her legs around his waist and pushed her tongue into his mouth. Her perfume filled the room.

Satin climbed on to the bed beside them, still wearing her stockings. She caressed her lover's back, his shoulders, his flanks. She squeezed the cheeks of his backside, gently bit his upper arm, poked one exploratory finger into his tight, puckered arse. He grunted. She got the impression he didn't want her to do it to him, not yet anyway. He propped himself up on one arm and, still continuing to pump in and out of Véronique, put his other arm around Satin and pulled her to him. She nibbled his ear, kissed him on the lips. She stuck out her tongue and he licked it. She could taste another woman on him and it excited her.

Then she turned her attentions to Véronique. She leaned across and licked each of her tender pink nipples in turn until the dancer moaned and rolled her eyes in a state that plainly was already bordering on ecstasy. She was still full of the Comte's cock, could feel his powerful movements in and out of her welcoming body. Satin was not sure whether she was entirely used to the idea of being made love to by another woman. For herself, she certainly liked to have sex with another of her own sex – at least once in a while. Some of her clients, back in the old days – although they were still not so many months distant – had liked her to go to bed with another whore.

One man, the owner of one of the largest vineyards in the Midi, had taken her to bed with his own wife on several occasions. There were friends, too, that she sometimes slept with, some who were whores, and others who were not. Women, she felt on the whole, were more considerate than men, had more finesse. She had several times had two men at once but on the whole had found it curiously unimaginative, as though the men – well-bred and well-mannered – were simply taking turns, out of politeness, as though they were playing boules. It had not been concerned in any way with her pleasure, but merely to help them achieve their own. Satin knew that she was now rich and powerful enough to have anything she wanted – including having two men to fuck her senseless if she so desired.

At one stage in their frantic coupling all three were kissing at once, tongues and lips intermingling. Satin pushed her hand down to where Véronique and the

Comte were joined, and felt the lips of her vagina hot and puffy as they welcomed the great nobleman's vibrant and thrusting penis. She was surprised at how big it looked from this angle. For a while, evidently to gather his breath, he withdrew from her, and she noticed how hugely erect he was, how the sticky purple dome at the end of his great shaft seemed to be almost bursting with desire, like an over-ripe plum. Was he perhaps more turned on by Véronique than by her? She felt a stab of jealousy but then realised it was her imagination.

As the Count re-entered Véronique, this time from the rear, Satin once more entered into the spirit of things. She kissed Véronique and rubbed her own cunt against the other woman's thigh, the feel of her soft and crinkly pubic hair creating a delicious frisson between them. Then she knelt up, pressing her breasts against the Comte, her tongue seeking his even as he powered into the other woman's open body. Véronique came loudly and suddenly and then the Count's own climax quickly followed.

They lay back, spent, exhausted. Satin licked the nipples of the Comte de Loury while Véronique put her hands between Satin's plump and stockinged thighs, her fingers playing gently with the swollen lips of her vagina. When Satin turned round and took his cock in her mouth, he writhed about on the bed, knocked a half-full bottle of champagne off the table by the bedside and on to the floor. Everyone laughed and ignored it. It would ruin the carpet but Satin could just buy a new one. She carried on sucking him. He came off in her mouth while Véronique continued to masturbate her.

Night had drawn on as they made love. The window was open, and there was a distinct coolness in the air.

'Close the curtains, will you?' said Satin, as she took hold of the Count's prick and tried to coax him back to stiffness.

Véronique got to her feet and crossed the room. Satin

could see why men liked her body – and she did too. She was small, lithe and exquisite. Her breasts were perfect, just bursting to be licked and sucked. As she rose to pull the cord, her buttocks clenched up delightfully.

The three of them snuggled down under the covers while, outside, they could hear the sounds of the distant city, the traffic moving along the boulevard down below. Satin lay on one side of the Comte, Véronique on the other. He had his arms around them. She pushed out a hand towards his groin and was surprised to find Véronique's was there already. The two of them traced little patterns up and down his penis, twirled their fingers in his crinkly pubic hair, drew teasing fingernails across his balls. Now it was Satin's turn to have the Comte inside her.

With an almost intuitive understanding, each woman began slowly to tongue his nipples. As Satin well knew, he found this extremely arousing. She felt his cock stiffen in her grasp and she slithered down under the bedclothes and began once more to lick him. Véronique was lying half on her side, one leg crooked. Satin leaned across and kissed her soft pubic hair, then returned to his cock.

Through her nostrils she caught the scent of Véronique's own highly aroused sex. The Comte let go of her shoulders and, in the dim half-light beneath the sheets, she could see his hand snaking in between Véronique's legs, the fingers working their way inside her sex. Lucky bitch, she thought, and went back to sucking his prick.

Having spent twice in the course of the last hour, the Comte was understandably less urgent. But Véronique seemed visibly on heat, almost pulling him on top of her. He had other ideas, pushing her round on to her front. Perhaps to refresh his jaded palate, he took her from behind, abruptly and with less than his customary decorum.

'Fuck my arse,' Véronique hissed, and her words took Satin by surprise.

'I want your cunt,' he said in reply. 'That's tight enough for me. I'll have your arse another time.'

'No, no. Fuck me first,' cried Satin, urgent and imperious. 'Then you can fuck her up the bum.'

The Comte did as he was told. He climbed up behind her on the bed, pulled her to him quite roughly. She could feel how hot and wet his cock was against her, as she pressed her buttocks against him, urgent in her lewdness. This was no time for subtlety.

He slid massively into her, made her gasp. God, he was huge, even bigger than Frédéric de Fleury had been. Why did she always seem to attract men with such large penises? She laughed, giddy with lust and champagne.

Satin knelt up on the bed, trying to cram as much as she could of him inside her. She liked the idea of performing for Véronique, who was watching them intently from the side of the bed, sipping champagne, her hand straying involuntarily between her legs.

Satin knew how much the Comte enjoyed her legendary tightness. He had praised her many times as he explored her. She could sense now how intense his pleasure was, how overwhelmed he was, just by the way he slammed into her. He was like an animal on heat, a stag in rut. And she was opening up for him like a flower, taking him deeper and deeper inside her until an orgasm swept over her that was so fierce and so unremitting that she had to beg him to stop. She lay then on the bed, quivering still, while he knelt over her, trying to catch his breath, his great cock bobbing, his balls heaving with aristocratic spunk.

Véronique's eyes were heavy-lidded with desire, her breast rising and falling. She had obviously become extremely aroused by watching the two lovers. Quickly the two women changed places.

The Comte was still kneeling on the bed, where he had pulled himself unwillingly out of Satin's tumultuous pussy.

Now he was pulling Véronique towards him, eagerly seeking his own release. Satin in turn was behind him, almost straddling him, her arms around his waist, rubbing her pussy against the small of his back and his backside. She was still wearing her stockings and she noted with alarm that they were both badly laddered – and only new on that morning. What the hell, she thought, her mind afloat in a sea of erotic possibilities.

She could see Véronique's ripe breasts swinging loose as the Comte fucked her, her face red and her pretty bee-stung lips open, panting, quietly mouthing obscenities. She caught the scent of their bodies, the mixture of sweat, secretions and cosmetics, the faint tang of his shaving cream – or was it his cologne? – mingled with her own expensive perfume and Véronique's cheaper scent.

'Give it to her,' she urged. 'She wants your spunk up her arse.'

She leaned forwards and kissed him on the neck, bit him so hard it made him wince. That would leave a mark by morning, sure enough. He twisted his head round and his tongue came slithering towards her mouth. She put her hand down between his legs, felt the thick root-stem of his penis penetrating the slick and swollen wetness of Véronique's body. Then she pressed her finger into the furrow between his buttocks, found his anus and pushed her finger in.

'God, you're so full of spunk, aren't you?' she breathed. 'I bet you've got enough for both of us.'

There and then she felt his balls contracting. She could both see and sense his orgasm, the look on his face, the pulsing of his loins, Véronique's muffled shout of release. Then she found herself lying curled against Véronique's backside, his sperm seeping out of her and on to her own stockinged thigh, the Comte lying facing the other way, his breathing short and ragged, bottles on the floor, clothes everywhere, and not a care in the world.

She felt almost as good as if she had just swallowed a phial of Thierry Albert's tinctures.

Satin wanted the house the minute she set eyes on it – and what she wanted, she generally got.

They had driven out in the Comte's private carriage, just the two of them and her little dog. To put him in a good mood, she had permitted him a certain measure of intimacy on the journey. Now, as he discreetly wiped the stains from the upholstery with a silk handkerchief, she looked out at the surrounding countryside.

How long had it been since she had last left Paris? Months, perhaps even years. The countryside seemed like an alien landscape to her city-bred eyes. Where were the shops, the cafés, the sense of excitement? Where were all the people? Where was the money, and the things to spend it on? But she didn't want to buy the land. She just wanted the house.

She looked out across fields, a distant plume of white steam along a railway line. From time to time they saw groups of labourers – harvest time was approaching fast – and passed carts in the narrow lanes. It was one of those exceptionally bright, clear, August days. She could feel the heat in the air and was glad of the shade and shelter of the endless lines of poplars.

These days, she scarcely even left her apartment until after dark. She was becoming a creature of the night, out until dawn and then sleeping through the day. The Comte paid for almost everything, of course, and she had managed to wheedle money out of Alain Hubert, now the holder of the grandiose title of her business manager, as an advance against her earnings from the next play she was to appear in. Rehearsals were due to start in two weeks' time and the play would run at the Gaiety until after Christmas. She had even read the script.

She gazed out at the unaccustomed sunlight, stroking the

dog's ears. The land seemed to go on for ever – so very different to her own vista of city streets and corridors. She could see the clouds in the sky, the sense of open space. To her, the heavens were something you glimpsed only briefly between tall buildings.

The Comte patted her on the knee – a proprietorial gesture. He was, for the moment, the only man she was sleeping with. She knew that Antoine, her young exquisite from the Academy, was dying to make love to her, but for the moment she refused all his importuning – which was not to say that she would always do so. Véronique, though, was another matter. She and the Comte had enjoyed her favours several times. And from time to time, without his knowledge, the two women had spent the night – or, to be more accurate, the day – together at Satin's luxurious new apartment.

'We're nearly there,' he said, a broad smile on his handsome, patrician face. He tapped the roof of the carriage with his cane, and called out some words to the coachman.

The carriage slowed and turned into a narrow drive. Satin craned out of the window, easier for a glimpse of what she hoped would be her new property. It had been the country home of the second son of a marquis who had died of drink, not quite as grand as the chateau that Satin had secretly been hoping for, but a desirable residence nevertheless. The Comte had described it to her in some detail but she had already formed her own impression of what it would be like, and refused to move from it.

They came out from a long avenue of trees into a wide crescent and there, all of a sudden, was the house. It was smaller than Satin had imagined but undeniably elegant. It was quite a new house, built of stone, in a style that was fashionable thirty years ago and was still reasonably au courant. The entrance in particular impressed her as the carriage drew up. She could imagine the rich and famous coming here for dinner parties and country weekends – it was quite easy to reach from town. And the windows, it seemed to have lots of windows.

The agent was there to greet them. They were ushered inside. The place smelt damp and stale – it had not been lived in for nearly a year, he explained. A year, thought Satin. A year ago – well, getting on for two, if truth be known – she was still a streetwalker, an habituée of the Café des Artistes. How times and the circumstances of her life had changed – and she was still only just one-and-twenty. The Comte had promised her the house as a birthday present – if she liked it. It would be in his name, of course, but she would be its mistress.

They walked through rooms that were only partly furnished. The walls were quite bare. Light patches showed where pictures had once hung. The chairs and tables could, by negotiation, be included in the selling price, the agent informed the Comte, but the best pieces had already been removed by the marquis's family.

Their footsteps echoed on the bare wooden floors, long since stripped of rugs and carpets. The house was on three floors, with a spectacular central staircase. Confronted by its bare treads and dusty balustrades, Satin could nevertheless imagine herself making a spectacular entrance down that very flight, her long gown trailing behind her. She could see the hallway in which they now stood packed by friends and admirers, the men in formal evening clothes, the women looking ravishing – but none quite so ravishing as her. She looked up, and there – just as it had been in her imaginings – was the crystal chandelier, heavily swagged now to protect it from the dust but a crystal chandelier nevertheless.

They walked through the upper storeys. There seemed to be a huge number of bedrooms, perhaps as many as a dozen – ideal for a house party. And all the time Satin was getting the feeling that the place was right for her. It would need painting, of course, and the Comte would need to spend a lot of money on refurbishing most of the rooms – some of the surviving furniture was dreadfully old-fashioned, in the styles of fiifty years and more ago. But the staircase, and the reception rooms – a pity there wasn't a ballroom, but it wasn't quite that sort of house – all this seemed to suggest infinite possibilities.

They had reached the top of the house.

'The servant's quarters are in the attic, of course,' said the agent, pointing to a dark and narrow flight of steps at the end of an equally dark and narrow corridor.

'I don't think we need bother with those, need we, my dear?' said the Comte, making up Satin's mind for her as usual. He murmured something to the other man.

'Yes, certainly,' he said. 'I'll be downstairs if you need me for anything. Perhaps you might like to meet the housekeeper later – she is here this morning.'

He went down the stairs, his footsteps echoing.

'Well,' said the Comte. 'What do you think?'

'I think it's marvellous,' said Satin, quite spontaneously. 'I think it's the loveliest house I've ever been in.'

She hugged him. Then, arm in arm, they walked down the flight of stairs and looked again at the rooms on the first floor.

'I think I'd like this as my own suite,' she said, pushing open a door. 'I liked it when we first saw it.'

The windows at the end looked out over the grounds and at the line of poplars that marked the drive. In front of the house was a small terrace, ideal for drinks on hot summer evenings. The more she looked, the more she found and the more she was pleased by what she saw.

She stood by the window. There was a little balcony outside, just like the one back at the Boulevard de la Madeleine. They were, she realised, directly above the main entrance to the house. She wanted to go out there and see how the world looked from that vantage point.

She tried to open it but it was evidently locked. It was directly facing the noon sun and the air in the room was stuffy and overheated, full of dust. And yet, to Satin, the world seemed alive with possibilities. A sense of excitement was coursing, unbidden, through her veins. She felt exhilarated, very much alive. And it was his wealth that was making it all possible.

The carriage was waiting for them down below. She looked down on the fabric of its roof, at the horses shuffling their feet. The coachman had taken her little dog for a walk while they were looking around the house.

Soon it would be taking them back to Paris. But that wouldn't be the end of it. They – the Comte and herself – were going to go on a much longer journey.

She turned away from the window, looked again at the two smaller rooms that led off on either side of the chamber. They would be ideal for clothes, dressing, a small sitting room perhaps. Then the Comte de Loury was by her side. She turned to him and then, without conscious effort, they were in each other's arms.

In the still, jaded air of the house she felt flushed and intoxicated. Sharp urgings of desire began to explode inside her as she returned his kiss with passion, her arm slipping inside his coat, feeling how warm and firm his body was under his clothes. He was dressed in a suit of fine grey cloth, a rose in his buttonhole.

Time stood still as their tongues mingled together. She felt his erection, sudden and urgent, pressed hard and meaningfully against her thigh. Then they broke away from each other, breathing heavily. She felt a prickly kind of heat. Her head was beginning to swim, she wanted to sit down. Was it the air in the room that was making her swoon, or was it the rising and irresistible tide of lust within their bodies?

She was aware of a sense of recklessness, as if she had fled her everyday world and escaped to this island where every whim could be satisfied. She cared nothing for the green countryside that stretched out to infinity beyond the railings. It was what the house represented to her that was making her drunk. She imagined the tinkle of glasses, the flash of wit, the brilliant plumage of the women and the gorgeous flesh of the men who would visit this house and worship at her shrine. But everything around her was absolutely silent save for the occasional creak of the floorboards – they could hear the agent moving around downstairs – and the sound of their own movements in the muffled air of the room.

She looked around. They were alone, cut off from the rest of the world. No one knew who they were and what they were about. The sense of power it gave her was absolute. She felt a girlish thrill, was aware of the reckless and imaginative possibilities of the moment. Was this the way it would always be in this house? She hoped so. She always wanted it to be like this, a house where every desire could be indulged. Carefully taking off her hat and gloves and placing them on the window ledge beside them, she dropped to her knees in front of the Comte.

'You're mad,' she heard him whisper, and she believed him. In that rash, delirious, uncaring moment she felt herself capable of anything, and she surrendered herself to the pleasures of her body, and that of the Comte.

With deft hands she unbuttoned his fly, reached inside and took hold of his penis. It was not yet fully erect but she could sense it growing and stiffening with every pulse of her heart. She uncapped the tip, leaned forward and, holding it in one practised hand, ran its smooth, spongy surface against her cheek.

'What if someone comes?' she heard the Comte say, but she ignored his anxiety, so great was the thrill of the moment for her. 'The agent. He's waiting for us. I can hear him. He wants us to go and talk to the house-keeper.'

'Nobody will come,' she breathed. 'He knows better than to come barging in on people. No one will disturb us.'

She looked up at him and smiled. She loved the faraway look that came into his eyes at times like this. His stoic common sense, normally so marked in him, flew out of the window and the urges of their bodies took over instead. She had seen it at her apartment, on the first occasion when he had fucked Véronique while she watched, even that very morning when she brought him off in her hand in the carriage.

Then she dipped her head and took the tip of his penis into her mouth. She cupped her lips around it, letting her tongue probe its surface, infiltrating the tiny slit-like eye. She loved to lick him and play with him like this, building up his expectations. Sometimes he came off there and then, in her mouth or all over her face, but it only served to excite her all the more.

He was very big now, the blood coming pulsing through his veins. Her practised ministrations had already had their effect – as she knew they would. She had never sucked any man until she had begun to work in the Café des Artistes, so many years ago now it appeared to be and yet it could have been no more than two at the outside. How many cocks had she sucked in that time? From the very start, it seemed to be the skill she was most proficient at – certainly if she judged by the way her clients always responded to her ministrations. Best of all was doing it with someone like the Comte, an artist of the flesh, a carnal gourmet. He, a man who had buggered English duchesses and licked the cunts of a thousand courtesans, knew the quality of her work. With some men, it was like scattering pearls before swine – except it was their pearls that, ultimately, were scattered.

She wondered sometimes if the wives of the men who had been her regular clients ever performed it – their husbands always seemed so uncommonly grateful for what she did to them. It seemed to be the English who appreciated it most – did they not suck each other in England, those high-blooded men and women, with their mincing manners and bodily smells. Or was it, perhaps, seen as something naughty, wicked even? The kind of thing that only women like Satin would possibly do. The kind of thing that, in some way, was 'not nice.'

She had learned how to suck a man effortlessly until he came in her mouth – or over her breasts – inside a couple of minutes at the outside. At first, it had left her with an aching jaw and a sore mouth. Now she could – and did – keep a man's cock occupied for half an hour or more. Her special skill was to keep going, nice and slow, building up a steady rhythm, a hypnotic wave of sensuality that might go on for ten, fifteen minutes, sometimes longer, depending on who she was with and what she stood to gain out of him in terms of money or favours. No one knew better than her how to do it, and no one enjoyed doing it more. In the old days, men sought her out specifically for this. She charged them an awful lot of money for the privilege of having their whims gratified.

'Suck me off, you bitch,' the Comte breathed.

She had taken almost all of him into her mouth now, opening wide to swallow him in. She could taste the come on him from that morning, salty and ammoniac. She swirled her tongue over him and swallowed until he was nice and clean – that was something else the English could learn. She slowed down the pace, relaxing her grip on him, making her mouth go loose and allowing her tongue to rove over him, up and down the length of his erect penis, tracing every last line and vein, the smooth and aristocratic skin turning to velvet under her wet and succulent caress.

She took the end of his penis between her teeth and bit him very, very gently, not so much as to make him wince but sufficient, when she next washed over the tip with her tongue, to let him enjoy the soothing sensations she knew it would induce. She could hear him moan his appreciation, was aware of his hands on her shoulders, touching her collar, drawing her closer to him. She nibbled him again, could hear his short intake of breath and knew the pleasure it was bringing him.

Finally, she paused, expectantly. She desperately wanted to be penetrated by him but she wanted him to take the initiative now, for him to be the active partner and her to be the object of desire. She didn't always want to be the seductress.

She looked up at him, willing him to make a move. He got to his feet, clumsily rearranging his clothing. There was a bed in a corner of the room, pushed there out of the way. It was covered in dust sheets but it would satisfy their needs.

Satin lay down on the bed and parted her legs, an openly lewd and provocative gesture. She knew, even without looking at him, that he could see right up her skirts. She parted her drawers, let him see her dark places, wet and ready for him. He came and sat beside her and put his hand under her skirt. She moaned, even as his fingers brushed against her damp and mossy labia. Then she let him enfold her in his arms, kissing him wildly and passionately. They were both panting but whether it was from lust or from the heat and stuffiness of the room neither of them could know.

From where they were lying on the bed in the dusty room she could see over his shoulder, out past the tree-tops and over the park itself, a distant church spire. It was a Friday and there would be little groups of figures walking to and from mass. There was a village they had come through, not a bad-looking sort of place. But here, in their love-nest, they had the world very much to themselves.

The Comte took off his coat – it was already far too warm in the bedroom and Satin could see the thin film of sweat over his upper lip – and draped it over a chair. She fixed him with her most provocative gaze, challenging him, inviting him to make the next move, flaunting herself to drive him wilder and wilder. He took her by the waist and turned her round, pushing her forward against the head of the bed so she had to hang on to it with both hands to prevent herself falling over the edge. She knew what was coming next.

With confident hands he hiked her dress up over her hips. She could feel him drinking in the sight that greeted him, the coral-coloured lingerie, the stockings held up with pretty lace garters, the firm roundness of her backside, the shapely legs on which so many men had complimented her. She sighed; he seemed to catch her impatience.

He slipped his hand in between her legs, under the silk, his gentle fingers smoothing over the warm slickness of her labial lips. Then he pushed her underclothing aside.

'Come on and fuck me, you bastard,' she heard herself saying. She was desperate for a cock. She wanted him to drive into her but instead his hand played with her and tormented her, making her buck her hips against him, impatient to be impaled on that great twitching prick of his. Again and again his expert fingers brushed her opening and penetrated them but slightly. She knew she was going to swoon, whether from lust or the stale air she did not know, but she could not help herself. She surrendered herself to the wanton desires of her body .

Again she urged him to fuck her but still he was busy with his fingers, touching and teasing, stringing her along, until she was almost ready to beg him – and she knew that was what he wanted. She wondered if the agent down below could hear them – apart from him they seemed to have the whole of the house to themselves. But such niceties seemed an irrelevance compared with the desperate longings that she felt within herself.

And then, quite suddenly, he was inside her, all the way up in one smooth and slippery movement, and she gasped and immediately felt filled, sated, complete, joined with the Comte in the mystical union of their bodies in this place that was soon to be her own. This was what it was all about, she realised, as he began to pump into her. All those endless hours with fools like Moscato, those fumbling fucks in the doorways – this was where the road had ultimately led her. And she had done it all by herself.

His cock filled her utterly, plunging deep inside her. Her senses were alive with the strange scents of the room and of their own bodily secretions, strong now in the sunlit air, the motres of dust that danced before her eyes. Her eyes, half-unseeing, followed the Chinese patterns of the wallpaper – that would have to go, for a start – the figures and bridges, the little lakes and trees. It was another imaginary landscape for her and she entered utterly into this rich and sensual world, the mysterious perfumes that filled her nostrils even as the Comte pierced her to the very root and she felt, squirming and shameless and aroused beyond belief, the encroaching climax beginning to fill her loins like the rumble of distant thunder, the heat intense enough now to make her feel like fainting.

'Cock,' she called out. 'Cunt. Fuck. Arsehole. Suck me. Fuck me.'

She grasped the delicately gilded railings of the bed as hard as she could until her knuckles began to turn white and then she was falling, falling into the whirlpool of her senses, the Comte joyously pumping his seed into her, heedless of all consequences. She opened her eyes and, for a second, she did not know where she was, waking in a strange room with a man beside her. But this, to a woman such as Satin, was a familiar and momentary anxiety.

Chapter Six

The next six months, through the winter and on into the spring, were among the happiest and most contented that Satin had ever known. The Comte bought, on her behalf, the property at Campignon-Bois and she devoted much energy to furnishing it in the grandest style. They would spend time there together whenever they could – the Comte de Loury, of course, enjoyed the favours of several ladies as well as his wife in the distant Vosges – and the house would be alive from Friday until Sunday, after which the peace of Campignon-Bois would descend again.

Satin still had her apartment on the Rue de la Madeleine, of course, and this became her home during the week and whenever she was in performance. Véronique was practically living there herself, enjoying the warmth and luxury and showing little inclination to return to the uncertainty of her career as a dancer – at least, not while the generosity of Satin and the Comte de Loury provided her with a bed to sleep in (sometimes alone, more usually not) and food in her belly.

Satin's stage career continued to thrive. True, it did not propel her with quite the same velocity as that with which she had come to stardom – but this was only to be expected. But her relentless momentum was well maintained. She appeared in three more plays that were carefully set up by the calculating Hubert. Two were new plays, one was a revival of the old favourite, *The Vagabond*. In each her talents – limited as they were –

were stretched as far as they would go, but no further. Everything had to be built around her. The supporting cast would be chosen with great care, lest Satin be eclipsed both in terms of acting ability and of physical beauty. Her weaknesses and failings were brilliantly accommodated by the people who surrounded her at almost every hour of the day and night. To anyone who had not heard of her – and there could be few in all of France who, by the end of that year, had not – she would have seemed an actress of no mean ability.

Of course, there were those who doubted her. Patric Esteve, the drama critic of *Paris-Expresse*, the man who had cruelly wooed her and then written caustically about her role as Aphrodite in *Love's Plaything*, had been particularly cutting. It was, he wrote of one of her appearances, as if an idiot had been taught to play a single tune on the fiddle, over and over again, until he were note perfect. Set him up in a market place, make him play his piece, and people would admire his talent. But ask him to play anything else, and he would be all thumbs.

Satin longed to find a way of getting her revenge on Patric Esteve, much as she had on La Cabache and, subsequently, the doomed promoter Moscato. She found herself compelled to read all her reviews, even the ones she knew would be unkind. Always there was the hope of flattery and approbation. Often it came, sometimes it did not. She did not know that the hacks were being well paid for their complimentary remarks.

All this was the work of Hubert, ever watching, ever calculating. He was aware that Satin's success in *The Vagabond* had not been perhaps quite so outstanding as it had been in the other two plays. People had begun to make unfortunate comparisons with previous performances. *The Vagabond* had played in Paris no more than five years previously, with La Cabache. She had taken the city by storm and Satin, so restricted in her ability, could never hope to emulate her success. So he took to offering the drama critics little favours – a little financial inducement here, the company of a lady there – to build up a steady stream of good notices. Sooner or later, he reasoned, people would start to believe what they were told, not what they thought themselves. If everyone was saying how brilliant she was, how subtle her gifts, how vivacious her presence on stage, then surely it must be true, and the doubters had been mistaken.

She fared much better in new plays, with roles created specifically for her. But new plays cost money to develop, and Hubert wanted to be certain well in advance that he would recoup his investment many times over. And so he entertained lavishly, and greased the right palms. He exploited Satin – and her audience – as audaciously and as plausibly as a quack doctor selling patented remedies.

It was a difficult time for him, if not for Satin. He had done very well out of Bichfoucauld, the author of the first two plays. Bichfoucauld was an experienced playwright with a string of fair-sized successes to his name. But with recognition had come complacency, and with complacency – and money – had come a predilection for drink. It had been touch and go whether he would complete his last play in time. Now he was drinking more than ever but the new play he was writing for Satin – a classical extravaganza based around the story of Orpheus and Eurydice – had scarcely got beyond the first act.

'When can I see something?' Hubert had demanded.

'All in good time, my dear boy,' he would say. 'Don't you know you should never lift the lid on the pot while the casserole's cooking?'

'Just the first act, you know. That's all I want to see.'

'All in good time.'

'Why not, if it's finished? It is finished, isn't it?'

'Not as such. Or at least, not entirely. But maybe by the end of the month.'

'The end of the month. But we're almost due to start rehearsals then.'

'That is true.'

That much he admitted to but the cynical Hubert believed that the drunkard had not yet committed a single word to paper. He was not going to pay him any more of his advance, he decided until he saw at least half the play. Writers, he had begun to realise, were all the same – show them a bank note and they drank it. He wondered sometimes why he had allowed himself to be seduced by the lure of the theatre, when he could have made a comfortable living for himself buying and selling railway shares.

That was marked up to the debit account. On the credit side, the Comte de Loury – on whose personal fortune Hubert was coming increasingly to depend – still remained a steadfast supporter. It was, admittedly, for as long as his relationship with the mercurial actress survived. Hubert, sometimes, had his doubts. He long ago had lost all hope that he might be able to steer the voluptuous actress towards the bedroom himself. But there were compensations. Through the Comte, Hubert had met Levinson, a wealthy American with interests in the shipping trade. He travelled frequently between his native country and the continent of Europe and considered himself a thorough cosmopolitan. De Loury – ever the speculator, like Hubert, and ever on the alert for new sources of investment, despite the resources of his own considerable fortune – all but pounced on him. He recalled the circumstances of their first meeting.

A weekend party was being held at Campignon-Bois to celebrate the final performance of *The Vagabond*. There were perhaps a dozen guests altogether, all chosen by Satin. There was the Comte, of course, and Hubert, and the faithful Véronique, who had been rewarded for the pleasure she had given the Comte – and Satin – by a small cameo role in the performance. Now, she and Satin were almost inseparable and she had all but taken over the apartment. The Comte might have cavilled at the expense of keeping two separate establishments for one woman – his other mistresses made do with just the one – but, with his every whim indulged, he saw no grounds for complaint.

Bichfoucauld was there, steadily drinking his way through the extensive cellars of the house. With him was some tart or other that he had picked up on the streets – a surly and insolent bitch with flaming red hair, mercifully not known to either Satin or Véronique. The Comte knew of their past, of course – in fact, it quite excited him – and yet despite the more than somewhat tarnished image of the theatre there were those who might have cavilled at the thought of associating with those who were known, or had been known, as prostitutes of the streets.

None of those prim-lipped puritans, however, were present at the house. It was exclusively a gathering of friends and intimates who were associated with the play or with its backers. All in all, a highly select group.

And then there was Levinson. Hubert had met him at a reception at the American embassy and the two men had immediately struck up a rapport. When Levinson intimated his fondness for the theatre, the impresario lost no time in securing him the best seats in the house for one of the final performances of *The Vagabond*, in so doing decanting the President of the Board of Deputies – who had reserved the box – into the third row of the stalls.

The American, predictably, was utterly smitten by Satin's performance on stage that night. It was then that Hubert, acting in association with the Comte, played his trump card. Would he, Levinson, like to meet the lady? Levinson was agreeably surprised and did not demur for one moment. They enjoyed a discreet dinner à quatre – Levinson, de Loury, Hubert and of course the lady herself – at an exclusive restaurant frequented by leading diplomats. Every head in the place turned when Satin made her entrance.

Hubert did not ask what happened later that evening. The impresario/banker had no sexual peccadilos himself. Business ruled his life and he was a man of few other passions. He was unmarried and did not keep a mistress. If he needed a woman, which was only very occasionally, he would visit one of the better class bordellos in the suburbs of Paris. He rather looked down on the wanton extravagances of Satin and her coterie but he knew better than to bite the hand that fed him.

All he could gather was that Satin had, in the company of the Comte, taken Levinson back to her apartment where he had been introduced to Véronique. The two of them had subsequently departed for his hotel. Véronique had not returned until the following afternoon. It had been made plain to the American, though, that Satin herself would not be available at any price.

'What's he like, then, this American?' Satin had asked as soon as Véronique returned. She looked exhausted.

'Insatiable,' she said. 'I lost count of the number of times we did it. The sheets looked a complete mess this morning.'

Satin was intrigued. 'Tell me more,' she insisted.

'Well, he's really strong and he knows just what a woman likes. He doesn't just do it. He likes to take his time, make sure you're feeling good. When he gets going, though, he's wonderful. He can keep it up for hours. And he's huge, I can tell you. I don't think I've ever had a man so big – or with so much spunk in his balls.'

'What kind of thing does he like?'

'Everything. I love the way he tongues me out. And he likes me to get on top, too, to fuck him that way. And from behind. Once, we did it standing up on the balcony, looking down on the boulevard. I thought I was going to fall over the edge, he was fucking me so hard. And yet, at breakfast, he was the perfect gentleman. I'm seeing him again tonight, I hope.'

'He sounds interesting,' said Satin. She was glad she had invited Levinson to her little soirée.

The whole place was ablaze with light. The crystal chandeliers twinkled and the smell of perfume and of fresh-cut flowers mingled with the aroma of polish and new fabrics. A buffet supper was laid on for the guests. Levinson and the Comte arrived shortly after Hubert did. The guests, including several men of influence as well as a number of ladies of fashion, were immediately struck by the American's firm handshake and warm, open manner.

The Comte talked casually with Levinson for some while of the theatre. There was an atmosphere of gaiety about the gathering, a hint of promiscuity and wickedness. There were rumours of some little entertainment that Satin had arranged, a private matter for their eyes only. No one knew quite what to expect.

The evening promised much. Véronique had been dropping little hints to him all week, suggesting Satin had something up her sleeve. Levinson was no prude but he was surprised at the profligacy of the Parisian theatrical world. Everyone was so blasé about it – women would give themselves quite openly, and gentlemen would frequent the city's brothels as naturally as they might visit a Turkish bath or a smoking divan.

Despite the sensuality that hung heavily in the atmosphere, the conversation veered, inevitably when men of means are gathered together, towards the financial side of things. Hubert and Levinson, the Comte was pleased to note, spoke the same language.

Véronique sat opposite him during dinner. All the while she kept winking at him, tried to reach under the table and touch him with her foot. The way she ate a plum – knowing his eyes were on her – was positively lascivious.

He wanted very much to be a part of this libertine world. Its cost, to a man of means such as himself, was an irrelevance.

After dinner, aware that he was not entirely sober, Levinson let it quietly be known that funds might be available for a future production with Satin, subject to the usual percentages being agreed. The Comte, though he was leaving all the negotiations to Hubert, felt an inner glow – everything was working to plan. His terms and conditions seemed perfectly acceptable to de Loury, although very little was said directly. A word, a nod, an unspoken agreement – this was the way business should be conducted between gentlemen. But inwardly, de Loury was as excited as a man who had just backed the winner at Longchamp. He made his excuses and left to attend to Satin.

'Have you any ideas for the next play?' said the American in his quiet, unassumptive voice.

'Oh yes,' said Hubert, rather too quickly. He looked across at where Bichfoucauld and his trollope were sitting on a sofa, practically devouring each other. The great playwright, it was plain to see, was extremely drunk. He had been loud and extremely unfunny all through dinner. Even Satin – who normally tolerated his loud excesses – was beginning to get more than a little embarrassed by him.

He gave Levinson a brief outline of the story. He seemed impressed. He was, it appeared, well versed in the literature of antiquity.

'Who is writing it?' he asked.

'Bichfoucauld,' admitted Hubert. He could see Levinson wince.

'Bichfoucauld?' The voice was cool and level.

'He's very good, you know. He wrote *The Farmer's Wife* and *An Accident of Fate*.'

'That was ten years ago.'

'But he's still very good. That's why he's here tonight, to give you a chance to meet him, talk some things over. Would you like a word with him?'

'The guy's a drunk.'

'What writer isn't?'

Levinson laughed.

'I'll level with you. I've seen some of his plays. They're good. I saw *An Accident of Fate* in Pittsburgh last year. It toured fifteen states, sold out everywhere. But the guy is a souse. I don't think he's up to it.'

'I assure you, I have every confidence in him.'

There was a loud guffaw from across the room, where Bichfoucauld was telling risqué stories, and giggles from the women. A tray of glasses was knocked to the floor and several were broken. Levinson ignored him.

'You want this play to open in December, right?'

'That's what we said.'

'That means we're into rehearsal by September. The end of September at the very latest.'

'Two months is usually all right, to get a new play ready. I'm hoping to line up a first-class cast.'

'I'm sure you are. But my question is, where is the script? How far has he got with it?'

There was another loud peal of laughter. Satin and Véronique were evidently highly amused by the outrageous tales the playwright was telling them. Levinson turned back to Hubert.

'How much has he written? How much of it have you read?'

Hubert knew it was pointless to lie.

'He tells me he's getting on very well.'

'How much has he shown you?'

'Very little.'

'The first act?'

'Not all of it. Not as such, no.'

'So he's hardly started? I mean, look at the guy. From

what I hear, he's like that every other day of the week. He's never sober long enough to write a line of dialogue. The last few plays he's done are just reworkings of things he wrote ten, fifteen years ago. He's hoping people will have forgotten about them, that they won't recognise the same tired old ideas. That's what he's trying to do with you.'

'For an American, you know an awful lot about the French theatre, Mr Levinson.'

'I've been coming here, sometimes twice a year, for twenty years. I make it my business to know what's going on. I love the theatre. It's my second home.'

'What are you saying? That we drop Bichfoucauld?'

'You said it, not me.'

'And what would you do instead? Plays don't grow on trees, you know.'

They took fresh drinks from a passing waiter, lit cigars.

'Do you know the name of Etienne Valéry?'

'Etienne Valéry? He writes revues, little sketches. I know the name, but not much else.'

'How much else?'

'Well, that he's very difficult to work with. He has very high ideals. Small-scale stuff, I'd say.'

'Etienne Valéry is going to be the biggest name the French theatre has ever known. And within five years, I'm telling you. I hear good things about Etienne Valéry. He knows the popular mind. He understands what people want. He's a man of the people himself.'

'You've met him?'

'I've spoken to him, through an intermediary. We've exchanged ideas. I'm very interested in some of the things he has to say.'

'I'm not sure about it, to be honest.'

'Look – all these spectacular effects, these tricks and illusions. It's had its day. You're going round in circles. How far can you go? They've already fought the Battle of Waterloo on the stage of the Comédie Francais. Etienne

Valéry writes real plays about real people. They're like comedies of manners – that's where the future lies, I can assure you. Forget all these explosions and shipwrecks and things. The guy's a genius, I'm telling you.'

'Has he written a play? Nothing's ever been performed.'

'Not under his own name he hasn't. But did you see *Her Last Letter*? That was him, writing under another name. Savarin's name went on the playbill but it was Etienne Valéry who wrote them. That was one of the biggest-grossing plays last year. Now he's written two new plays and he wants to do them under his own name. I've talked to people who've read them. I respect their opinions.'

They were interrupted from any further discussion by Satin rising to her feet and clapping her hands.

'Ladies and gentlemen,' she began, her face glowing with pleasure. 'I'm so glad you could all come to my little house to help me celebrate the end of the play. In return, I've arranged a little entertainment for you – just a little amusing diversion for my friends. So, if you'd like, we can all go through to the Arabesque room . . .'

Everyone rose at once to their feet – what could this mean? The Arabesque room? This was something entirely new to everyone, except the Comte, who had paid the bills.

They passed out of the room where they had been seated and through a doorway off the main hall. Immediately, it was as if they had been transported to another land and another place. The room was large and decorated in a lavish Moorish style, with arches and strange mosaics, an exotic retreat. Intricately patterned rugs were scattered on the floor, and heavy cushions. Not entirely sure what to expect, Levinson sat down on a spectacularly upholstered sofa next to a giant urn – one of several that were placed around the room. It was like being in the soukh – he had been to Morocco once and had seen this kind of dance at a house of ill-repute.

He was joined by Véronique. She sat next to him, sipping champagne, expectantly. He was excited by the sense of intimacy that filled the room.

There was a piano at one end of the room. Duruflé, who had been in charge of the orchestra during the production of *The Vagabond*, was seated at the piano stool, playing soft, gentle music. There was a strong scent of incense in the air.

When everyone had taken their place, Satin gave the sign for the performance to begin. Duruflé began to play again, a melody that fell strangely on the ears, with its hints of the orient and exotic climes. Two girls appeared from archways at either side of the room, clad in loose-fitting, gauzy clothes. Their bodies moved sinuously, in time with the music. They were barefoot and they moved silently across the floor.

The girls looked foreign – Moroccan, perhaps, or Turkish. Levinson, for all his cosmopolitan upbringing, could not be quite sure. He craned his eyes to see better. He loved the way the girls used their bodies to act out a story in dance.

It was like some strange Eastern ballet, this performance they were watching. There was evidently a narrative, a simple story about lost love. There seemed to be a lot of sighing, an air of poignancy. The two girls in their floating, shimmering costumes, went their separate ways around the room, amid the pillars and the huge, mysterious urns. One lay down on a couch while the other continued to dance alone.

And then, there seemed to be a sudden uplifting of the spirits. Levinson couldn't quite catch what had happened. All of a sudden, the two girls were together on the couch. The one kissed the other, very gently, on the forehead. They were meant to be a boy and a girl, right? He was sure he'd got the story straight.

The girls stood up and continued their dance. Suddenly one of them freed herself of her voluminous garment and stood in front of the audience, bare-breasted. There was a sharp intake of breath. Then the other one did the same, the two of them pirouetting and circling around each other, their young breasts jiggling, and all the time that arabesque music.

The performance came to an end – or rather Levinson perceived that it had come to an end. All of a sudden the girls left the stage and everyone was clapping like mad, exchanging comments and shaking their heads.

A beam of light speared the darkness. They were looking at an image of a naked woman – Cleopatra, evidently, from the snake, a real one by the looks of things, that was coiled around her arm. And then another, three or four women altogether, dressed in those same diaphanous costumes that the dancers had worn. He was conscious of a longing starting up in his loins, was aware of the perfume of Véronique next to him in the darkness. He could hear her breathing, could see silhouetted in the lantern's beam the heavy rise and fall of her breast.

Another picture, the same woman. It was a harem, he understood it now. They were looking at tableaux, photographs. The detail in each picture was incredible. Someone must have gone to a lot of trouble to provide a setting for these women. They were beautiful, too. Aroused already, he was looking forward to sharing his bed with Véronique that night.

He followed the sequence of pictures. Now they were braiding each other's hair, holding up mirrors. But the women didn't look at all eastern – this was some photographer's licence. And another picture – the women were in déshabille now. Through the open window with its pointed Moorish arch a crescent moon could be seen. They were making ready for bed.

More images. Bare breasts now, and thighs. Then the

women were splashing water about from a jug, naked, rubbing each other's bodies. Satin was sitting in front of him. He heard what she said in response to an enquiry from her neighbour.

'A friend of mine, a painter, he gave them to me. He had many pictures like this.'

The people lounging on the sofas and cushions of the arabesque room were beginning to relax now. They were responding to what they saw, laughing and jocular. Levinson had seen images like these before, blurred and indistinct, crude images of nakedness photographed in the back streets of Chicago and Delaware. This was something different. It was unmistakeably erotic but it was also, indubitably, artistic.

Most of the women were naked now. Some were openly caressing one another. One image successed another in slow sequence. He was particularly taken by a short, dark girl with luxuriant hair.

Then a man appeared on the scene – the sultan, evidently, a large man with a swarthy complexion and a heavy moustache that was patently false. And then, good heavens, he was naked too. Levinson was as conscious of his own erection as he was of the man on the screen. Hell, what a brute. And yet there was the dark-haired girl, lying on her back, and there was the man between her legs. He could hardly believe what he was seeing and yet all around him everyone was so relaxed, in high good humour. You had to hand it to the French, he told himself. They certainly knew how to enjoy themselves.

The sultan was seen with two or three of the girls in turn, licking and sucking, each of them taking it in turns to fondle his monstrous tool. And then, all too soon, they reached the end of the sequence. The piano music started up and, after a brief pause, the two girls appeared again. This time both of them were quite naked.

Levinson craned forward, his eyes not missing a thing.

And did Véronique's hand just brush his crotch for a second? He was sure it did. He smoked furiously as he watched the girls, dancing faster and faster now, a whirl of limbs and breasts and glimpses of dark pubic hair – and more. It was, he was sure, exactly the sort of thing one might see in a real harem, that heavy air of mystery and delight, the unashamed revelling in the pleasures of the body.

There was something almost mystical about their ethereal beauty, the way their delicious young breasts shimmered in time to the rhythm of their dancing. The music slowed until it was barely a pulse. Dropping to their knees, they scooped up a handful of gauzy scarves and wraps – evidently placed there for the purpose – and rose to their feet once more. Levinson took in the dark pubic mounds, the breasts like ripe fruit, the jutting, purple nipples.

He sipped his wine, aware – not for the first time – of a curious excitement that it seemed to bring on. His heart seemed to beat faster, his skin felt prickly. Was the wine drugged? He didn't doubt it for a moment. But his eyes were drawn, irresistibly, back to the dance.

The two girls had begun to drape each other in those soft and filmy fabrics. Their hands lingered gently over each others bodies. They circled around one another, each step carefully choreographed, in perfect time to the music. The taller one of the two wrapped the other's neck in a shimmering scarf of mauve silk, knotted below her magnificent young breasts. Then she wrapped another, pale peach this time, around her waist so that it trailed over her delectable pubic region. The effect was as if the Ballet Russe and the Folies Bergere had merged. Was it about art, or love, or both? Levinson found it hard to decide, aware only of the steady pulsing of his blood, his increasing breathlessness and the enormity of his own erection. He forgot all about the business deals he had struck up with Hubert – that would have to wait until they got back to Paris, and he could wire his bankers in New York. Nothing mattered now but the spectacle before him.

He began to anticipate what those fabrics of silk and chiffon would feel like against naked flesh – very different, he imagined, to the hard chafing of his own starched linen. The women stepped elegantly across the room, trailing such pretty colours behind them, revealing to the rapt audience a tantalising glimpse of bare arse or rampant nipple. A woman partially clad, Levinson realised, was infinitely more alluring than one totally naked.

The shorter one stood still now, swaying gently from the hips. Then she began slowly to lean backwards from the waist until her long black hair was almost touching the floor. Her pubic hair, in so doing, was totally exposed to the gaze of the watchers. She flexed her knees, began to bob up and down, her legs spread slightly so he could catch a glimpse of her coral pink lips nestling among the bushy darkness.

He had never seen anything like it in his life, not even in Kitty Malone's whorehouse on 82nd Street in Chicago, which was generally reckoned to be the most lascivious of them all. But Kitty Malone's was pure burlesque. This was more like a temple dance and the goddess they were worshipping here tonight was Aphrodite. The same role, he recalled, that Satin had once played.

As the girl moved, the scarves around her waist shimmered and glowed, parting from time to time to offer tantalising glimpses of her body – a generous, gentle curve of breast, a shadowy belly button, the deep cleft beneath. And always those momentary glimpses of a dusky pinkness.

The other girl watched, almost stationary, her eyes like smouldering coals. Then the other one held out her hands to her and she began to move towards her, slowly and without urgency, gradually circling nearer until just their fingertips were touching. Levinson was aware of the close and intimate proximity of the women's bodies, the seductive glow of the wine he had drunk, the exciting scents that filled the room. He wiped a film of sweat from his forehead and was aware for the first time of Véronique's hand in his lap.

Now the women were dancing together, bathed in a pool of light. Their embrace was soft and gentle, even when the dark-haired one parted her legs and drew the other one right in close to her. Hands reached out and clasped flesh, the scarves and fabrics with which each was draped now revealing all, now maddeningly hiding their caresses from prurient view.

Véronique was openly stroking Levinson's cock now, through the light fabric of his trousers. He felt a momentary anxiety, lest anyone be watching, but everyone's attention was on the aphrodisiac dance before them.

The girls were kissing now, tongue seeking tongue, breasts and pubic bushes pressed closely together, dark hair on pale flesh. Levinson felt he would go insane with desire. What the hell was in that wine? He had been with many women in his three and thirty years, but he could never recall feeling as aroused as he did at that moment.

One of the girls sank to her knees, burying her face in her partner's lap. From the movement of the other girl's backside, it was obvious what was going on, a rhythmic undulation that had a universal significance to everyone in the room. They changed places without breaking time, this time facing forward so Levinson could see the dusky pink of the dark girl's sex and then the tongue of the other girl, fully extended, came snaking out and buried itself deep in the other's cleft. She had her arms round her as she licked her, kneading the soft, dimpled flesh of her arse, which continued to writhe and shiver in time to the music, almost inaudible now, so that the breathing of the two girls could be heard quite clearly.

Levinson came at the same time as the girl did, heedless as his seed spilled out into his drawers under the delicate ministrations of Véronique who, entirely nonplussed, stared fixedly ahead. Such was his confusion that he scarcely saw how the dance came to an end, nor did he witness the departure of the girls, their scarves trailing as they shimmered into invisibility.

When he came to his senses everyone was applauding. The Comte, Bichfoucauld and several of the others were congratulating Satin on her ingenuity, her impeccable taste, her infallible sense of what was right for the occasion. The women in the room, too, were looking flushed, their breasts heaving, their eyes dark. Véronique, he was sure, would be on fire that night, judging by the way she was acting towards him. Her body, Satin's presence, the lantern slides, the dancers – he was sure, in his heart of hearts, that it was all a part of the plan.

People rose from their seats, accepting glasses of wine. The performance, it seemed, was at an end. At the Comte's instigation, the pianist stood up at his instrument and graciously accepted their applause. But then Bichfoucauld came up beside him and put his arms round his shoulders, as if to steady himself.

'I don't know,' he began, his voice thick with wine, 'I don't know whether our friend here knows that lovely old tune, The Oak Tree by the River.'

The pianist nodded.

'Well, I'm very glad of that. Because, if you will excuse me, I would very much like to give you a little song that is very much in keeping with the nature of our entertainments this evening. And which, I hope, will round off our revels in a suitably jovial way.'

Levinson wondered what on earth he was going to subject them to. The man was plainly drunk and impervious to any embarrassment he might cause. He had his arm around Véronique, wondering just how soon he might decently steer her away from the gathering and upstairs to their soft feather bed.

Bichfoucauld had to steady himself against the piano for support, lest he fall over. He spoke in animated fashion with his accompanist, who began to pick out the well-known tune.

'Not too fast, now,' warned the playwright with a wink and then, his tie askew and his hair falling down over one eye, he began to sing in a surprisingly rich baritone, sparing perhaps of melody, economical too with timing and intonation, but with a relish that was all too evident to the audience:

When desire first enters a sweet maiden's breast
She longs by her lover to be well caressed
She longs with her lover to pull off the trick
And in secret she longs for a taste of his prick!

And when, if cruel fever her spirits do shock
What she wants best of all is a nice stiff-standing cock
While her cunt will be itching from morning till night
When the prick of her lover will yield her delight.

So please give her a prick – it will soon make her well
And don't worry too much that her belly might swell
For she longs to be fucked once, and fucked twice and more
And anything else to a young maid is a bit of a bore.

She would like very much to be laid on the grass
And to feel his fine bollocks bounce against her arse
It's a pity if a fine girl a-hungry should go
For all girls like a nibble, as well you might know.

So if all you young men would be ready and free
We'll be up with our skirts in a trice, as you'd see
We long to be fucked, but to ask brings bad luck
So get your cocks out, lads – she'll give you a suck!

When the song came to an end, everyone applauded, Levinson included. He was standing in a group that included Satin and the Comte. Bichfoucauld came over, weaving alarmingly, and spoke at some length about his plans for the new play. Levinson pretended an absorbing interest in a mosaic near the door. The guy was an arsehole, plainly, and yet there was something not unappealing about his oafish delight in his song – one of many, no doubt, in his repertoire. But the guy just didn't cut it with him. He would have to go. Hubert was going to tell him as soon as they got back to Paris. No one wanted a scene.

Mercifully, any intention the drunken playwright might have had in mind of giving them another song was quashed by Satin suggesting they move back to the drawing room, where a little light supper was awaiting them. Levinson stayed as long as decency allowed and then made his way upstairs, a trifle unsteadily perhaps. Véronique was waiting for him in his bed, naked.

Véronique seduced Levinson. This was a part of the plan. Levinson's money seduced Hubert. That was also a part of the plan. What did not go according to the script, however, was Satin's designs upon seducing Etienne Valéry.

She had wanted him from the very first second she had set eyes on him. True, she was sorry to see Bichfoucauld go. Like Levinson, she had a soft spot for him. She knew he could be coarse, vulgar even, but he had no airs and graces, he didn't set himself up to be any better than he ought. And that gave him a head start over some of the people she found herself associating with, for a start. She had never particularly warmed to Hubert, except in terms of what he could do for her. He was a cold fish, a man largely devoid of sexual chemistry. That he should never show any inclination to want to take her to bed with him was no great source of distress to her. Hubert didn't seem much interested in anything apart from making money.

But Valéry, he was something entirely different. He was tall, very Breton-looking, dark skin, dark eyes. Words were money to him and he used them carefully. Levinson had brought him to her apartment to discuss ideas for the new play. She had in mind to be difficult that day, but one look into those coal-black eyes changed all that. She sat opposite him on a sofa and simpered for the whole afternoon.

She hardly took in a word of what he and Levinson were saying when they met to discuss the play which the young playwright had been commissioned to write. The play was about two sisters, one a few years older than the other, who are separated when very young. One grows up on a farm, the other is adopted by an aristocratic family. One learned to value thrift and industry, the other led a life of indolence and personal gratification. In later years, when their circumstances had changed, they meet again. Each resents the other and, at the same time, is attracted to her. Only later do they discover they are long-lost sisters.

'What are you going to call it?' asked Levinson.

'I don't know,' replied Valéry. '*Sophie and her Sister*, perhaps. But I've not really thought about it. I don't think the title matters much, to be honest.'

'Which one is Sophie?' asked Satin.

'She's the aristocratic one,' said Valéry.

'Doesn't she come to a bad end?'

'Well, she does. But she has a lot of fun on the way.'

Satin's face visibly brightened. 'I'm not sure I like playing nice girls,' she said. Everyone laughed.

'And she is so much younger than her sister, Giselle,' added the young playwright, knowing how this would flatter Satin.

She thought about this. 'How much younger?' she said at length.

'Oh, four or five years, at least.'

'And is she pretty?'

'Very.'

'I mean, is she prettier than the other one? The sister—'

Levinson and Valéry exchanged glances.

'They're both pretty,' Levinson began but Valéry cut him short.

'Sophie is a lot more fun than Giselle,' he said. 'She loves dancing and parties. Giselle always has a nose in a book. She would like to be a teacher one day.'

'Oh dear. That doesn't sound like me at all.'

Levinson smiled. He was glad Satin had got what she wanted, and wouldn't be difficult.

The second meeting they arranged, Satin unavoidably had to cancel at the last minute. Later, a messenger arrived at Valéry's apartment, summoning him to meet the great lady. He arrived at her apartment in something of an ill-humour. He had been busy re-writing the script to accommodate some whim or other of Satin's, and did not wish to further burden himself.

But, when he got there – having taken the precaution of bringing with him an enormous bouquet of flowers – he was relieved to find her in a very agreeable mood.

She was sitting on a sofa, stroking her dog. Though it was only three in the afternoon, she was wearing a very revealing gown of organdie and lace, cut low at the front.

She bade him to sit down beside her. Mathilde brought tea. She fed the dog with little crumbs of cake.

'I was wondering,' she began, once the formalities were over, 'whether there might be some kind of dance in the play that I could perform.'

Valéry, who had not seen Satin's legendary early performances of a couple of years back but had heard all about them, was not taken entirely by surprise. Clearly, the woman would lose little opportunity to show off. Inhibitions, it seemed, she had none.

'There is the masked ball, of course,' he said hastily.

Satin had her script with her. 'Where is that?' she said, dreamily.

He told her the page. She looked at her dialogue for a few minutes.

'Well,' she began at length, 'it's not very exciting, is it?'

'It depends what you mean?'

'Well, I wondered if she might not do something a little more, how can we put it, interesting. Like Salome, for instance.'

'You mean, take most of your clothes off?'

'Something like that.'

He was nonplussed for a moment. 'I hadn't thought of it quite like that, you know.'

'But it is a masked ball. People are in costume. She could go as Salome.'

'What an extraordinary idea.'

She patted him on the knee.

'I knew you'd like it,' she said, leaning forward to pluck up another crumb of cake for the dog and allowing a further generous glimpse of her cleavage.

'Yes I do. But I just wonder, you know, if it's entirely right for the play. At that moment, I mean.'

'You don't think I can dance?'

'I'm sure you dance beautifully, Madame. And I'm sure you would make a marvellous Salome.'

'Shall I show you?'

'Let me put it to Hubert. He is, after all the promoter.'

But Satin was already on her feet. Humming to herself in a surprisingly tuneful voice, she began to move around the room. Her eroticism was undeniable and Valéry began to feel a growing confusion. Of course this would be exactly what people would expect of Satin. Word would soon get around, and the success of the play – his play, mind – would be assured. What did it matter if it were her idea, and not his? And yet, and yet. This wasn't the kind of play he had written, this erotic spectacle. It would be out of place, somehow, and he did not know how to make it plain to her in a way that she would understand.

He was spared further embarrassment by the arrival of the Comte de Loury. Satin seemed surprised to see him too.

'My sweet,' she said. 'What on earth brings you here?'

'I happened to be passing,' he said simply. 'I knew you would be at home this afternoon and so I called.'

'Too divine,' she breathed. Valéry felt uncomfortably aware of the Comte's questioning gaze, of the way Satin had hurriedly rearranged her décolletage when her paramour and principal benefactor was announced. The two men exchanged civilities but he was aware of a momentary steeliness in his manner.

'We were just talking over a few ideas for the play,' he ventured.

'Yes,' said Satin, rather too quickly. 'I want to dance Salome.'

'Salome?' said the Comte, raising an aristocratic eyebrow.

'Yes. At the masked ball. You remember.'

'Salome?' he repeated. Valéry, not liking what he saw, pulled out his watch, drew in his breath and rose to his feet.

'I'm afraid I have another appointment,' he said, trying not to appear too flustered. He gathered up the various papers that were scattered around the couch, thrust them into his case.

'No, don't go on my account,' said de Loury. 'I'm interested in everything concerned with the play. After all, it's my money behind it, as well as Mr Levinson's.'

But Valéry would not be deterred. Mumbling his excuses, he rose to his feet, shook hands and made for the door. He managed to tread on the dog's tail, setting off a furious yelping. He apologised still further, and made good his escape.

Once he had gained the street outside the apartment, he breathed a sigh of relief. A cafe was open nearby. He went in and, though it was barely four-thirty in the afternoon, ordered brandy and soda. While he sipped it he reflected on his narrow escape. The woman was a predator, that much was true. Of course, he was as aware as any red-blooded man of her beauty and undeniable physical attraction – she was positively dangerous, so highly developed was her sensuality.

He had thought, often, of her, and of her body, and of the pleasures it would yield. He was convinced she wanted him and he knew he would have to fight hard to resist. He was sure she was making overtures to him, had been ever since they had met.

But for him to become involved with her in any kind of romantic way – why, that was sheer foolishness. Not only would his career as a playwright be at stake, there was also the Comte to consider. A man of his wealth and power could destroy an unknown like Valéry as simply as swatting a fly. There was too much at stake to risk everything for the sake of one night of passion with this latter-day Cleopatra. He was, he realised, best advised to stay well clear of her.

'What was that about?' said the Comte, trying not to sound too angry. Of late, he and Satin had begun to argue quite a good deal.

'What was all what about?'

'Just then. Valéry, and this Salome business.'

'It was just an idea, that was all.'

'You know about Salome, don't you? And what she represents?'

'Of course I do. I find it very appealing.'

'What will people think? About you?'

He knew nothing, of course, of her past history.

'I think they'll enjoy it and everyone will have the most tremendous fun.'

'I just don't think it's right, that's all.'

'Why not?'

'Because I would be compromised.'

'By what?'

'By you.'

'What about me?'

'Playing Salome.'

'It's only a character in a play. And it's not even the whole play. It's just one tiny bit of the play. Besides, who knows about us?'

This part, at least, was true, the Comte had to admit. Their association had lasted some considerable time now and yet they had succeeded in being very discreet. They only associated openly together when they knew they would be safe. And yet, somehow, the idea of what she proposed was distasteful to him.

'It was his idea, of course?'

She saw her opportunity.

'Yes.'

'You like him, don't you?'

'He is nice. He is kind to me.'

'Was he trying to make love to you? When I came in?'

She laughed, tried to brush his remarks aside. Sometimes the Comte was just too ridiculous.

He repeated his request.

'Of course not,' she said. 'We were just talking about the play. He was showing me some changes he had made to the script.'

'He didn't say anything about that when Hubert spoke to him this morning.'

'That was because he's only just made them. He came right over here to show me.'

Her hands reached out to him, imploringly, her huge eyes opened wide.

'Don't be angry with me, my sweet,' she breathed. She reached out, touched him.

'Tell me the real reason you came here,' she whispered.

She drew him closer to her. Then he was beside her. She took his hand, placed it on her breast.

'You wanted to make love to me, didn't you, you wicked man. And at four-thirty in the afternoon.'

He took her there and then, without preliminaries, on the floor of her apartment. He crushed out his cigar roughly and then fell upon her. She felt his hand under her skirts, on her knee, moving up her thigh. She had worn pretty satin garters with the intention of seducing Etienne Valéry. All the time she had been talking to him, she had been willing him to make the first move. She wanted his tongue in her mouth, between her legs. She kept looking at his groin, thirsting after his body. She wanted to undress for him, just like Salome, for him to see her pretty new garters and silk stockings. But it was not Etienne Valéry who was touching them now.

She looked at him. 'Ought we to be doing this? Here?'

'I think we should,' he replied with the effortless charm that is so often born of nobility.

Now his hand was under the waistband of her dress, feeling the soft flesh of her legs, gliding slowly and smoothly back and forth but moving inexorably towards the sensitive skin of her upper thighs.

'I need to pee,' she said.

'Pee later,' he said. 'I'll come and watch.'

'Wicked man.'

'We've done that before.'

He took her hand, placed it on his cock.

'What if Mathilde comes in? Or Mu?' she murmured, though the fear of that never normally rose in her conscience.

'All the more exciting for us,' said de Loury. 'Besides, Mathilde knows better than to come barging in on us when we're together.'

He certainly has magic fingers, Satin thought to herself.

She sensed her breasts thickening and the nipples growing hard with desire. They were practically spilling out of her dress, she had so wanted Valéry to suck them. But now, as the tide of desire began to rise in her, she needed the Comte de Loury, if only to satisfy her own burgeoning and unrequited bodily lusts.

His hand was at the top of her thighs, brushing against her drawers. Half of her wanted him to stop, the other half to go on. The urge to pee was becoming stronger with her growing arousal. His fingers caressed her sex gently through the cream silk of her lingerie, catching and stroking a stray wisp of pubic hair, outlining the unseen shape of her lips. She was aware of a growing dampness in her crotch.

She moved slightly on her chair and allowed his finger to enter her vagina. She couldn't, at this stage, look at him directly. She was still thinking about Valéry, imagining it was his fingers that were probing her. She thought of his cock, how it would be strong and hard in her mouth. She looked at the Comte. He smiled, but there seemed to be little warmth in his eyes. He seemed angry, somehow.

He had three fingers in her vagina now, and she felt full and stretched. He was being quite rough with her now, which was unlike him. The pressure against her bladder was becoming almost unbearable. And yet despite herself she parted her legs more to accommodate him, leaned backwards in the chair, thrusting out her pelvis. I just hope I don't wet myself, she thought.

She was surprised when he suddenly withdrew his fingers. He held them up to his face, wet and glistening with her secretions, inhaling deeply and appreciatively. He licked the tip of his index finger, the one that had been doing all the work on her clitoris. Then he offered the finger to her. She licked it too, tentatively at first and then drawing it in deeper into her mouth, holding his palm as she did so. It tasted salty and musky, a bit like anchovies.

But it's not like sucking his lovely big cock, she said silently.

He stood up and drew her to him. But instead of the anticipated kiss, he turned her round, pushing her face forwards over the rear of the sofa. It was Louis XVI, blue and gold, one of her favourite pieces. The Comte had bought it for her himself. He drew her dress up around her hips and his hands caressed the silken globes of her buttocks. There was a pause, a hesitancy – was Mathilde coming? she wondered with a stab of alarm. But then the footsteps receded, and she could relax.

And then he was inside her, pushing and thrusting, forcing her down until her breasts were crushed flat against the brocade trimming of the sofa. His penis felt big within her sheath but she knew that she was not yet fully aroused, that her own vagina was still tight and tense.

'I've got to pee,' she cried out, even as he powered into her.

'Pee all over me, then,' he said. 'Remember that time at Campignon-Bois? After the party with the dancers?'

She ignored him. She had been very drunk that evening, had hardly known who had fucked her or what she had done with anyone. It would never be like that with Etienne Valéry, she told herself. Oh, but he was beautiful. Maybe it was a good thing she had not been able to seduce him before the Comte arrived. She had been so excited, she wondered if she might have been too wet for him, that he might even find it embarrassing. She caught a whiff of the Comte's penis, subtle and musky and unobtrusive, mingling with her own effusions, and she saw smoke rising from his crushed cigar as it smouldered in the ashtray.

Her own passion smouldered too, without ever quite catching fire, not even when he withdrew his penis from her vagina and pressed it back in again with considerable force, over and over again, faster and faster now. She heard him saying things under his breath. She couldn't catch the words but she was sure he was angry with her. He didn't believe what she'd said about Etienne Valéry, she knew that – and why should he? Well, now he was fucking her out of anger and she was fucking him back.

She closed her eyes and thought again of the handsome young man who had so lately quitted the apartment. Could she catch just a hint of cologne on the cushions where he had been sitting. She buried her head in them, breathing deeply. Yes, it was him, it was! A wave of lust swept over her – it was as much as she could do to stop herself calling out his name. She felt no guilt about what she was doing – fucking one man while she was thinking of another. But she thought again of Valéry the playwright, his muscles and his mind, those handsome Breton features, and suddenly it wasn't the Comte making love to her at all any more, it was Valéry. It was Valéry who was inside her, Valéry's balls brushing against the backs of her thighs, Valéry's hips pressed against her backside.

Valéry was fucking her like she had never been fucked before, strong and hard and masculine, and she wanted him like she had wanted no other man before. Her illicit lusts went spinning round in her mind like a whirlpool and she came, noisily but powerfully, a woman totally out of control of her body and her mind.

When she came round and opened her eyes, she saw herself reflected in the mirror above the fireplace, her hair dishevelled, her dress up around her waist. She knew where she was and whom she was with. The Comte was busy rearranging his clothing, smoothing out his moustache with the tips of his cunt-smelling fingers. His anger appeared to have subsided. She turned around to a sitting position, pulled up her drawers where he had so hurriedly tugged them down. One of her pretty new garters, she realised, was missing. Perhaps it was under the sofa. But she hadn't time to worry about that now –

she was going to burst at any minute. It must have been all those endless cups of tea she had drunk with Etienne Valéry – if they'd have had champagne, the whole thing would have been much easier.

She was aware, as she hurried to the closet, of how wet she was. She hadn't even noticed, at the time, whether the Comte had finished or not. Men usually did, in her experience.

Chapter Seven

Besotted as she was with Etienne Valéry, Satin threw herself into preparations for *Sophie and her Sister* with a vigour that surprised all who knew her – from the humblest wardrobe assistant to Hubert and even the Comte himself. They recalled her lassitude, her indifference to the needs of others, her moods, her legendary lack of punctuality. All that had changed.

She would often be the first one to reach the theatre, though this was, in truth, more in the hope of a chance meeting with Valéry than the opportunity it afforded her to rehearse her lines and stage movements.

The play was developing quickly. Satin, it seemed, was revealing hidden depths of ability as an actress. In the past, what had too often caught the eye was the depths of her unreasonableness.

She was even unusually civil to Violette, the actress who was to play her sister. Violette was one of those actresses – perhaps less commonly found among the theatres of Paris than in the provinces – who promised much without ever, in the event, really fulfilling her potential. She was pretty, but not too pretty, talented but not excessively overwhelmed with ability, vivacious without being incandescently so. Her career was the exact opposite, in many ways, to Satin's meteoric rise to fame. She had built her parts – and her career – slowly and cumulatively. The Comte had become a great admirer of her work, as had Valéry. But Satin was sure enough of her own position now not to feel herself threatened by this.

A small part had been found, too, for Véronique, whom she now counted as one of her oldest friends. The two women shared a dressing room during rehearsals and, not infrequently, a bed afterwards. Véronique often told her about Levinson. The two of them were not true lovers – and never would be – but he had sometimes visited her at Satin's apartment in town, when its owner was away at Campignon-Bois, and she had visited him in his suite at the Ritz.

'I'm surprised he hasn't made more of a play for you, my dear,' said Véronique one evening as they were sitting by the fire.

'Why do you say that?'

'He's rich, he's good-looking, he's all the things you like about men.'

'He doesn't really do anything for me.'

'So it seems. Has he ever tried anything on with you?'

'No, not really. I catch him looking at me sometimes and I wonder. Sometimes I think that might just be what's on his mind but, then again, it might just be his manner. I think, in a curious kind of way, he respects me. And I quite like that. And there's the Comte, of course.'

'Mr Levinson is a gentleman.'

'Of course. He would never do anything that would compromise the Comte.'

Satin, stroking her little lap-dog, was faintly irritated that Véronique should have mentioned the Comte. Of late, she was perhaps beginning to grow a little bored with him. She liked all the things he paid for, of course, from the house at Campignon-Bois to her own stage productions, which had been growing increasingly expensive to mount, what with the elaborate scenery and effects that was so often called for. The apartment, however, was entirely her own now.

As was almost inevitable by now, she found some way of introducing Valéry's name into the conversation.

'Oh, I do like him,' said Véronique. 'Isn't he so wonderful? Such ideas that he has – and so very good-looking.'

Had she glanced up at that moment, she would have seen Satin shoot her a look. But she carried on, quite innocently.

'I know I've only got a small part but he takes a lot of care. Far more than the director. I can't say I care much for him.'

'Voissard? No, I don't like him much either. He's too full of himself. A pompous ass.'

'But Etienne – he rewrote some lines of script that I was finding difficult. Voissard didn't even notice they'd changed the lines. I don't think he's even aware of me when I'm on stage.'

'They say he prefers the company of other men.'

'It wouldn't surprise me in the least. I wonder if he fancies Etienne?'

'Doesn't everyone?'

There – it had slipped out.

'Do you fancy him?'

'He's so nice – and so good-looking. How about you?'

'Oh yes. I mean, well – yes, of course I do.'

'Do you ever think of him?'

'How do you mean?'

'Well, about you and him, you know, doing it? Being together?'

Véronique smiled, a mysterious, sphinx-like smile. Even in the firelight Satin could sense the glow that lit up her features.

'You won't tell anyone?'

'Who could I tell?'

Véronique drew closer, until she was almost whispering in Satin's ear. There was no one else in the room. Mathilde and the other servants had long since been dismissed for the evening.

'Well, sometimes I think about him coming round here, unexpectedly.'

'Where am I?'

'Oh, off in the country or somewhere. I'm just here on my own.'

'You're lucky. And then—'

'And then what?'

'What happens next?'

'Oh, you know. We start talking. Maybe we have a glass of wine.'

'Does he come on to you?'

'Oh yes. I can tell he's really excited by me. I can see how stiff he is, through his trousers.'

'I bet he has a nice prick.'

'I do too.'

'Nice and thick.'

'I bet it is. I like a nice thick one.'

'I wonder if he likes having his prick sucked?'

'I'm sure he does. Don't all men?'

'Do you imagine what it would be like to suck him?'

'Of course I do.'

'So what do you do, when he's with you?'

'He starts to kiss me, really soft and slow. He's so gentle with me but I know that underneath he's on fire with passion for me.'

'Go on, go on.'

'Then he starts playing with my tits.'

'I envy you your tits.'

'You've got lovely tits, Satin. Really big, the way men like them. Mine are so small.'

'But not that small. Nice enough to suck and lick and such a lovely shape. I bet Etienne would like them. I bet he wants to rub his cock against them.'

'Mmmmm, I'm sure he would. I'd really like that. And I imagine him licking me while I'm stroking his cock.'

'Has he taken his trousers off yet?'

'No, that comes later. When we go into the bedroom.'

The dog started struggling in Satin's lap. It distracted her attention.

'Don't stop. Tell me what happens next.'

'We lie down on the hearthrug by the fire. I take his lovely long cock out and lick it.'

'What's it like?'

'Lovely. I love the taste of his cock in my mouth.'

Satin reached out and began to caress Véronique's bosom. The two women were in their negligées, as was their custom in the later part of the evening, when they would sit together and sip champagne and discuss the day's news. Items of scandal and gossip predominated.

'Then we go through into the bedroom. He undresses me very slowly. He keeps murmuring all these lovely compliments, like he really means them. It makes me feel good.'

'Sure it does. What does he say?'

'Oh, about how much he likes me and how he loves my body. And all the time he's stroking me and playing with my tits and sucking my nipples—'

'Let me suck them for you.' Satin leaned forward and deftly undid the silken cord that bound Véronique's robe. It fell open, revealing her luscious, strawberry-tipped breasts.

'Goodness, that feels lovely,' breathed Véronique as Satin took her nipple into her mouth. 'I hope Etienne can suck me as nicely as you do, my love.'

'Of course he can. And he's got such a lovely big prick too.'

'Mmmmm – his prick. I often dream about his prick, you know.'

'Has he got it in you, in your dream?'

'Not yet, not yet. That's what I like about him so much. He takes his time. He waits till I'm ready for him.'

'I can feel you getting wet just talking about it.'

'Am I wet?'

'Oh yes, you're just soaking.'

'Put your fingers right up me, my love. Oh, that's nice. Do it harder.'

'Is that like Etienne would do it?'

'Oh yes, that's just like his prick. Frig me up and down like he's fucking me. Tell me what he's doing.'

Satin drew a deep breath. Her own pussy was on fire and she wanted to be satisfied herself. For the moment, though, she was enjoying pleasuring her friend. Her own time would come later.

'He's got his cock in you and he's playing with your clitty with his thumb, really gentle. Can you feel that? Isn't that just like a man?'

'Oh yes. Don't stop.'

'And with his other hand he's squeezing your nipples, really gentle, so gentle you want to come just because of the way he's doing it to you. And his tongue, he's licking you all over, like this.'

They were sprawled on the sofa in an attitude of utter abandon, their words ceased now, everything silent now but for the silken sound of hands on flesh, of lips gently touching and parting, of kisses given and exchanged. Their breathing was becoming harder and more insistent, half-formed sighs and endearments, the fire blazing and popping away beside them and bathing their half-naked bodies in its warm glow.

And then, suddenly, Véronique began to pant and gasp, and to call out first Satin's name and then that of Etienne Valéry, and then she forced her squirming body against that of her friend and ground her hips against her, with Satin's fingers still buried deep inside her, and she came tumultuously and triumphantly, her own wicked tongue seeking out Satin's, her robe spilling wide open to reveal her wanton charms to her imaginary lover.

Later, in bed, it was Satin's turn. They had a familiar

routine for times such as this. Imagining that Véronique was Etienne Valéry gave it added spice, a thrill of the unusual.

Satin was sitting up in bed, impatient and at the same time savouring the urgency of the moment. She watched as Véronique took off her long, elegant robe of oyster silk, revealing the full beauty of her body. She was tall and lithe, almost like a man in some ways, but her sex was proclaimed with her long, colt-like legs and small breasts.

Satin stirred impatiently. Véronique was teasing her. It was all a part of their game.

From a drawer Véronique took out the ebony dildo, the same one Frédéric de Fleury had given Satin when they had been lovers, so many months ago now. It had been a good companion to her ever since, whether she was alone or with a friend.

She held it up, admiring its perfect contours, the beautiful shape. In the soft light of the boudoir, the inlaid silver bands gleamed dully. Véronique ran her finger over the exquisitely formed godemiche, which had found her innermost recesses again and again. She held it up to her mouth and kissed it gently. Be patient, she mouthed to Satin.

Then, from a drawer, she took out something that was half garment and half harness, fashioned of soft black leather. It fastened around her hips with tight buckles and belts that pressed into her smooth white flesh, leaving her sex exposed. Through Véronique's soft downy bush, Satin could see pink lips glistening moistly with her secretions.

Véronique tightened more straps. Now the black dildo was fastened to her body, jutting arrogantly forward like a man's penis. She stood there, her eyes fixed on Satin, one hand holding the root of her strange ebony manhood, the other caressing her own nipples.

The two women looked at each other in silence, eyes longing. Véronique spoke first.

'I want to fuck you now, my sweet,' she said, her voice deep and dark, almost like a man's.

Satin squirmed with excitement.

'I'm dying for you,' she breathed. 'It's been too long. I can hardly wait.'

She pushed back the sheets, revealing her nakedness. Though Véronique had seen her friend unclothed many times, the beauty of her body never ceased to inflame her. She was like the Aphrodite that she had been in one of her earliest roles, voluptuous and full-bodied, her breasts ripe and heavy, her thighs and belly womanly. Frédéric de Fleury had twice begun paintings of her in this pose but each time had allowed himself to become distracted by the demands of his own body – and of his sitter's. Neither painting was, in the end, ever more than a sketch. In his rage at losing Satin for another, still more wealthy lover, he had burned them both.

'Come and fuck me now, Etienne,' she said, her eyes closed. Véronique came and stood by the bed, the black dildo heavy and potent.

'Suck me first,' she said, still in that deep voice. 'And I'll lick you at the same time.'

They lay down together, reversed. Satin caressed the ebony godemiche, tasted it with her tongue. She could smell Véronique's pussy and she could see it too at the same time, the lips puffy and aroused. Down below, her lover began to lick and lap at her own labia, teasing them expertly, the tip of her tongue darting and probing.

Satin took the whole of the dildo into her mouth and, at the same time, inserted just the tip of her index finger into Véronique's arsehole. Her friend was very fond of that particular insertion, and she began to moan and whimper as her wanton tongue explored Satin's inner folds.

Her tongue seemed to push Satin to higher and higher levels of pleasure and yet, somehow, she was still not satisfied. She wanted the dildo in her, wanted Véronique to fuck her hard with it, as hard as a man with a real cock, but it wasn't Véronique she wanted inside her, it was Etienne Valéry.

Yet when she parted her legs and Véronique climbed on top of her, she found it remarkably easy to maintain the pretense. Véronique knew exactly what to do, her body now so muscular and strong. She fucked her as any man would have done, gentle at first, but then with increasing vigour, until at length she was pounding into her with all the force she could muster, the dildo crammed right up inside her one moment and then, at the next, withdrawn almost to its fullest extremity.

They kissed, burning kisses fiercely exchanged, and their tongues danced around each others', and their breasts were crushed together as Satin parted her legs and brought them up and around behind Véronique's back, clutching her around the waist, trying to draw her body inside herself.

She could feel the black leather of the harness against her own flesh now, the warmth of the material and the cold silver buckles. It too had been the gift of the celebrated portraitist, who had had it made specially for her. Sometimes she wore it, sometimes Véronique. Sometimes one or the other of them had worn it when they went out together. On one memorable occasion they had fucked each other in the ladies' convenience at the Louvre while the Comte, who was on several of its many committees of administrators, ushered a visiting head of state around the most important paintings in the collection.

Satin wondered if it would be like this with Etienne. She would like him to be fierce with her, rough even, but she would also like him to show tenderness. She wanted to try different positions with him, wanted to bend down in front of him and present her lewd arse for his lascivious delight. But most of all, she wanted to feel his weight on top of her, to smell his masculine scent, to be aware of his beard and hair and the aroma of the Turkish tobacco he smoked. When she came, it was with the dildo inside her and Etienne Valéry's face imprinted on her imagination.

She lay back on the pillows, naked and sated. Véronique crouched between her legs still, the black dildo slick and wet with her own juices, bobbing there between her thighs as she caught her breath.

'Oh, take the damn things off,' Satin said suddenly.

Véronique looked confused, even hurt. Normally, Satin enjoyed the sight of the other girl so attired.

'I'm sorry,' she said at length, reaching out and stroking Véronique's hair. 'I shouldn't have said that. I just wish it was the real thing, that's all.'

'I know,' said Véronique. 'I know just how you feel.'

They lay together, arms around one another, under the covers, and drifted off to sleep in each other's arms. Outside, the bells of the church of La Madeleine chimed the midnight hour. They were both restless and neither of them, though they fervently wished differently, dreamed of Etienne Valéry that night.

'I wonder,' said Satin, 'if I might invite you to dine with me on Saturday. Just a very small gathering, of course – a few friends.'

Etienne Valéry smiled, showing handsome white teeth.

'I would be delighted,' he said. 'I'm afraid I don't really care for large, noisy gatherings.'

'Nor do I,' replied Satin, quite untruthfully. Véronique heard her words and suppressed a smile with difficulty. 'But really, there will just be a very few of us, I can assure you. And we all just love your work.'

He smiled modestly. He was, in many ways, a surprisingly modest man in a world where people tended to have monstrously inflated opinions in general and of themselves in particular. And yet, as everyone said, he was one of the most gifted young playwrights to have emerged in years. Levinson predicted great things for him, as did the Comte, who had rapidly become one of his most fervent admirers. *Sophie and her Sister*, it was confidently predicted, would be a sensation even without Satin's Salome routine, which the Comte had insisted be dropped.

'And will you come too?' she asked Levinson, knowing full well that he would have to be away. It was all a part of her plan.

'I would love to,' he said, 'but I have a business appointment in Lyon and I will not be back until Monday.'

'Oh, what a shame,' said Satin, with an exaggerated pout of disappointment. 'Still, there will be another time, I'm sure.'

She had chosen her moment carefully. There was just the four of them sitting in the stalls, watching the rehearsals of the final act, a scene that did not involve Satin. The play was due to open in two weeks' time and it had been running like clockwork. Some of the most important critics of the day, including Oisy of *Figaro* and Brillat of *Paris-Soir* – but not that appalling man Patric Esteve from *Paris Expresse*, who would have been denied one anyway – had been clamouring for a glimpse of the rehearsals, but without success. Nothing would be revealed, everyone involved with the production had insisted, until opening night.

'It'll be the last opportunity we'll have until the play finishes, I'm sure. After that, I want to travel. I feel like I've not been further than Campignon-Bois in ages. Have you travelled?'

Distracted from watching Violette in her final soliloquy, Valéry conceded that he had travelled to Italy and to the northern shores of Greece.

'Italy! How beautiful,' cried Satin. 'Yes, I shall go to Italy.'

'You must come to America also,' said Levinson, in his paternal way.

'Yes, I would love to. But I must see Italy first. I hear so much about the lakes, the glory that was Rome. I love all that kind of thing, you know. That English poet, Byron. Yes, Italy it must be.'

But Etienne St Valéry would not be drawn. He was making copious notes in the margin of his script and none of Satin's efforts would distract him.

The Comte was bored, it was plain to see. He sat in the window of the great drawing-room at Campignon-Bois and gazed out over the autumn landscape. Already the trees had begun to yellow and fall. Gardeners were raking the grass twice a day, to keep them clear. Satin knew better than to try and deal with him when he was in this kind of mood.

She wanted to ask him for money.

Money – or her lack of it – was her most pressing concern for the moment. But she wondered, too, if she were perhaps beginning to tire of him, for all his wealth. He knew of her affair with Véronique, tacitly approved of it and, indeed, sometimes joined them in their sport. But he would react very differently to another gentleman in her life. She had, without his knowledge of course, once or twice taken a fresh lover to her bed. It was no one he knew, of course, he would have been far too proud to have tolerated such a disgrace. But just once in a while Satin felt the need to dally a little. She and Véronique had even made a joke of it – maybe the way to solve Satin's mounting debts, the ones the Comte didn't know about, over and above the ones he did, was for them both to go back on the streets.

Once, in disguise, she had returned to a spot quite near to her old haunts by the Café des Artistes. She'd done it just for a laugh, to see if she could still pull the old bell-ropes. She had turned down four or five men who came by – none had recognised her, thanks to the dark wig she was wearing and the clever use of make-up.

And then this particular man had come along, quite young, with the most lovely almond eyes. She was surprised a man such as that would need to go looking among the flaring gas lights at the girls of the streets but she knew better than to ask questions. Perhaps he had a girl-friend who had jilted him, who could have known. They went to a hotel she used to frequent and they coupled quickly and passionately.

She enjoyed the experience, enough to want to do it again. But not for the moment, not with her dinner with Etienne Valéry coming up. She had been paid for her services, of course, but it was nowhere near enough to cover even a tiny fraction of her debts. It might have paid for the last pair of gloves she had bought on credit, or a new hat. She would need to go with hundreds, if not thousands of men in order to be free of her financial obligations for once and for all.

What she needed, of course, was to have several lovers at once, each of them of the stature of the Comte. Unfortunately, she knew only too well how jealous he would be of the merest whisper of another man in her life. Why, only last month at a reception she had attended at his side at the Tunisian legation, he had looked daggers at her because she had joked with a handsome young equerry. He was too important to her, in so many ways, to risk compromising anything.

The Comte paid for everything at Campignon-Bois but it was her town apartment that was causing her difficulties. The upkeep, the interest payments – it swallowed up what little she had. There had been an unfortunate argument with a dressmaker whose bill had not been paid for six months and more. Satin needed new clothes every week – she was, she maintained, expected to be in the very van of fashion – but she could not ask the Comte for more money, on top of that which she already had from him, which was a very considerable amount indeed. When the new play opened, of course, everything would be fine but she was certainly feeling the pinch at the moment.

The Comte had always been so indulgent with her. Anything she asked for, she could have. She knew – or suspected – that he had other mistresses, but he had never been anything less than generous in meeting her increasingly frequent demands. He was, after all, an extravagantly rich man.

But even the vintner was asking for payment now. Why did they always come direct to her for these things? She should have someone who would handle these boring everyday matters on her behalf. Surely Hubert, if he put his mind to it, ought to be able to help. Maybe the Comte could provide her with the services of a book-keeper, or an agent, or something. There was an agent who looked after the day-to-day running of Campignon-Bois, saw that the gardeners were paid, made sure the repairs to the roof were in hand. Why couldn't she have someone who would deal with the dull things in life while she, a creative artist after all, got on with the more important matters? Bills, bills, bills. She could see she was going to get nowhere with the Comte, so she didn't even bother trying.

She left the drawing-room and made to go upstairs. In the hall, a servant approached her carrying a silver salver. There was a letter on it, addressed to her. She did not recognise the handwriting.

In her room she tore the envelope open. It was from Levinson.

I have to return to the United States unexpectedly. I sail from Cherbourg this evening and it may be some months before I can return, by which time *Sophie and her Sister* will have finished its run.

May I wish you every success with the production?
I will write more fully when I have more time – we
dock at Southampton tomorrow. For the moment
these few lines must suffice. I have a great many
matters to attend to.

Your admirer

Henry Levinson

Her feelings were mixed indeed as she folded the note
and put it back in its envelope. It was kind of Levinson to
write to her in this way. She did not doubt for one moment
the sincerity of his feelings. She enjoyed his patronage,
the way he encouraged her talents and abilities without
asking for anything in return other than the honour of her
acquaintance – and, of course, the income that she would
produce for him. He was more like an uncle to her, a kind
uncle. She knew he had slept several times with Véronique – she had described their exploits in considerable
detail – but had shown no desire for a greater intimacy
with Satin. With most men she would take it as an insult,
but, as far as Levinson was concerned, she viewed it as a
compliment, a mark of respect. She was obviously more to
him than a body, however voluptuous it may have been.

And yet, and yet . . . It was to Levinson that she hoped
to turn to help her out of her current financial plight. She
wasn't asking for vast amounts of money, she just needed
enough to tide her through, just this once. She was sure
she could have counted on him. But now he had been
called away – what could she do? She had been quite
faithful to the Comte for some time now, had no intimacies close enough to warrant the gift of large sums of
money. It was a worrying time for her.

She left her room, frustrated and unfulfilled. She stood
on the balcony looking down on the distant fields and
hedgerows, her lines from *Sophie and her Sister* running

through her head in a random and confusing way. The play would open next week but she did not know quite when she would be paid for it – by the month, she had been led to understand. The day was overcast and grey. She felt almost unhappy, but then she thought of Etienne Valéry coming to dinner the following week and her spirits improved considerably.

Even by Satin's standards of extravagance, the rooms in the apartments had been decorated in remarkable fashion. It was like a small theatre set in itself, dark and intimate, candles glittering on polished silverware, heavy fabrics contrasting with filigree lace.

She and Véronique were dressed in equally stunning fashion, Satin in a close-fitting dress that revealed far more than it concealed, Véronique in spectacular red silk. They had plotted this evening for days past. No detail was too small to escape their attention.

They drank apéritifs, both of them excited beyond measure. And then Mathilde was at the door.

'M Valéry,' she announced.

He came in. The two women rose. He took their hands in turn, kissed them. Satin could sense his eyes on her, taking in the stupendous amount of cleavage she was revealing. He accepted a glass. Satin had a small phial of the tincture for later, in bed. She would slip it into Etienne Valéry's wine when he was not looking.

He stood by the fire, admiring the room. He had not been there before.

'This painting,' he said, glancing up. 'It's by Fleury, isn't it?'

'That's right,' replied Satin. 'Do you know him?'

'Really only by reputation, though I've met him a couple of times. A delightful man.'

'Yes,' said Satin, rather too quickly. 'Yes, we knew each other quite well at one time.'

'Through his friend, La Cabache, I should imagine.'

'How very clever of you. Yes, she and I were in a play together, quite some while ago. *Lovers' Vows*, did you see that? By Cocon? I came to know them quite well.'

'Do you still see them?'

'Not very often, I'm afraid. But he did give me the painting, as a keepsake. I'm very fond of it.'

Valéry studied the other pictures but found little of interest.

'So,' he said, turning back to Satin. 'Who will be dining with us tonight? I hope you've managed to find someone agreeable. I'm sure you have, of course.'

Satin and Véronique exchanged glances.

'I'm awfully sorry to have to say this,' she began, 'but there's just the three of us. Mr Levinson, as you know, was called back to the United States and cannot be with us. Likewise, my other friends – delightful people, the Canards – have had to cancel at short notice. She is having a baby next month and is not feeling too well at the moment. So I'm afraid we will be rather an intimate little gathering, tonight.'

Véronique glanced at her again, a playful expression crossing her face. She was watching Etienne Valéry intently. Did she detect a little flicker of lust there, as he considered the possibilities? She rather hoped she did.

At any rate, the conversation went well enough. Satin talked enough for three, while Valéry was the personification of good manners. They made their way into the dining room.

'I say,' said the playwright, when he saw the exquisite care with which the room had been prepared. The room itself seemed to glow with life, the flicker of the many candles, the fire burning in the hearth.

They took their seats. A fish soup was served, the servants discreet to the point of anonymity. Valéry passed some quiet compliment, allowing Satin to lean forward to catch his words and in so doing to display even more of her spectacular décolletage.

There was wine of the finest quality. Satin was surprised at how much the playwright drank, and the evident relish with which he despatched it. He was evidently in a fine mood. She hoped the wine wouldn't fuddle him too much. She had other plans in mind than a flow of anecdote and reminiscence, pleasant though that might have been.

They were talking about Bichfoucauld. His new play was not going well at all, Valéry had heard. It had had to be rewritten twice on the director's insistence. The poor man was drinking more than ever.

'He is a good writer,' said his young contemporary, 'but he no longer makes the effort. He thinks his reputation will save him. The trouble is, he no longer knows what kind of a reputation he has.'

'Have you known him long?' asked Véronique.

'Two or three years. I never knew him in his heyday. Then, they say, he would dance all night and go home and write all day, go out in the evening and dine with the best, go from theatre to theatre and party to party, keep it up for days at a stretch. Not any more.'

'Why does he do it?' asked Satin as the main course was served, haunch of venison on a bed of wild mushrooms. 'I'm very fond of the man. But it's like he's trying to destroy himself.'

'I don't know,' said Valéry. 'I wish I did. I think he doesn't like himself very much. But he can be very funny. I saw him once in a bar, as drunk as a lord. He was in fine voice, shouting and laughing and telling stories. And then he'd go all quiet, and his face would fall. He'd look serious, almost gloomy. "What is it?" I asked him. "I've just remembered what it is that I'm drinking to forget," he said, as quick as a flash.'

They laughed. The venison was delicious, from the Comte's estates. It almost flaked off their forks.

'Another time,' went on Valéry, speaking with his mouth full, 'I was having real difficulty with something I was writing. I had only done sketches and short pieces then, I think it must have been my first play, or perhaps my second. I didn't use my own name then, as you know. Through a friend of a friend I went to see him, to ask his advice on what I could do.

'It was only about ten or eleven in the morning but he was drinking already. I told him my problem. I think it had something to do with the way one of the characters was developing – it just wasn't coming out right. I asked if he could help.

'He looked at me with that leering eye of his.' Valéry screwed up his face until he looked just like the old soak. Satin and Véronique could hardly eat for laughing. Valéry was laughing too.

'He got up, opened a drawer in his desk and took out a bottle of absinthe. He put it in front of me.

'"Here's your answer," he said.

'"How is this going to help my play?" I asked, trying to guess his meaning.

'"Who said anything about the play?" he said deadpan. "This is for the playwright."'

Satin laughed so much that she almost choked. Valéry had to pound her on the back, her shoulders bare in the candlelight. It was the first time, she realised, he had ever touched her. She felt an inner glow begin to steal over her.

Véronique told some story about Bichfoucauld's other shortcomings. His sexual appetites, it was well known, were monstrous. He would start off an evening in the highest society and end it in one of the notorious stews by Les Halles.

Satin added a reminiscence of her own, all the time drawing the conversation round, in the glow of so much good food and wine, to the sensual. When the meal was over, Valéry was three parts drunk, Véronique even more so. They were grouped together at one end of the table, both women as well as the gentleman smoking cheroots. A decanter of fine brandy was before them.

Satin reached for the basket of fruit that formed the spectacular centrepiece of the table. She took a grape, peeled it and placed it between her lips. Véronique leaned across and took it in her own mouth. It was a game they had played together many times.

She peeled another grape, and another. She was aware of the slight hesitancy in Valéry's conversation, the little catch that began to appear in his voice. Good, she thought. He's noticed. Now we're starting to get somewhere.

Still, even as he watched, the two actresses continued to feed each other fruit. He saw their tongues touch as well as their lips, the vestige of a kiss growing ever more prominent with each exchange.

Satin turned and looked at him, a wanton smile on her face. She nodded towards the fruit basket. Valéry indicated his cigar, reached for the decanter, his hand noticeably unsteady.

'Would you excuse us a moment?' said Satin, her voice as even as she could make it. Her mind was reeling and her heart was racing – she wondered whether she might have overdone it with the tinctures. She and Véronique stood up, giggling together, and left through the small door at the side of the room.

Behind it was a small retiring room that might have been used for reading, drawing or some other harmless pastime. Instead, Satin and Véronique undressed as quickly as they could. Soon Véronique was naked apart from her boots and stockings, and the black lace garters she wore. Satin was bare-breasted, her spectacular bosom as proud and arrogantly uplifted as that of a teenage girl. She too was naked apart from a pair of filmy drawers in palest pcach lace.

Both women were breathing heavily, the fires of lust aflame in their eyes. They looked at each other, smiling mysteriously and with hidden significance. Their clothes were scattered all around them. There was a small mirror above the fireplace in the retiring room and Satin studied her reflection, the elegant chignon of her hair, the way her drawers emphasised rather than hid the voluptuous curve of her backside. How could he resist?

And Véronique, she was all but naked too. Those small, pert breasts that she had sucked and fondled so many times. The long, colt-like legs. The thick, luxuriant hair. She was a girl absolutely in her prime, a rare beauty and a prize for any man. Surely Levinson would not mind if she played around a little while he was away?

The women kissed, momentarily, amid the tangled dresses and the froth of undergarments that were scattered around them. Then, triumphant and secure in their sensual power, they threw open the door that led back into the candlelit chamber they had so lately quitted.

But the dining room was empty. Of Etienne Valéry there was no sign. Only the butt of a cigar, still smouldering in an ashtray, was evidence of his presence here that evening.

Satin was confused, standing there half-naked in the doorway. What could be going on?

And then she heard a man's cough. Of course, it was a game. Anticipating the frivolities to come, Valéry was playing hide and seek. Where was he? Behind the curtains? Under the table?

'Come out, you wicked man,' she called.

Véronique stepped out beside her, the two women sharing the gay mood of the moment.

'I know you're waiting for us,' she said. 'Come and see what a nice surprise we've got for you.'

They stood there, expectant. In the corner of her eye, Satin caught a sudden movement. She whirled round, a playful smile on her face.

But her eye did not light on the handsome, youthful features of Etienne Valéry. There, in the dark shadows by the door, stood the figure of the Comte de Loury and there was anger written deep in the lines of his face.

From the further reaches of that over-furnished apartment, she heard a door slam and the sound of footsteps on the stairs.

Satin could never have realised just how vitriolic the Comte could be, now that their long affair was over. Passionately jealous by nature, he seemed to take an almost wanton delight in destroying everything that associated him with her.

The first thing to go was his involvement in *Sophie and her Sister*. He sent a curt note to Hubert, withdrawing his financial support for the play. At first, it seemed the play must be cancelled entirely. Several anxious days elapsed, with the opening night barely days away. But then, miraculously, a new backer was found, a prosperous bullion dealer called Labatte. Everyone was mightily relieved but then came the second bombshell.

The new sponsor, having attended the final rehearsals, proved to be no admirer of Satin. Unless she were removed from the cast, he would not support the production. In vain did Hubert protest that Satin was arguably the greatest attraction that the play could offer to the paying public. She could not act her way out of a paper bag, countered Labatte. She had to go.

As fortune would have it, Satin – quite unaware of these backstage machinations – was indisposed for the second dress rehearsal. Her understudy, a young girl called Babette, took over her role. Everyone agreed she was marvellous. True, she lacked Satin's fire and passion, but she could actually deliver her lines as written. All of a sudden, the play seemed somehow better balanced without Satin's presence. Even Hubert had to admit it.

There was just a week to go now to the opening night. Satin's sudden temperature caused her to miss two more rehearsals. Hubert, after consulting Labatte, had a discreet word with her doctor. He soon got the message. A sum of money changed hands.

She must rest, he subsequently announced. For a month at least, preferably two. The long series of rehearsals had exhausted her. It would be two to three weeks before she would be fit enough to resume her part as Sophie. Long enough, Hubert realised, for Babette to establish herself in the role and have the critics and paying public alike eating out of her hand. He would decide what to say to Satin later.

Satin, of course, was furious. There was absolutely nothing wrong with her, she thundered, apart from a sore throat. She could be ready to take the stage at an hour's notice. Hubert, as wise and deceptive as a snake, made soothing noises. Both of them probably knew the true nature of the situation.

Satin, incarcerated in her apartment, read the reviews of the opening night. Babette had been a sensation. Satin's rage verged on the apoplectic.

The Comte let it be known to her that, while the apartment on the Rue de la Madeleine was in her own name, she would no longer be able to visit Campignon-Bois. She could see that coming – he was such a small-minded, petty man. She had never liked the place much anyway, always so dark and damp. She had spent a lot of time there in the summer and it had been so boring, nothing to do, nothing to see, nobody to visit or be visited by. Only when her friends came down from town, which was infrequent, did she even begin to enjoy herself in the country. No, she told herself, she was well rid of Campignon-Bois.

But what was she to do about money? Her lawyer, a choleric Marseillaise named Vincent, held out little hope of extracting anything further from the Comte. The possibility of her resuming her role in the play that had, in great part, been created especially for her was looking increasingly uncertain, now that Babette had assumed the leading role. It was all too much to bear, she told Véronique. Soon she would be reduced to wearing rags and dining off scraps.

The business with Valéry had been the hardest to bear. Just what had happened there, that night in the apartment? She had not seen him since, though he had sent her a polite note of condolence when she fell ill. Why didn't he come and see her? What did the Comte make of it all?

She learned the truth of the matter from a contact at the theatre. The playwright had made a clean breast of things to de Loury – how he had gone to Satin's apartment expecting to be among a small social gathering, but had become alarmed at the increasing intimacy that the two women had shown towards him. He had decided that, in order not to compromise the Comte, he should make his excuses and leave. At the very moment when Satin and Véronique were undressing, the Comte had arrived unexpectedly to be confronted by Valéry in a state of considerable confusion. He had been so honest and open about his motives and his desire to leave the apartment as expeditiously as possible that the Comte had no option but to believe him.

Satin cursed herself for ever having lusted after him. He hadn't been aroused by her after all – indeed he had all but spurned her advances, with the biggest prize that all of Paris could offer practically spreading her legs in front of him. How arrogant he was, underneath that cool exterior. Still, she reflected, it was a good thing that things had turned out the way they did. Had the Comte arrived even half an hour later, he may well have murdered them all, a crime of passion upon which no judge would seek a conviction.

* * *

In the event, stripped of the Comte's considerable support, she managed to raise quite a substantial sum of money by selling various items of jewellery that men had given her. It was enough to keep the wolf from the door for the time being, to pay off the most pressing of her creditors. When it became plain that she would not be returning to *Sophie and her Sister*, she, Véronique and Mathilde – the other servants having been dismissed – took the train for Nice.

They took rooms at the Hotel Splendide – not the grandest of all the Mediterranean resorts, but very high-toned nevertheless. She decided, after much agitation, to travel as herself and to pose as an invalid.

'Yes,' she told the unctuous little manager, 'I am very sad to miss *Sophie and her Sister* – but dear Babette is such a friend, and is doing so well in my role. I have to rest, to look after myself. Maybe in the new year we can think about something new. But not now.'

She seemed in good enough health to him, the manager privately reflected. But he was sufficiently used to the whims and caprices of the very rich not to probe too deeply into her motives. Of course he was able to let her enjoy the best apartments in the hotel, and at no charge to herself. Once or twice she graciously consented to appear in the hotel dining-room. He felt her presence would add tone to the place.

But Satin and Véronique were growing restless. The Cote d'Azur may have been delightful in the summer months but in winter it was a grave disappointment. Where was everybody? Where were the lavish parties, the grand balls?

The months passed. Winter turned to spring. The manager, having understood that Satin wished to stay only until Christmas, began to drop uncomfortable hints.

Finally, to general relief all round, the two women plus the faithful Mathilde packed up their belongings and moved into a much smaller apartment at the hotel, for which they would pay on a monthly basis. The dreadful little man even had the temerity to suggest that it might be more convenient for her arrangements if she were to pay for the first month in advance. That took care of the pair of diamond drop ear-rings that Frédéric de Fleury had given her. The gilt jewellery box was now all but empty.

Paris – if only she could go back to Paris, where she was known. But to do so would have been to have admitted defeat, to show everyone that there was nothing wrong with her health, to confirm the success of Babette in the play that, she was still convinced, had been written largely as a vehicle for her own talents. No, she would have to stick it out, at least for the time being. But what could be done? They had to eat.

After some enquiries, Véronique established the location of the most exclusive brothel in Nice. She went there, spoke with the Madame, made arrangements. She worked there on three afternoons a week, bringing in some much-needed francs. At night, she shared Satin's bed. The faithful Mathilde made do with a tiny box room along the corridor.

It was discreetly made known, to those who might be interested at the house on the Rue des Palmes, that Satin herself might be available – at a price. Even to men to whom money mattered very little, it still seemed an exceptional price to pay. A small and exclusive gathering was held at the house, to give the buyers the opportunity to preview the goods. No one was disappointed by what was on offer. Arrangements were made.

The following evening a carriage called at the Hotel Splendide. Satin bade goodbye to Véronique and Mathilde and drove off into the darkness. She had left the hotel only rarely during her six-months' stay in the South of France. Even in daylight she would have had difficulty recognising the streets along which she was driven.

They left the town behind. Now they were by the coast.

Occasionally, through the windows of the carriage, she could glimpse the lights of a large house, set well back in its own grounds.

They reached their destination, another of those houses, imposing but anonymous behind its screen of cypress trees. The carriage wheels crunched along gravel. Then Satin was ushered quickly inside.

A gentleman was waiting to greet her, not tall but well proportioned, and handsome in a Mediterranean kind of way. He was wearing evening clothes. He took her hand and she noticed how soft and warm his flesh was, the nails well manicured.

'I am pleased to meet you,' he said. 'My name is Édouard Pernice. Would you perhaps care for some refreshment?'

They walked through to a drawing room where a fire crackled in the hearth. A servant took Satin's wrap. Underneath, she was wearing a long gown in burgundy silk cut, as usual, very low at the neck, to display her wondrous bosom.

She accepted a drink, nibbled at the food that was provided. They made small talk. She was gracious and amusing. Slowly, as was often the case on such occasions, their conversation became more intimate.

At length, Édouard Pernice rose to his feet.

'Shall we?' he said, with a gesture towards the door. Satin rose in a swish of garments, drew herself up to her full and impressive height. She was wearing a silver choker around her neck and it twinkled in the candle-light.

They walked side by side up a grand staircase. All around her she could see family portraits hanging on the heavily panelled walls. The house smelled of beeswax and money.

They reached the first-floor landing. A door was open at one end. Satin turned to Édouard Pernice and smiled her best coquettish smile. He smiled back at her, touched her arm lightly, ushering her through the open door.

A man was sitting in a high-backed chair at one end of the room. He looked up as Satin entered.

'My father,' said Édouard Pernice, and he suavely closed the door behind him as he withdrew.

Satin was, for the moment, nonplussed. She thought he was the client and now, it seemed, he was not. The older man made no attempt to move, but merely sat there in his chair in front of a pair of tall, velvet-draped windows. The room was decorated in an old-fashioned way and was lit by a pair of heavy oil lamps on a table. A fire crackled in the hearth. The atmosphere was hot, airless and oppressive. Orchids would have grown well in these conditions.

He looked up, a man of perhaps five-and-sixty years, his eyes grey and tired. For a moment something stirred there, for only a blind man would have failed to have been moved by the sight that confronted him. He sat without moving, drinking it all in. Satin's face was pale and still, her eyes dark and brooding under the heavy film of kohl. Her full, bee-stung lips were painted in scarlet and her hair cascaded over her neck in a series of delectable ringlets. She smiled, showing perfect white teeth.

The man murmured faintly. A tongue flickered out from beneath parched lips, and then withdrew. She could see his little reptile eyes scanning her, moving from her face and hair to the generous curves of her alabaster breasts, as pure and rounded as a snowy hummock. Her dress was cut almost to the nipples to reveal as much as possible of her firm, soft body.

'Undress,' he said. The voice was quiet and rasping, the words coming out with difficulty. Satin did as she was bade. Not without difficulty, she undid the buttons and hooks of her mulberry-coloured dress. It lay in a tangled heap around her ankles and she stepped out of it.

She could sense rather than hear the old man's sharp intake of breath. She was wearing a minuscule set of stays that left her breasts all but totally exposed, a pair of loose drawers fashioned of black lace and very little else apart from her stockings and shoes. She smiled at him, encouragingly. But there was very little expression on that pale face.

She stood with her thighs slightly apart, then she gently pulled down her drawers, exposing the dark and mysterious cloud of her pubis and giving him a tantalising glimpse of her pudenda, slick and swollen already, dusky with desire. It was not the man she was excited by, but the opportunity to display herself and be applauded for her beauty.

She could smell herself too, the dampness that exuded from her like a miasma. It hung in the air as boldly as any perfume, unmistakable and almost arrogant. She wanted him to breathe in her scent, to become conscious of her essential womanliness.

She could see him swallow, watched his eyes follow her hands as they traced a line down her body and over her hips, her thighs bare and marble-pure, the dark line of her stockings.

'What would you like me to do?' she purred, fixing him with a soft and playful gaze.

He shivered, despite the heat in the room. The fire hissed and crackled. The air was almost suffocating; Satin felt her body was covered in a thin film of moisture. And yet he kept that rug clasped to him as though, without it, he might freeze to death.

A frail, claw-like hand emerged from underneath it and made a beckoning motion. On her high, pointed shoes, Satin stepped forward. He reached out his hand, touched her thigh. It felt desperately cold.

His fingers, with their long, uncut nails, roved over her thighs, playing with the delicate lace of her garters. The man's eyes were closed and he was breathing heavily. Satin could feel the heat of the fire on her bare flesh. For a few moments they remained like that, not moving.

Then his hand began to rove over her again, tracing little circles and patterns on her thighs. His touch was surprisingly delicate, despite his age and obvious infirmity. He found the cleft between her legs and she parted her legs for him. His eyes were almost level with her labia.

Gently he stroked her lips, feeling the slick wetness of her folds. There was no violence or aggression about him. She felt her labia embracing him, settling comfortably around his probing fingers. She had never seen this man before in her life and probably never would again but she felt curiously safe with him.

He withdrew his hands, brought his fingers up to his face and sniffed deeply and appreciatively. He looked up at her and a faint smile crossed his cold, grey features. She smiled back, encouraging him, ground her hips a little. His tongue flickered out again, chameleon-like, and licked her juices from his fingertips.

He gestured for her to come nearer. Now her bush was only inches away from his face. She could hear him breathing now, not entirely regularly. Suddenly he pressed his face against her and his tongue was between her legs, seeking her hidden places.

She pushed her hips forward against his face. His tongue parted her lips, probed along them. His touch was as delicate as that of his fingers. She gasped, involuntarily. The sense of pleasure that he gave her was exquisite. He was rolling his tongue around her now, leaning forward as best he could in his high-backed chair.

He found her clitoris, barely brushing it with just the very tip of his tongue. Satin came, suddenly and unexpectedly, her loins fluttering like a butterfly's wings. Her heart was racing and she gasped for breath in the tropical heat of the room.

He paused. He knew the effect he was having on her. He stopped and inhaled, seemingly drunk with the scent of her, the womanly perfume that must have been as over-

whelming to him as the tropical heat of the room was to
her. Again, he extended his tongue slowly, running it
along the warm wet channel between her anus and the tiny
pink cherry of her clitoris. He wore a beard, trimmed
short, and her pubic hairs snagged on it. She liked the feel
of his facial growth against her most sensitive parts.

'Poke me with your tongue,' she said. 'Stick it right up
me. Fuck me with it . . .'

He found the dark opening of her vaginal cleft and
pressed the tip of his tongue against it. It yielded, and he
pushed beneath the soft wet folds and up between those
smooth walls that parted obligingly for him. She could feel
his tongue probing inside her, going surprisingly far inside
her – there was as big a difference in the length of men's
tongues as there was with the size and thickness of their
pricks.

He needed to do very little to bring fresh waves of
pleasure flooding over her. She thought of the young men
she had been with and how little they really knew about
bringing a woman to the point of rapture. Fresh ripples
began to spread out through her abdomen. She seemed to
be coming almost continuously, slowly and gently.

The tonguing seemed, eventually, to tire him. He drew
away from her. She could see how wet his beard and
moustaches were. He lay back against the cushions, his
eyes closed, drawing in breath. The firelight danced on
Satin's trembling body.

Tentatively, she drew back the rug with which he was
swathed. He was wearing a nightgown under a thick,
quilted jacket. She crouched to her knees, her bare
breasts lolling, and drew the nightgown up around his
hips. His penis was the largest she had ever seen in her
life.

For a moment she could hardly take it in. It stood there,
proud above his belly, ivory white and potent. She
reached out a tentative finger, stroked the sensitive glans,

drew back his foreskin a little. Then she leaned forward and took just the tip of it into her mouth. It was like trying to eat a plum whole. Her tongue roved over its ridged underside, her lips closing around him. Then she gently began to bob her head backwards and forwards, backwards and forwards, cradling his heavy balls in the palm of her hand.

She could not take very much of him into her mouth without feeling she was going to choke. She had never known anything like this in her life before – just wait until she could tell Véronique. She would have been happy to have sucked that huge cock all evening, the fire gently roasting her marble flesh.

Eventually he reached out a hand, touched her hair, made a gesture. She got his message. She withdrew, climbed on top of him there on his chair and spitted herself on him. His cock slid straight inside her, massive and potent. She gasped, and again the little butterfly fluttering resumed deep inside her.

Her breasts were almost level with his lips as she began to buck up and down on top of him. His cock remained ramrod-straight and as hard as iron. It filled her as completely as she had ever been filled in her life, pushing her lips outwards almost to the point of distension. She had to move slowly, almost gingerly until she could accommodate as much of it as she dared. And then, very slowly at first, as his magical tongue flickered out once more and caressed first one inflamed nipple and then the other, she began to fuck him as though this were the moment she had been practising for all her life.

Chapter Eight

The money, inevitably, began to run out, because the supply of gentlemen willing to provide it also began to run dry. It was, as she now realised, the wrong season to be in Nice. No one was there. Everyone was in the country, or in Paris. The pleasure-seekers, for the moment, were elsewhere, and would not return for some months. Now the Riviera was home only to those who were too old or too young, too wasted or too pure to want to know a woman such as herself.

Satin knew that, sooner rather than later, she would have to return to Paris. The idea of returning to her old life at the Café des Artistes filled her with horror – it would have represented the ultimate humiliation. No, she would not go back there, however hard she had to struggle. She would try and resume her career in the theatre, try and snare herself another wealthy lover. After all, she had nothing to be ashamed of. Nearly penniless she may have been in terms of ready cash, but she still had the apartment on the Boulevard de la Madeleine.

She still knew one or two people of influence – that bastard de Loury had not been entirely able to kill off her circle of friends. Once or twice a month she had received visits from travellers who gave her the latest news and gossip. The world of the theatre, however, seemed to have dropped her entirely. She had thought, when she first left Paris, that it would be only a matter of time before producers, playwrights and impresarios began beating a path to her door. But in that hope, as in so many, she had been sadly disappointed. No letters came, summoning her to audition. No admirers besieged her with irresistible offers. No playwrights besieged her with future master-pieces.

She felt hurt and rejected at first, and later her feelings turned to bitterness. It was not because of her, but because of who she was, and what she represented. Once a tart, always a tart, she could almost hear them saying. Well, everyone knew about La Cabache – except for that fool, de Fleury – and that hadn't stopped her making a name for herself, or from mingling with the highest in the land. So why not Satin too? And who, in any case, were these people whose snobbery prevented them from giving her the respect she deserved, who were so toffee-nosed that they failed to recognise her abilities? She was convinced the Comte de Loury had poisoned people against her.

Only Levinson had kept faith with her. Evidently ignor-ant of the true nature of her rift with the Comte and with Hubert, he had written to her several times from the United States and had been unstinting in his praises. She had responded to him with equal fervour – he was like a favourite uncle to her, as he remembered the times they had spent together. She was surprised that theirs had never been a closer relationship although Véronique, too, was the occasional recipient of a note from him, of a rather more intimate nature than her own.

However settled she may have become at the Hotel Splendide, despite her difficulty in paying the bills, Paris, at least, was still a kind of home to Satin. In Nice she had been always an outsider, despite her fame, cut off from the nourishment from which she had for so long drawn her sustenance. But Paris – that was in her blood. As someone had predicted to her many months before, for her to leave Paris would be like the pigeons leaving the Place des Vosges.

She knew, in her heart, that one day she would return. A chance meeting convinced her of the inevitable. She and Véronique were walking one day along the Avenue d'Antibes. It was a cold, blustery day, the wind whipping whitecaps along the water. Only that morning that wretched hotel manager had been more than usually direct about the settlement of her bill. She had, if he but knew it, little hope of being able to fulfil her obligations to him and to her many other creditors. Almost all the jewellery, and quite a substantial part of her wardrobe, had now been sold. Once or twice she had even entertained notions of selling up her apartment. True, she was able to earn considerable sums from M Pernice and some of the other wealthy gentlemen of Nice, but there were so few of them at this time of year. If she had been able to entertain two or three of them every week, she would have had no problem. But as things were, even though Véronique, too, was able to sell herself without undue difficulty at first, things now were not looking quite so promising as they once had. As it was, there were times when they might almost have been glad of a bowl of onion soup.

They were talking, as they strolled along the promenade, with the great white buildings towering above them and the palm trees whipping in the breeze, of the old days, of people they had known in the theatre. Then they caught sight of a familiar figure walking towards them. It was Bichfoucauld.

Rarely had Satin been so pleased to see a familiar face in a strange environment. Her name was not unfamiliar in Nice, of course, but her reputation was so much stronger in Paris. She had never travelled, had never become a touring actress. Had she done so, she might not have been facing her present predicament.

She had never been especially fond of the old roué but they fell on each other like old friends. He was very well, he told her, very well indeed. They went to a small café where he was known. After the cold wind, Satin was glad of the warmth.

'And you are recovered too?' he asked felicitously, already ordering another cognac. He had heard of her 'illness', then. Whether he knew it was just a convenient excuse or truly believed it, she could not tell.

'Oh yes,' she said. 'We will return to Paris soon. I'm longing to see all my old friends again.'

He told of his own doings over the past months, ever since he had been unceremonially deposed by the arrival of Levinson. He dismissed the American with an airy wave – there was nothing wrong with his play, he had insisted. The problem was merely that the wrong people were involved with it – always excepting Satin, of course. No, she would have been perfect as his Eurydice. It was the rest of them who didn't have a clue about it. He had put it to one side, worked on it from time to time. A couple of people were very interested in putting it on, he knew. Maybe next year, if he could find the time to finish it.

While Satin had been away, he had had a couple of plays put on at small theatres in Paris. They had done quite well, he said, but Satin – eagerly scanning the Paris papers when they were brought to her, two and three days out of date – remembered the poor notices they had received. But Bichfoucauld, she knew, was never a man to let misfortune stand in his way. Any disappointment could rapidly be turned to advantage.

'In fact,' he said, leaning closer and blowing cigar smoke, 'I have a new play right now that you might be very interested in.'

A new play, thought Satin. That could be just the answer she had been praying for.

'Oh yes,' he went on. 'It's very probably going to be put on at the Royale.'

The Royale, despite its misleadingly imposing name, was a small and run-down theatre in Montmartre, well known

for its popular farces and burlesques. It was definitely a
step down from the Theatre des Etoiles but, Satin
reasoned, she was in no position to choose.

She put on a show of vague interest.

'Oh yes?' she said, trying not to sound too keen. 'I don't
think I ever played at the Royale. Of course, I have so
many offers, you know. In fact only last week Hubert
wrote to me, asking if I would be interested in touring
with *The Vagabond*.'

There had been no such letter from Hubert, of course.
With her impresario, as with all the rest, it had been as if
she had never existed. She had not heard a word from him
since she had been dropped from *Sophie and her Sister*.
She had consoled herself with something Frédéric de
Fleury had told her in the early days of their courtship.

'When you're on the up,' he had said, 'everyone wants
to know you. But once you're established, people assume
that you're going to place impossible demands on them.
So they look for new stars, because they don't ask for so
much money. There's always an endless supply of young
hopefuls. Talent comes cheap in the theatre.'

That was all very well, she thought, but what about
someone like La Cabache, well into her thirties now but
still with a regular list of engagements? How did she
manage it, with her reputation and her meagre talents?
Moscato had once intimated to her how royally the older
actress was paid.

'Well,' said Bichfoucauld, 'I'm sure you've got lots of
things lined up, now that you're back on your feet again.
But I thought that *Madame Angot's Daughter* might be
just the thing for you.'

Again, the show of bored indifference. Satin would be
so very busy, now that she had decided to return to the
stage. She was having such difficulty making up her mind.
Hubert and others were constantly asking to look at this
script and at that. Her apartment was entirely filled up

with them – they were piled almost right up to the ceiling. But she might, purely as a favour to her old friend, have a look at the script, see what it was like, maybe help him with a few ideas and comments. If he could send it over to her at the Hotel Splendide, she would be happy to read it through, when she could find a moment. But the chance that she might be involved in the production herself seemed, as she candidly informed him, a very remote one – much as she would have liked to have renewed their working acquaintance on the boards.

They left it at that. Bichfoucauld seemed quite pleased with the arrangement. They left him eating soup and drinking brandy.

'You've got to do it,' insisted Véronique.

'But it's dreadful,' said Satin. Bichfoucauld's script was scattered all over the sofa.

'What's it about?'

'It's difficult to tell. A girl, Antoinette – that's the part he had in mind for me, presumably – is sold into slavery. She is transported to Arabia. She becomes the sheikh's favourite. All the time she's plotting how to get back to her dear old mother. So she disguises herself as a boy or something, smuggles herself away from the palace on to a ship bound for Marseilles. They're captured by pirates. She reveals herself to the pirate chief. He falls in love with her. Then there's a shipwreck. It goes on like this for page after page. Every other scene seems to involve her having her clothes ripped off her back. I can't do it, I tell you. It's beneath me.'

'But you must.'

'Why?'

For answer, Véronique waved a sheaf of unpaid bills that were lying on the table. Satin shook her head wearily and went back to the narrative.

That evening she and Véronique had an engagement, the first for some days for either of them. An Englishman, long resident in Nice for the good of his health, had been seeing Véronique for purposes of pleasure in his suite at the Hotel de Ville. A sporting friend of his would be staying with him for some days and would be glad of a little female company. Did Véronique perhaps have a friend she might like to bring along?

'He won't know you,' said Véronique. 'Besides, he might be good looking. Who knows, he might even be rich and single.'

'All the rich, single Englishmen are pederasts,' said Satin, gathering up the pages of Bichfoucauld's script and dumping them in an untidy heap on top of the pile of bills so they were hidden from sight. 'What I need is to find myself some lord or other, with a great big prick and a big pile of money. And preferably one who prefers pussy to arsehole.'

But she agreed to come – she needed the ready cash. She and Véronique spent a long, long time getting ready for the evening ahead. Véronique wore a black gown trimmed with sequins and pearls that had been one of the Comte's gifts to Satin. It flattered her trim figure, made her look elegant and sensual. Satin herself wore a dress that she had often worn at partics at Campignon-Bois. Scarlet in hue, it had been fashioned from the plushest velvet. Brief even by Satin's lascivious standards and emphasised by the severity of her long black evening gloves, the bodice was boned and strapless, revealing not only the wearer's superbly sculptured shoulders but also a great deal of her breasts and upper torso. It stopped just short of her carefully rouged areolae, hinting at the delights to come.

The velvet clung to her hips like the embrace of a lover's arms, stretched over her body as tightly as a second skin. Then it cascaded to the ground in a veritable waterfall of scarlet material, trailing behind her as she walked. The effect had stunned even the Comte de Loury, accustomed to the most expensive couture and the most expensive women that Paris could offer. What the two Englishmen might make of it was something that only time could tell.

A carriage arrived for them punctually at nine. Satin noticed the crest on the side. The Hotel du Ville was not far from the Splendide and she gazed out at the almost deserted streets of the town as they clipped along over the cobbles. Where was everybody, she thought, drawing her wrap more tightly around her. If she had known that Nice was going to be as dead as this, she would have gone somewhere else entirely – Deauville, even, would have had more life to it. She swept majestically through the lobby and up the grand staircase – eyes turned to look, some with admiration and others with shocked contempt. Did anyone recognise her? Did it matter? She doubted it – she was wearing a hat that shaded most of her face and she looked intently ahead, for once not particularly wishing to see or be seen.

A tap on the door and they were ushered into the Englishman's apartment. They were received by Véronique's friend, the Honourable Charles Fairfax. Satin had not met him before. He was tall and distinguished, with a reputation as a gambler and man about town, a creature of the night much as Satin was. His companion was much fairer, with a delicate skin.

'My friend, William Bawden, the poet,' said Fairfax, introducing them.

William Bawden. William Bawden!

'Are you *the* William Bawden?' she asked. His reputation had preceded him and, for a moment, Satin almost lost her practised poise. She had read his verse, of course. She loved its reckless extravagance, the shimmering couplets, the sense of a life lived to the full. It was more like Baudelaire or Rimbaud than any of the other English poets she had read, who – with the honourable exception of Byron – all seemed so pallid by comparison. None of them could have written anything so monstrously and wickedly sensual as his poem *Strange Fruits*, an evocation of passion and wantonness on an epic scale. It was just as impressive, in its own way, as Baudelaire's masterpiece, *The Flowers of Evil*. That great work had been too much, even for the liberal standards of Paris, and its author had been prosecuted for obscenity. This was a fate that had also befallen William Bawden, who was now condemned to a life in exile. There had been a scandal, a whole series of scandals – an elopement, a scion of the royal family compromised, even rumours of bastardy and buggery in high places. They did not nick-name him 'Bawdy' Bawden for nothing.

'I am a William Bawden,' he said at length, in a voice of exquisite languor. 'But whether I am the William Bawden you have in mind, madame, I am not in a position to tell.'

How clever he was! And how good-looking! He had not, it appeared, heard of her. But then, why should he have? Less than two hundred miles separated them, but there was a world of difference between the salons and theatres of Paris and London.

A great deal of wine was drunk in a short space of time in that over-furnished and over-heated hotel room. There was food, too, in great abundance, but Satin and Véronique showed even less interest in it than the gentlemen did. It was impossible, of course, to make love on a full stomach.

Soon William Bawden was sitting next to her on the sofa. Véronique and the Hon Charles Fairfax had already gone through into the bedroom.

'I do admire that dress of yours,' he said, his eyes drinking in the lascivious sight that greeted him. 'The colour of blood, you know. Flesh and blood. I love it.'

There was a wicked gleam in his eyes. Like his compatriot, he spoke the language effortlessly. Satin loved the way his long, fair hair flopped over his forehead, the skin that seemed to be untouched by the Mediterranean sun. She would have been happy to have slept with him for nothing. Already she was longing for him to take her to bed.

He produced a small silver bottle from his jacket pocket and opened it.

'Tincture of laudanum,' he said. 'Would you care for some?'

Satin smiled at him dreamily. Tincture of laudanum – that was what her old friend Thierry Albert used to give her in those mysterious purple phials. Her supply had run out many months ago now. She would love to have some again.

William Bawden rose to his feet and brought over a couple of liqueur glasses. Into each of them he poured, with great ceremony, a three-finger measure of the tincture. In the yellow gas-light of the room its deep brown colour seemed to glow, to hint of the inner secrets of its chemistry that would make themselves known only to the initiates.

She raised her glass, toasted him silently. They each drank it off almost at once. He poured her another measure, and one for himself.

Slowly, inexorably, the familiar feeling began to steal over her. She relaxed on the sofa, made herself comfortable. Bawden was next to her, alone with his thoughts. His eyes seemed to settle a little deeper into his head, his skin to become distinctly paler.

How long his hair is, she found herself thinking. From a centre parting it seemed to fall in two waves down the side of the face. She loved the way it curled around his ears, tumbled down over his collar at the back. Each time he moved, his hair seemed to shimmer like it was alive. And those eyes – they seemed to pierce her to the very root of her womanhood.

The tincture that the poet had given her seemed much stronger than anything Thierry Albert had prepared. She seemed to be floating now, high up in the atmosphere of this overheated room, looking down at herself in her scarlet dress slashed open almost to the navel, and the handsome young poet who was sitting next to her. Her mind seemed disconnected from her body so that she scarcely noticed when their familiarities began. One minute they were talking idly of this and of that, the next she was in his arms and his tongue was seeking hers.

She let herself relax into his arms. It was all so natural, like falling asleep. She could tell how mesmerised he was by the snowy white protuberance of her bosom, the way she practically came spilling out of her dress – as was the intention of the dressmaker who had created it. His hand slipped inside her bodice, cupping one luscious breast. His fingers felt incredibly soft and warm, his touch almost ethereal.

She could feel how quickly her nipple seemed to swell up like an over-ripe fruit in the hothouse atmosphere of the hotel room. They broke from a kiss, panting, and he bent his head and delicately applied his lips to her areolae. A fresh wave of pleasure shimmered through her, especially when he began to tongue her nipple with infinite gentleness.

She put her hand on his shirt front, pushed it inside through the studs. She could feel his chest rising and falling against the palm of her hand, the small nipples. His body was firm and well muscled. She knew he would fuck her well, and passionately.

Her nipple seemed to swell up inside his mouth. She was alive to the sensitivity in her nerve-endings, immeasurably enhanced by the effects of the tincture. The wine had loosened her inhibitions – if she ever had any – and the drug had sharpened and refined her sensibilities. She was aware of a slow, steady burning in her loins.

Somehow they managed to get to their feet and into the adjacent bedchamber. Though her heart was pounding and she could feel the fullness of his erection against her thigh, he undressed her without any semblance of haste. The slowness of his movements was almost like a dance, hypnotic and ordered. He peeled the scarlet dress away from her shoulders, holding her by the waist as his eyes took in the spectacular breasts that so many had admired in the past.

She turned, indicating the line of buttons down the back. He undid them one by one with deliberate slowness, kissing her bare shoulders, nuzzling against her sensitive earlobes. She sighed, rubbed herself against him, aware of the feeling of arousal in both of them.

He pulled her dress down over her hips – not without difficulty, for it clung to her hips like a skin – and she stepped out of it. She was clad now only in her long black evening gloves and her stays, black also, her breasts spilling out from the lace of her chemise. Her drawers too were of exquisite black lace, loose and floating, her silk stockings shimmering in the firelight, the high heels of her lace-up boots making her almost as tall as he was.

They kissed again – their lips could not keep apart. She was floating in a purple cloud of desire, enjoying the intensity of every moment and yet longing for the next, to see what pleasures it might bring. She did not have long to wait.

William Bawden sank to his knees before her, pressing his face against the delicate Chantilly lace of her drawers, breathing in the musky aroma of her womanhood. His hands cupped her buttocks through the gauzy material. She looked down at him, aware of the way his hair spilled over her thighs. Her nipples, she noticed, were uncommonly erect.

And then his tongue began a slow, lascivious exploration of her body. It probed along the outer labia, delicately stroking her warm slickness, tasting her salty womanhood. She noticed what a delicate touch he had, with both his tongue and his hands. She hoped he would be equally as exquisite with his cock.

She changed her position and parted her legs slightly, to make it easier for him. Now he was tonguing her vagina open-mouthed, piercing her, his tongue reaching up into her. Slowly, tantalisingly, he began to lick her, her labia spread wide for him now, his tongue probing her soaking furrow from one end to the other. She pressed herself down on to his face, never wanting the moment to stop.

He found her clitoris and a shock of electricity went through her. He had barely touched it with the tip of his tongue and yet the intensity of feeling had been breathtaking, almost unbearable.

He paused, rose to his feet. She could see the wetness on his face. She ran her tongue along his upper lip, tasting her own secretions. She squeezed his cock through his trousers. He was as hard as a rock.

Her eyes never leaving his for a second, she lay down before him on the bed: He tore off his collar, threw it to one side, and then his shirt. He stepped out of his trousers, tossed them heedlessly on to the floor on top of her scarlet dress. Then he was naked before her, his penis erect and hungry.

She parted her legs for him even as he came to her. He was on top of her in an instant and she could feel his penis against his thighs, urgent and uncompromising. She guided him home. He slipped in at once up to the hilt, filling her to the brim, and she wrapped her legs around his hips the better to experience the heavenly sensations that went coursing through her body.

Slowly, inexorably, he began to fuck her. He raised himself up on his powerful forearms and she reached forwards and began to tongue his sweet nut-brown nipples, a gesture that evidently excited him still further. He began to pump in and out of her, his naked flesh pressed against her own, her layers of lace and silk chafing against him as he took her with sublime passion. Her breasts were naked like snowy mounds, shaking with the power of his movements. She pushed at him with all the strength of her back muscles, raising her hips off the bed to meet him at every thrust.

She peeled off her gloves, tossed them heedlessly on to the covers. Her tongue roved over his chest, his neck, his shoulders. Then he too was tonguing her, kissing her forehead, her eyes, penetrating her ears in a manner that was guaranteed to bring her to a climax.

She opened her eyes and peered over his shoulder, could see her stocking-clad legs wrapped around his firm rump, could see the ripple of his muscles. He was so strong and powerful and yet his body gave no hint of athletic prowess – here, plainly, was a man who lived purely to indulge his own senses, and to feed the imaginations of others.

She could hold out no more. Her hands were raking over his back, her nails digging into his beautiful flesh. She squeezed his body with her arms and thighs as hard as she could, ground her hips against his and in that instant her lower body became seized in the grip of a series of spasms, opening and closing, until she cried out in pleasure and in pain and felt his own pulsing release deep within her, the waves of passion that went shimmering from one to the other of them until both were stilled and exhausted, their breathing ragged.

Gently she lowered her legs and he rolled off her. Her hand stole down involuntarily between her thighs, to check perhaps that she was still intact after the pounding he had given her. Her pussy was almost overflowing with their juices, his and hers mingled together, seeping out now over her legs and on to the sheets. She was still wearing her stays and stockings, even her lace-up boots with their high heels. Her drawers lay beside her where William Bawden had all but torn them off her in his excitement and desire for greater intimacy with her body.

She kissed him gently on the forehead, stroked his tumescent penis that lay against her hip like a plump sausage, touched the delicate eye with a fingertip and drew out the last little globule of semen that lay there. She held her finger to her lips and licked it, the man taste clean and salty on her tongue. The heat from the fire matched the warm inner glow that suffused her whole body. It had been a long time since she had enjoyed a man as much as she had enjoyed being with William Bawden, poet and carnal gourmet.

He brought in some more of the tincture. As it spread through her, it seemed to both relax and stimulate her at the same time. They lay on the bed, both of them naked now.

'Your friend Véronique,' he said at length, once the first intoxication of pleasure had passed.

'Yes?' replied Satin. He seemed to be speaking to her from very far away. This tincture really was most extraordinarily powerful – no wonder he wrote the kind of things he wrote while under its influence. She reached for the carafe that he had brought in with him as well, poured herself some wine. It helped to clear her head a little. She had the impression that William Bawden lived like this almost every day of his life.

'She is an actress too, I gather?'

'Yes, she's been on the stage. We were in a couple of plays together, even. But when I first knew her she was a dancer.'

'How very interesting. I love the dance. And you have an apartment in Paris, I gather. Which you share with Véronique.'

'That's right. On the Boulevard de la Madeleine. Do you know Paris?'

'I do. There are some very grand houses on the Boulevard de la Madeleine.'

Satin smiled at him. He knew the prestige of her address. She sensed a vestige of respect in his attitude to her. Though he was unaware of her fame, he sensed that she was no ordinary actress, and certainly no common streetwalker. Only someone of exceptional fortune could have an apartment on the Boulevard de la Madeleine.

'I'm not a kept woman, you know,' she said, sitting up against the pillows. 'The apartment is in my name.'

'I didn't doubt it for a moment, madame. So you live there with Véronique?'

'Indeed I do.'

'And do you entertain there?'

'No – at least, not very often, not in the sense you are meaning.'

'But you keep one another amused.'

'What a way you have with words! I'm sure I don't know what you're implying.'

'I rather think you do.'

'Well, perhaps you should ask Véronique about that.'

'You think we should?'

'Why not? I wonder how she's getting on with your friend Charles.'

They finished their wine, went through to the other bedroom. William Bawden opened the door slightly, enough to give them a grandstand view. They stood at the door, both of them naked, and took in the sight that greeted them.

Véronique was kneeling up on the bed, straddled sideways across it, her breasts hanging down like beautiful ripe pears. Charles Fairfax was behind her, slowly rocking backwards and forwards as he fucked her from the rear, burying himself up to the hilt in her welcoming flesh. Véronique's eyes were closed and a smile played on her lips. It was obvious that this English gentleman, for one, knew how best to pleasure a lady.

Gradually the pace of Fairfax's fucking increased. Through the crack in the door they could hear his gasps, see the way he clasped Véronique firmly around the hips to give him better purchase. Both of them were breathing heavily, calling out lewd words to each other. Then Fairfax, red in the face now with exertion, pushed himself hard up against her and shot his seed into her womb.

'My turn now,' said the poet, suddenly entering the room. It was plain that Fairfax, to say nothing of Véronique, was no stranger to such familiar intimacies. As he disengaged, the other man took his place. Véronique, dreamy-eyed, sighed with pleasure as she took him into her right up to the hilt.

'God, but you're absolutely full of spunk,' said the poet. 'It's a wonder that bastard Fairfax hasn't flooded the floor. Maybe the people on the floor below will complain.'

Fairfax laughed, as he poured himself a glass of wine. Satin came and sat next to the couple on the bed, kissed Véronique lightly on the cheek.

'My friend William asks if we keep ourselves amused together,' she said in a playful voice.

Véronique, arching her back to take in more of William Bawden's miraculously reanimated cock – like Thierry Albert, he seemed to be another of those young men who can spunk twice in half an hour without difficulty – looked at her friend and smiled.

'What a cheeky man he is,' she said. 'Perhaps we should show them how we have fun in Paris, then.'

She winked. Satin leaned over and kissed her again, and then their lips met in a passionate embrace, their tongues roving. Satin could see the reaction this was having, even on a dissolute roué like 'Bawdy' Bawden.

'What's the matter?' said Satin as she broke from the kiss. 'Haven't you seen two women kiss before?'

He smiled, his eyes alone telling of his desires.

She climbed up on to the bed beside them, parting her legs for Véronique and pushing her pubic bush – still matted with William's spendings – right up to Véronique's face.

'Lick me out, there's a darling,' she breathed.

Véronique needed no second bidding. Her tongue flickered out and then her lips were pressed against Satin's overflowing sex. William, pushing into her from behind, could see her hair spread out above Satin's voluptuous thighs as she tongued her.

'Yes,' he said as he thrust into her with renewed vigour. 'She tastes good, doesn't she?'

Satin was half-sitting up now, her large breasts jiggling, her knees drawn up so that Véronique could tongue her better.

She threw her head back in abandon.

'Oh, it's so good,' she breathed. And, in a very few moments: 'Oh God, I think I'm going to come again.'

Véronique licked on as Satin pushed towards her, wild-eyed with desire. Her legs were wide apart now, and Véronique's face was almost buried in the tangled mass of their bodies. Tongue, labia, pubic fur – all was matted into one lascivious whole. She found Satin's clitoris and nibbled on it delightedly. Almost immediately, it brought Satin off.

The actress lay back on the pillows as, for the second time that evening, William Bawden found his own rapture inside the welcoming folds of Véronique. He cried out all manner of strange words that only a poet would use and the next thing that Satin knew, Charles was crouched next to her, his cock only inches from her face.

Half-turning towards him, she took hold of his already erect member and licked her lips provocatively.

'Are you full up again already, you wicked man?' she purred. 'I'll have to give you a good sucking, then, to make you feel better and bring you off!'

236

She ran her tongue over his bulbous purple glans. Then, sensing his urgency, she began to bob back and forth with it in her mouth. He wasn't going to last long, she was sure, even though he'd only spunked Véronique a few minutes earlier. He was urgent and insistent, thrusting himself between her lips so that she almost choked on his cock.

She and Véronique were certainly giving them their money's worth, she reflected. She took hold of his balls to try and still him, gave him a gentle frig or two along the length of his shaft with the other. She could sense the movements in his heavy sack, could feel the balls themselves beginning to tighten.

She caught Bawden's eye. 'Lick my cunt,' she said, 'and I'll suck his spunk out of him.'

Almost instantly the poet buried his face once more between Satin's welcoming thighs. Despite her excitement, Satin was aware of his finesse, the delicate way his tongue teased her lips and found her clitoris, rolling it gently around and around. She knew she was coming – the feeling was on her almost instantly.

She took Charles Fairfax's cock between her lips once more and, at the same time as her womb contracted into a shimmering sea of spasms, his sperm came welling up out of his shaft and into her mouth. She coughed and spluttered – there was so much of it, and he was so far down the back of her throat and she let go of him. She caught a glimpse of a perfect arc of come flying through the air and landing on her breasts, where so many men had found their nirvana in the past, and many more would – she knew – in the future.

The apartment in the Boulevard de la Madeleine was exactly as it was when Satin had left it. Mathilde had gone on ahead to make arrangements for her return. When she and Véronique came through the door, they were greeted by vases of flowers on every surface and every light on in the place. Satin may have left Paris in ignominy, but she certainly returned in her characteristic style.

Friends were there to greet her – not so very many, these days, but enough to give her a warm welcome.

'And what are your plans, my dear?' asked Thierry Albert.

'My plans? Well, I've agreed to appear in this super new play that Bichfoucauld has written especially for me. We're doing it at the Royale – the one in Montmartre, you know. We had thought of opening at somewhere bigger, the Imperial maybe, or even the Opéra Comique, but I'm so terribly rusty. It's been nearly a year, you know, since I've been away.'

'And what kind of a play is it?' he asked.

'Oh, something very much in the fashion. I get to wear all sorts of exciting costumes. And there's a role for Véronique too, you know. She has a dance in each act. Everyone's terribly excited about it. The papers are going mad already. Everyone wants to come to rehearsals when they start next week.'

It was strange indeed for Satin to go once more inside a threatre, to breathe once again that once-familiar musty smell, compounded of damp upholstery, generations of dust and mice-droppings. The Royale was an old theatre, its fabric faded and crumbling, its painted walls and ceilings beginning to flake away. It was small, too – its main use had always been as a palace of varieties rather than as a temple to the thespian muse. The circle was tightly curved around the compact stage, the rows and rows of serried seats rising up to the gods with dizzying steepness. Everyone seemed to be on top of everyone else. She could stand at the rear of the stage and hold a perfectly intelligible conversation with the director seated at the rear of the stalls.

Bichfoucauld's drama was in fact more of a playlet, to be performed in three acts between the appearances of a novelty cycling act and the comic monologues of Biff and

Boff. Its plot was perfunctory, its character development was almost non-existent, but Satin remained firmly convinced that it was the surest way to revive her fortunes. She threw herself into rehearsals with unaccustomed vigour. By the end of the third week she had mastered most of her lines, not that there were so very many. Satin was required by the script not so much to act as to appear, and simply to be herself. And in that task she was as accustomed as any.

Her fellow actors were journeymen and women. None of them were particularly welcoming towards her, nor particularly cold. Acting, to them, was a job, and she was another wage-earner, like themselves. Still, she had Véronique with her and she drew great comfort from the fact.

Without an agent of her own for the moment – she did try to see Hubert, but he was always too busy, or out of town – she had been unable to negotiate quite the fee she had hoped for from the management of the Royale. Still, it was a great deal better than nothing, and it would be guaranteed for the fifty nights for which the performance was intended to run. Who knows what might come up in the meantime? Once her name became known again, she would have the choice of all the new plays that were on offer, and would be able to name her own price.

She still wasn't entirely sure about the play, though, although her name would appear at the top of the bills. Still, it was all good fun and a lot less demanding than her part in *Sophie and her Sister* had been. Young Babette, the actress who had understudied her and taken over the title role from her in that production, was now doing extremely well for herself, while Etienne Valéry's stock seemed to rise by the minute. She thought often of what might have been had not the Comte arrived so unexpectedly at the apartment on the Boulevard de la Madeleine but, she reasoned, there was no use her crying over spilled milk.

She could sense the excitement in the air even as the first night approached. There was the usual quota of catastrophes. An accident in rehearsal led to the novelty cycling act having to be replaced at short notice by a group of performing seals. The actor who was to have played the pirate chief fell victim to laryngitis and – refusing to quit the stage and consequently face the loss of earnings that would entail – had to bark his lines in a hoarse croak that, mercifully, was largely hidden by the report of pistols and cannons which accompanied almost every appearance he made on the stage. Even Véronique's costume failed to materialise in time and she had to make do with something quickly improvised by the wardrobe mistress.

Finally the opening night arrived. Satin and Véronique huddled in their tiny dressing room – it was damp and cold, despite the warm evenings outside – and made their elaborate preparations for the play. Satin's costumes were perhaps not entirely as daring as some that she had worn on stage but they were revealing nevertheless. Her slave-girl costume was a near-translucent confection and the lighting man had so arranged things that, whenever possible, she would pass in front of a strategically placed limelight, which would illuminate her curvaceous charms through her thin outfit for all the audience to see. She was to be cast away, at one stage, into a dank and gloomy dungeon, dressed only in rags, and these were arranged with such artifice as to conceal and reveal in almost equal measure.

The call boy, a young scamp called Victoire, put his head round the door. 'Ten minutes,' he said. 'The seals are just finishing.'

Satin did not turn round. She was too busy sticking pins into Véronique's hair. The young lad drank in her voluptuous body.

'What kind of a house is it?'

'About three-quarters full. But they're a good crowd. They enjoyed the seals.'

When Satin made her appearance – treading the boards of a theatre for the first time in almost a year – it was obvious that Victoire had been over-generous in his estimate of the size of the audience. There were conspicuous gaps to be seen in the stalls, like the teeth in an old man's head, and this despite the offer of reduced admission prices for the first week of the performance. There was a noisy crowd up in the gallery, whistling and shouting and generally doing all they could to put the actors off their stride. But none of this deterred Satin so much as the sight, there in a box by the side of the stage, of Patric Esteve, the man who had so cruelly rubbished her very first performance. He caught her eye and gave her a little wave, but there was irony and cruelty in his gesture.

It seemed to be saying goodbye.

The first act, however, went remarkably well. The audience, sparse though they may have been in numbers, applauded vigorously, their sporadic handclaps exploding around the half-empty theatre like firecrackers. Bichfoucauld came backstage during the interval and, though three parts drunk already, was very enthusiastic.

'See,' he said, breathing cognac fumes all over Satin and trying to look down her cleavage, 'they love it. I told you everything would be all right. And the best is still to come.'

He erred disastrously in his forecast, as he so often had in the past. All was going well until Satin, by now captured along with the rest of the pirates and thrown into gaol, pining away in her solitary cell, began her lament, the fifty-line soliloquy that she and Véronique had rehearsed together so assiduously until she was word perfect.

She drew her hand across her forehead and sighed deeply, remembering to let the audience get a good view of her shapely calves through her rags.

'Alas,' she pined. 'I am now alone, and in a foreign country, scarcely knowing when I will see my own dear home again. Is there none that can save me, some fair prince perhaps, or some bold crusader, come to these barren, choking lands on valiant quest –'

A sudden commotion caused her to pause. She looked up, and a sudden ripple of laughter passed through the audience. A seal had just flopped out from under the backscene and was waddling about on the straw of Satin's tiny cell.

A trouper to the last, she carried on as if nothing had happened.

'Is there none that can save me?' she repeated. 'Some fair prince perhaps, or some bold crusader, come to these barren, choking lands on valiant quest, someone who might hear my plea and restore me to that which is truly mine.'

The seal knocked over the flat that represented the stone wall of Satin's prison. It fell to the ground with a resounding crash and Satin had to jump out of the way. The audience roared. It started to move towards her, evidently wanting to play, or hoping she had a mackerel or a herring concealed about her skimpy costume.

She resolved to continue. She tried to shoo the seal away.

'For here I sit, saddened but not forlorn at heart, a damsel who has truly wronged no one, an innocent aboard, a stranger in a strange land.'

Two men burst upon the stage and tried to corner the errant animal.

'Someone left the door of its cage loose,' one of them whispered at Satin. 'You carry on and we'll try and get rid of it.'

But she had lost her thread, her equilibrium was fatally disturbed.

'Is there none that can save me,' she began again, but now in considerable confusion. 'I am a fair prince who has truly wronged no one, an innocent abroad, a stranger in a strange land.'

She faltered, realising she was lost. What came next?

'Prompt,' she hissed but no answer came. She carried on, blindly stringing words together. Eventually the men managed to usher the wandering seal off stage, barking vociferously, but no one was listening to what Satin was saying any longer. Entirely oblivious to the misfortunes of the poor slave girl, despite her near-nakedness, they were too busy enjoying the unscripted disaster that was unfolding before them.

Somehow Satin got through to the end of the scene and the curtain came down. She stormed off stage, absolutely livid with anger.

'What the hell happened there?' she screeched at the manager, who was the nearest person in authority whom she could find. 'And where was the prompt when I needed it? It was humiliating. I've never seen anything like it in my life. How dare you treat me this way?'

The poor man could only shrug his shoulders and try to apologise, but the rest of the play fared no better. Weak, under-scripted and ill-rehearsed as it was, the audience seized on every last error and used it as an opportunity for general hilarity. By the end of the third and final act, the actors' words could barely be heard above the general pandemonium that raged from the gallery to the by now almost-deserted stalls. Bichfoucauld slunk off long before the final curtain and made his way sadly to a bar along the street, where he drank cognac alone until the small hours.

The notices in the following morning's papers were even worse than she had expected. *Le Figaro* ignored the performance completely, as was its wont with such poor stuff, but Patric Esteve in *Paris-Expresse* had a field day. Satin could only read the first paragraph before bursting into tears. He made a mockery of the whole thing and some of the other papers were almost as cruel.

That evening, she could hardly bear to drag herself back to the Royale, climb the narrow, dank stairs to her tiny dressing room and change, shivering, into the first of her minuscule costumes. The play's notoriety – for all the wrong reasons – had attracted a curious audience that night but the numbers were poor and on the third night they were worse still. At the end of the week the management decided to cut its losses and close the production. With nothing else on the horizon and all her fine hopes dashed, Satin was out of work and back on the streets again.

The next few weeks passed in something of a haze. Satin was as much a prisoner in her apartment on the Boulevard de la Madeleine as she had been in her canvas prison at the Theatre Royale. Her friends, apart from Véronique and Thierry Albert, seemed to have deserted her. The three of them spent long, slow days together, cocooned in the soft haze of his tinctures, oblivious to the world that passed them by outside in the Boulevard de la Madeleine. Mathilde cooked meals for them but they went largely untasted. Clothes piled up everywhere, empty wine bottles were on every surface. The oddest, most disreputable people began to visit them at the strangest hours. Finally even the ever-faithful Mathilde could take no more, and left her mistress to her own devices.

Bailiffs, eventually, repossessed the apartment. With what little money she now had after her many creditors had been satisfied, Satin moved back to within a stone's throw of her old haunts. She did not dare to show her face at the Café des Artistes, of course, but preferred to frequent the streets of the Tuileries and the Latin quarter.

One afternoon she found herself passing the house where, many months ago now, she had dressed herself in leather and straps and beaten Moscato. On an impulse, she climbed the short, crumbling flight of steps and rang the bell.

'Yes?' said the maid who answered the door, eyeing Satin up and down.

'Is your mistress in?' she asked. 'I wish to speak with her.'

Satin was ushered into the same comfortable parlour where she had sat before, facing the same twinkling-eyed old woman. She remembered her well.

'I don't have too much call for that kind of thing these days,' she said at length, 'and what I do have my other girls can take care of.'

'I do other things,' said Satin.

'I'm sure you do, dearie,' said the woman, and rang a bell.

A man entered the room, broad-shouldered, dressed in a flashy kind of way.

'We have a lady here says she'd be interested in our little establishment,' said the old woman.

'Oh yes,' said the man, looking Satin up and down.

'Says she can do all kinds of things. She was the one who beat that gentleman what used to come here, once upon a time. Do you remember him, the one who offed himself?'

'Oh yes I do,' replied the man, looking at Satin as if she were a piece of meat in a butcher's shop. 'And you're the one who did him that time, are you? Yes, I've heard all about you. Bit of a celebrity, aren't we? Come with me, then, and we'll see what you can do.'

He led her upstairs to a small room at the back of the house. There was nothing in the room except for a bed, a wash hand-stand and an old armchair. He sat down and opened his flies.

'Right,' he said, without any ceremony whatsoever. 'Suck me off.'

Satin did as he commanded. Taking off her hat and gloves, she knelt down before him, trying to avoid his eyes. That it had come to this! she thought. She leaned forward – he smelled none too clean but she stuck out her tongue and tasted him just the same.

245

'All the way in,' he said. 'Don't just lick it. Show me what you can do.'

Satin took hold of his now-erect shaft with one hand and ran her tongue up and down its length. She washed her tongue over the bulbous purple dome, catching it between her lips and sucking it like a child's lollipop.

'Nice,' he said. 'Do it some more.'

She squatted down to make herself more comfortable, kneeling there on the bare boards of the floor, she was afraid her stockings would be ruined. Then, opening her mouth wide, she took him into her as far as she could. He grunted, muttered something she didn't quite catch.

She swirled her tongue around his prick, caressing it with her full lips, bobbing her head up and down. She didn't need to put much effort into it but he liked what she did. She could tell by the way his breath was coming in short, ragged rasps that she was proving her point to his evident satisfaction.

'All right,' he said at length. 'Now get up on the bed and kneel over. Pull your drawers down.'

Once more she did just as she was told – a strange sensation for her. She was still wearing her skirt and coat. The bedsprings creaked. This was, she knew, quite an expensive house but it lacked the creature comforts that she had become used to.

He climbed up behind her, holding his prick in one hand. The bed shook with the weight of the two of them. Knowing what was to come, she spread her legs for him. His cock was already well wetted with her spittle and, though she knew she was unusually dry down there, he would have little difficulty gaining entry. She would soon get wet, she knew.

Instead, he wanted to bugger her. She felt his cock pressed against the tight little rosebud of her backside. Oh my God, she thought. She had taken quite a few men in her rear passage but never quite like this, when she was nowhere near ready for it. She wanted to stop, to tell him no, but the voice of reason told her why she was here in this small, airless room, with this ponce.

He pushed against her and a searing pain shot straight up her backbone and exploded inside her head. Tears welled up in her eyes. She tried to will her sphincter to open up for him but she was too tense and he was so crude, just pushing into her without a care.

She wanted to tell him to stop but she needed the work more. The pain was unbearable – if only she could relax. She bit the edge of the pillow, trying to distract herself. She hoped he would come off soon and spare her the agony. She couldn't bear to be fucked like this for another moment.

'Like it, do you?' he grunted. His breath smelled of beer and onions. She was glad he had not tried to kiss her.

'Yes, yes,' she managed to say, screwing up her eyes and gritting her teeth. 'Do it in me, for God's sake.'

In answer he pushed triumphantly deeper into her so that she felt she was almost splitting in two. Oh God, she thought, as the pain seared through her, he's going to kill me.

And then, miraculously, his cock pulsed and he shot his seed deep inside her, grunting and mouthing profanities. Satin lay there without moving, and her inner humiliation was as great as her pain. Even when he took his cock out of her, there was little relief from his agony.

He tucked his shirt back into his trousers, suppressed a belch.

'Right,' he said. 'You'll do. I'll just go downstairs and have a word with Mother.'

She walked through the lobby of the hotel, as she had done many times. She often seemed to come to the Excelsior. The head porter had an arrangement with the old woman and her son.

She climbed the stairs, her long dress swishing over the carpeted treads. She liked being here, enjoyed the sense of luxury and well-being. She had a new apartment now, better than the last, and a new maid, but she still pined for the old days.

A gentleman was coming down the stairway towards her. Through her wrap he could see the deep cleft of her bosom, scandalously exposed by the cut of the dress she wore. She gave him her warmest smile. He looked away, hurriedly. The little prick was probably on his way down to take dinner with his wife. Satin bet that she didn't suck him like she could, if at all.

She walked along the thickly carpeted corridor. Her feet made no sound but her dress rustled provocatively. She hoped the gentleman would like what she wore – if he was anything like any of the others she had worn it with, she knew he would not be disappointed. The dress of course, was as nothing compared with the lingerie she was wearing underneath it. She hoped he wouldn't get over-excited and try to tear it off her. She was seeing someone else in a couple of hours' time and she wouldn't have time to go home and change. She had been very busy these past few weeks.

She checked her hair in a mirror. It was piled high on her head, thick and luxuriant. Her lips were painted a flaming red, her teeth white like ivory. She smiled at herself. She was starting to get her old confidence back.

She tapped on the door. She could hear a man's voice humming on the other side, a popular song that was doing the rounds of the theatres at that moment. She knocked again.

The door was opened by Henry Levinson.

'Satin,' he said when he had recovered his composure. She stepped quickly inside.

Each was as confused as the other.

'I thought –' he began.

248

'I thought –' she began too, at the same time. They laughed. Her heart was pounding. Neither of them had been expecting this.

'I wondered where on earth you'd got to. I wrote to you from the States – didn't you get my letters?' They went into his suite, sat down on separate sofas. The sitting room alone was the size of Satin's apartment.

'No, no. I was in Nice.'

'I know that. You wrote to me, said you were returning to Paris.'

'And here I am.'

'And looking radiant, my dear. But why, why—?' He indicated her dress, the unsubtle erotic language of the whore.

'Oh, just to get me by, you know. We all do it from time to time, we actresses. Even La Cabache, you know, at one time.'

'So I gather,' he said quietly, and abruptly changed the subject.

'I came over three weeks ago, on board the *Carolina*. But when I went to the Boulevard de la Madeleine you weren't there. They said you'd moved out, months before, didn't know where you were. I couldn't find Véronique either.'

'Why were you so anxious to see me? And why are you here, in Paris?' she cried. He poured them both a glass of champagne in a crystal glass. It was more like the old days with every second that passed.

'I wrote to tell you – but of course, you never got my letter.'

'Tell me what?'

'That I've lined up a tour for you. Of America.'

'America?'

'Yes. New York, Pittsburgh, Chicago – ten cities in all.'

'Playing what?'

'*Sophie and her Sister.*'

'Did you see my last reviews?'

'I heard about it. All nonsense, of course. You were wasted in that part. That fool Bichfoucauld shouldn't be allowed near a theatre.'

It seemed almost too good to be true. Here was this man – about the only man in her life whom she knew well and yet had never slept with – who actually seemed to have faith in her. She had often thought about him in her long months of exile, had realised that he was quite besotted with her and yet realised that there was more to her than large breasts and voluptuous thighs. So often he had helped her and guided her when she needed him most and now, once again, he had come to her rescue. He was, she realised, like the father she had never known.

'Will you come? Everything is arranged. The theatres are booked.'

'But no one has heard of me in America.'

'That's precisely the point. You'll be a sensation, all over again, just as you were in Paris.'

'Wouldn't you rather have Babette?'

'Babette is married now and expecting a baby. Besides, I am asking you first. Please do not refuse me. We could sail in ten days' time.'

Satin had been staring at the pattern in the brocade of the sofa, scarcely knowing what to think. Her whole life flashed before her – the Café des Artistes, the hotel in Nice, the Rue de la Madeleine, the Theatre des Etoiles, the Jardin des Tuileries. She had nothing, really, to leave behind her.

'All right,' she said at length. 'I'll come to America with you.'